DECEIT *and* RESTITUTION

JACK NELSON

PAGE PUBLISHING, INC.
New York, NY

First originally published by Page Publishing, Inc. 2019

ISBN 978-1-68456-870-3 (Paperback)
ISBN 978-1-68456-871-0 (Digital)

Printed in the United States of America

INTRODUCTION

Warm summer's night on the streets of downtown Veracruz, Mexico, a brand-new 650 Mercedes Benz rolled smoothly through the rush-hour traffic. Halfway through the next intersection, a white panel van slammed into the Mercedes, dragging it to the side of the road. Four men wearing body armor and black hoods jumped out rushing the sedan. A woman screamed from a nearby balcony, crossing herself with the crucifix as the sound of automatic weapons could be heard a block away. Curious neighbors flooded the streets, just to return as quickly for they knew they wanted nothing to do with it. A nearby witness watched in horror as the body of a man shook as the bullets tore through flesh and bone. One man pulled opened the driver's door, pointed the gun at the man's head and emptied the magazine.

"Did you find it?" a man called out from the white van.

"No, not yet… I can't find it," the man shouted from the torn-up Mercedes.

"Did you find it?" the man yelled from the driver's seat.

"I need more time," he yelled back in a panic.

The sirens of the local police could be heard approaching in the distance.

"No time, no time," the driver yelled as the side door slid open.

"I DON'T HAVE IT!" the man shouted, holding out both hands empty-handed.

"LET'S GO!" the driver yelled as the man dove head first into the back of the van as it sped off.

CHAPTER 1

Past

"Desperta se. Desperta se," Marta De La Cruz called out to her two young sons, Juan Carlos and Luiz Fernando.

"Si, Mama," the boys yelled back.

Roberto and Marta De La Cruz lived on a small farm outside of the village of Santa Anna on the Bahia de Campeche in Mexico.

Their two young sons, Juan, eight, and Luiz, six, would help their mother pick, wash, and load a small buggy with fresh fruits and vegetables to be sold at the village market.

"Go directly to the market," Marta told her sons as they headed out on the three-mile journey into town.

The road into town would take them past their neighbors Marco and Rosa Fernandez and their young daughter Maria who was Luiz's age. The Fernadez's raised cattle, pigs, and sheep. Every day the boys stopped and chatted with Maria on their way to meet their father, Roberto, at the tienda, who was patiently waiting for the boys at the village square. Let's just say the fruits and vegetables didn't always arrive on time.

"Vamanos, muchachos," Roberto would call out as they ran the last one hundred yards, panting as if they had run the whole way. The two families would set up their own tiendas to sell their goods and services. The boys would run off and play with Maria throughout the day. The village square was always a busy place with farmers and merchants from all over, buying and selling everything from fruits, vegetables, meats, milk, grains and livestock, farm fresh eggs, home-made pies, and cheeses. By noon, the market would shut down, and the boys loaded up the buggy along with all the family's purchases, supplies, and profits from the day's work and headed back to the hacienda. The boys would repeat this same routine ten thousand times over the next five years.

On one warm summers day as he pulled the vegetable cart along the dusty three-mile trek back home, with sweat rolling down his face, Juan suggested to his younger brother, "Why don't we start our own business?"

Luiz looked back at him with a strange look. "Yeah…why not? You can take care of the sales, and I'll take care of the transportation," Luiz said smiling.

"Okay, it's a deal" they both said at the same time.

When the boys got home that afternoon, Papa was working hard on the old 1930s Chevy pickup truck.

"Papa, from now on, you don't have to repair the truck anymore," Luiz declared to his father with confidence as he grabbed the jack and helped his papa change the flat tire.

"And why is that, Luiz?" Roberto asked.

"Juan and I are starting our own business and we need a truck. This truck," Luiz said, looking back at his brother Juan giving him the thumbs up.

After talking it over with Mama and Papa, the boys were determined to start their own business and headed out on their own the very next morning. They painted a big sign on each side of the pickup truck. "Juan and Luiz De La Cruz Fresh Fruits and Vegetables."

With the truck, they could increase their profits by traveling to nearby towns and villages offering a variety of fresh fruits, vegetables from their farm, and a variety of meat, eggs, and milk from the Fernandez farm. On the longer runs, the boys would invite Maria and her mother, Rosa, along to help with the daily sales.

This was always a good thing in Juan's mind; it gave him a chance to sit next to Maria in the back of the truck. When no one was watching, Juan would reach over and try to kiss Maria.

"No, my mama is watching," Maria would say, slapping Juan lightly across the face and pushing him away.

"Oh, Maria," Juan would say with a slight wave of his hand. But that never stopped Juan from trying. He was persistent and never gave up. Every opportunity he had, Juan would try to kiss Maria, usually resulting in a slap across the face. This went on for several months.

Then one cold night, everything changed. Juan leaned over to steal a kiss from Maria. When he puckered up and closed his eyes, expecting his usual slap, Maria surprised him with a kiss instead. Juan opened his eyes with a surprised look on his face.

"I love it when you keep trying to kiss me," Maria said holding her two fingers up against his lips, then gently kissing him again.

"So why did you keep slapping me and pushing me away when I tried to kiss you?" Juan asked.

"Because no matter how many times I pushed you away and told you 'no,' you always tried again…and never gave up," Maria said smiling.

Juan looked deeply into Maria's eyes. "I love you, Maria," he said.

"I love you, Juan," Maria said as they kissed and made out in the back of the truck the rest of the way home.

Over the next several years, the new business grew larger and larger. The longer trips lasted two or three days. The deliveries were larger and more complex, and Luiz was getting frustrated constantly repairing the old truck. Veracruz was the largest nearby city, and the obvious destination to expand. Juan's plan was to set up a warehouse and distribution center there, get a new truck, and grow the business. The company was growing fast, and so was his love for Maria. Veracruz was a long way from Santa Anna and Maria, and Juan had promised Maria that he would be back for her once things got settled.

Veracruz was a huge culture shock for the two farm boys from Santa Anna with all the people and businesses on every corner, selling everything under the sun. The two boys took their savings and made a down payment on an abandoned warehouse on the outskirts of town and even had enough money left to buy a nicer newer truck, one that did not breakdown at every stop. Luiz was very happy about that. The boys lived in a small office above the warehouse they converted into a little apartment.

At first, they made weekly trips to Santa Anna and the farm for vegetable and merchandise they could sell in the city, but as the business grew, the trips back home grew farther and farther apart. The boys always looked forward to visiting Santa Anna, especially Juan who spent most of his time with Maria. Luiz loved visiting his mama and mama's home cooking.

"Juan is really good with figures, business, and money, but he makes really bad tortillas," Luiz would confess to his mom.

Luiz was sick and tired of hearing about Maria. "Did you see the nice present Maria got for me?" "Oh, did you see how Maria looked at me during dinner?" Juan would go on for days like that. Every time they left, Juan would promise Maria that he would come for her.

During the week, in the evenings, Juan and Luiz would spend their time in local diners, bars, and street corners looking for day workers for the warehouse. Luiz left the warehouse hiring to Juan, as he was more interested in all the ladies. Luiz was a playboy and picking up women for him was a big game and favorite pastime.

One night at a local restaurant, Luiz spotted a tall brunette at least five feet eight sitting at the bar by herself. Actually, all women were tall for Luiz, he was only five feet three, but that never stopped him from trying. Luiz looked over at Juan who was busy talking to a group of guys for warehouse jobs.

"Hey, Juan," Luiz shouted from across the bar, pointing at the brunette. Luiz always said he could pick up any woman in any bar at any time.

"No, Luiz," Juan shouted over the noise of the bar. "Not that one," Juan tried to warn him, not about the woman he was trying to pick up, but the six-foot-six, three-hundred-pound Chicano boyfriend with her. It was too late. Before Juan could make his way over to the other side of the bar, Luiz strutted over to her, sat down, and told her that she was the most beautiful woman in the world, bent her over, and kissed her. Luiz laughed as he looked at Juan who was pointing at something or someone behind him. Luiz felt this huge hand grab his shoulder from behind. Without hesitating, Luiz put both his hands on top of the big man's hand, then dropped to the floor. The sudden change of direction threw the big man off balance and pulling him toward the floor. When Luiz hit the floor, he bounced back up hitting the big man squarely in the jaw with his hardhead, knocking the big man out cold. Luiz just sat there laughing as Juan came over to see if he was all right.

Juan always knew his brother had a hardhead, Juan thought to himself as he picked him up off the floor.

The woman, clearly stunned, sat there and wondered what just happened. Luiz got to his feet, looked at her dead in the eyes. "*Wow,* you are the most beautiful woman in the world," Luiz said bending her over the bar kissing her madly. Everyone in the bar including Juan just cheered as if Mexico had just won the World Cup or something.

"Vamanos Chica," Luiz said grabbing a bottle of tequila off the bar leading her by the arm out the front door.

"Donde Vamos?" she asked giddily.

"Celebrate our first date," Luiz said heading next door to the Holiday Inn. They booked a room for the night, drank a few shots of tequila, and made mad passionate love all night.

The next morning, Luiz woke up to an empty bed and a terrible hangover, probably too much tequila the night before. He sat up in bed and wondered if it was all a dream. *Did he actually just make love to the most beautiful woman in the world last night?* Luiz wondered, rubbing the big knot on the top of his head. Luiz, rolled over and turned on the light, squinting as his eyes adjusted to the light. On the nightstand was a piece of paper with a heart drawn on it, with the words, "Love Natalia. It wasn't a dream." Luiz shouted out in the room, wondering where she had gone. He stood up quickly, too quickly apparently as the sudden urge to vomit overcame him. He lay back down and waited for the room to stop spinning then closed his eyes. The only thing he could remember was the little angel tattoo on her right shoulder blade. "But where did she go?"

CHAPTER 2

Past

As promised, Juan made a special trip back to Santa Anna, knowing that he could not live without her any longer. Juan's first stop would be to Maria's parents, Marco and Rosa Fernandez's hacienda.

Juan stood at the end of the long walkway leading up to the front door, his hands shook, his mouth so dry you would have thought he had eaten a bag of cotton balls. Juan walked up to the front door and, without thinking, reached up and knocked on the door.

Why did he just do that?" he thought to himself. Having second thoughts…as he turned…maybe he still had time to run. He was like family at the Fernandez hacienda. He never used the front door. *Run away. There's still time*, he thought just as the door slowly opened.

"Señora Fernandez," Juan said politely.

"Hola, Juan, que tal? Maria no esta," Rosa said waving him in, wondering why he was coming to the front door all dressed up.

"Mmmm, Señor Fernandez Esta?" Juan asked cautiously hoping that he wasn't.

"Si, yo busco," she said walking into the other room, wondering why he was acting so strangely.

"Que pasa, Juan, is everything okay?" Señor Fernandez asked as he headed for the front door.

"Si, Si bien," Juan said as the two of them greeted with a firm handshake, then headed for the kitchen area. Señor Fernandez sat at the head of the table, pulled out a roll of tobacco, cut off some of the shavings, and massaged them carefully in his hands, then rolled it into a cigarette. A quick lash of the tongue, and it was ready. The smell of the smoke and tobacco made Juan sick to his stomach.

Juan stood up briefly, looked out the window, and quickly sat down again.

"Estas seguro, Juan?" Marco asked wondering why he was so jumpy.

"Estoy esperando por mis Padres," Juan said quietly.

"Sus Padres Porque?" Marco asked.

There was a knock at the front door. Juan jumped, nearly falling off his chair.

Rosa answered the door, "Que paso…Marta?" Rosa asked her quietly.

"Juan, dise que necesitas hablar con nosotros juntos, es muy importante," Marta told her, inviting Roberto and Marta into the kitchen.

Juan was so nervous he could barely speak sitting across from his parents. "Señor Fernandez, Señora Fernandez…Con su permiso…yo quiero casarme con su hija, Maria," Juan asked in a low confident voice.

Señor Fernandez sat there for a minute, taking a long drag on his cigarette, quietly acting as if he did not hear the young man's request. Juan sat there, wondering what to do.

Maybe he did not hear me the first time? Juan swallowed whatever moisture he had in his mouth. *Should I ask again?* Juan wondered sitting quietly. Marco looked around the room, first at Rosa who was crying, wiping the tears from her eyes with a dish towel, then over at Roberto and Marta who both nodded quietly in agreement. Marco looked back at Juan who was sweating in his seat. Marco chuckled.

"Si, Juan tienes permiso," Marco said with a chuckle, then a big laugh "Si, mi hijo…it's about time," Marco said reaching for the tequila and shot glasses. Rosa walked over to Juan and gave him a big hug as tears ran down her cheek.

"Si, mi hijo."

"Maria, oh, Maria," Rosa called out loudly toward the barn.

"Si, Mama, ya voy," she said finishing her daily chores in the barn.

"Vamanos, Maria…a hora," Rosa said waving her hand at her daughter.

"Si, Mama," Maria said rushing for the door.

Maria walked in the kitchen door, followed closely by her mama. Maria was surprised to see Juan, drinking tequila and smoking cigarettes with her papa in the middle of the day.

Juan, walked over to Maria, with her tattered dress and dirty face and hands from working in the barn. Juan took her by the hand… and looked into her soft brown eyes.

"Maria, yo te amo. Tengo permiso de sus padres a casarse comigo?" Juan asked Maria as she stood looking around the room.

Her mother smiled and nodded her head.

"Si, Si," she said and gave Juan a big hug and a kiss.

Marco insisted about having the wedding at the hacienda. They were to get married two weeks from today. Juan and Maria wanted a very traditional wedding, inviting only close friends and relatives. Maria wore her mother's wedding gown, a traditional long white dress that she had stored in the attic since her own wedding. Juan wore a guayabera worn by his father, the dark blue slacks and vest with the traditional gold buttons. Rosa and Marta prepared a traditional meal of beef and chicken tortillas, spicy rice, refried beans, fruit salad, followed by doce de tres leches and all the sangria they could drink. The local mariachi band played till early the following morning.

Juan and Maria moved to the big city of Veracruz, far away from the little farming village of Santa Anna that they were used to. The office/apartment above the warehouse was dingy and small, but Maria knew that with a woman's touch, she would have everything looking great again. Luiz was very happy to have Maria living there. She was a much better cook than Juan any day.

Two months later, Juan and Maria had great news. Maria was pregnant and expecting their first child. With the new addition to the family, the small apartment was no place to raise a family. Juan took out a loan and purchased a 1,200-square-foot two-bedroom, two-bath ranch home a few miles out of town with a huge yard and plenty of land for a small garden. Later that year, Maria gave birth to a baby girl, Gabriella Maria Fernandez De La Cruz.

CHAPTER 3

Present day

Two police cars came to a screeching to a halt a few meters from the incident, four officers jumped out with their pistols drawn, expecting a confrontation with armed assailants, but instead, they found a 650 Mercedes Benz riddled with bullets and a dead body.

Capitan Lupe Benitez was one of those officers—a captain for over fifteen years at the local police precinct approached the Mercedes from the side, something seemed a little familiar about the sedan.

Was that Luiz De La Cruz's sedan? Lupe thought as he looked inside the driver's side of the vehicle, where a body or what was left of it lay across the seat. The bits and pieces of flesh and bone baked in the summer heat, emitting an almost sweet pungent smell.

"El Cartel," a woman shouted from her balcony. Lupe reached down and picked up one of the spent cartridges scattered all over the road, then looked at it curiously.

"El Cartel," the woman shouted again.

Lupe quickly slid the casing into his pants pocket.

Several official-looking vehicles pulled up to the crime scene, the federales. Lupe despised the federales; in particular, their commanding officer first Sergeant Roberto Costas. The most corrupt federal officer in Veracruz. In his opinion, all the federales were corrupt in one way or another.

"Federales," the woman shouted from her balcony.

In Mexico, no one knew who was more dangerous the "cartel" or the "federales." It was best to just not get involved with either one.

Lupe returned to the sedan to get a closer look. There was an open briefcase, scattered papers all over the car, as if someone was looking for something.

"Capitan Benitez," Sergeant Costas called out.

Lupe ignored the sergeant's call.

"Capitan Benitez," Costas called out again.

Out of the corner of his eye, Lupe spotted something shiny on the floorboard of the car, a microdrive. Lupe reached in and picked it up, just as Costas grabbed him by the shoulder and pulled him out of the car.

"Que paso," Lupe shouted pushing Costas away. "This is not your crime scene," Costas yelled. "This is a matter for the federales. We have it from here," Costas told him.

Lupe stepped back holding both arms above his head, waving his hands back and forth, then quickly slipping the microdrive into his pants pocket.

The ambulance pulled up a few minutes later. The medic threw up when he saw the remains of the body in the sedan. There wasn't enough of a man's face to make an immediate identification. The accident recovery crew loaded up the remains of the shattered Mercedes onto a trailer and hauled it away. The cleanup crew wasted no time sweeping up all the remains of the Mercedes—the spent cartridges, glass fragments all the evidence of the crime swept away, even the blood was washed off the street by the local fire brigade.

What is going on? Lupe thought as he watched from a distance. *What are the federales trying to hide?* This was totally against protocol. The coroner's office never took any pictures, of the body, or the crime scene. No evidence collected or witness's interviewed. In less than an hour, the pavement had dried, and the traffic resumed on this busy street in downtown Veracruz as if the accident or crime had ever occurred or taken place.

CHAPTER 4

Present day

The phone rang at JML Corporation Headquarters.

"JML Corporation… This is Esmeralda. How can I help you?" she asked pleasantly.

"This is Captain Benitez. I need to talk with Juan De La Cruz immediately?" he said anxiously.

"Sorry, he is in a board meeting at the moment. Can I take a message?" she asked.

"This is a police emergency. I need to speak with Juan De La Cruz right away," Lupe insisted.

"Please hold." Esmeralda got up and headed to the boardroom.

JML Corporation Headquarters boardroom was a large rectangular-shaped room with four massive crystal chandeliers hanging from the vaulted ceiling. The centerpiece of the room was a magnificent fifty-foot oval table made from one-hundred-year-old Brazilian cherry surrounded by twenty high back leather chairs. Juan was at the head of the table going over the latest crop reports.

Esmeralda walked over, interrupted him, and whispered something in his ear. Juan got up excused himself from the room and headed into the next room.

"Es La Policia… Capitan Benitez," Esmeralda told him. "Emergencia," she said crossing herself.

"Lupe… Como estas?" Juan said enthusiastically.

Juan and Lupe have known each other for fifteen years, ever since they all moved to Veracruz. Their children all went to the same school down the street from the warehouse complex.

"Juan, you have to get to Veracruz right away," Lupe told him.

"Why? What happened??" Juan asked.

"Accident… Juan, su hermano… Luiz está muerto," Lupe told him quietly.

"What happened?" Juan asked.

"I can't talk about it over the phone. You have to come down to the station." Lupe hung up the phone.

Juan ran back into the boardroom and told everyone that he had a family emergency to take care of, ran down to the parking garage, and drove off in a six series Mercedes. Juan drove the usual three-hour drive in a little over an hour. Captain Lupe Benitez, a large rotund man that was well respected in town, met his old friend in the lobby of the police station. The two men walked into Lupe's private office and closed the door.

"So what happened?" Juan asked as he sat down in front of Lupe's desk.

Lupe leaned over and opened the bottom drawer of his desk, pulled out a bottle of Mexico's finest tequila, two glasses, and several limes, then sat down next to his dear friend.

"Juan, Luiz esta Muerto," Lupe said quietly.

Lupe poured the tequila and handed it to his friend, a nip of salt, gulp of tequila, and a squeeze of lime. The tequila flowed down the back of his throat slowly warming his whole body.

"What happened?" Juan asked.

"Juan, a Mercedes registered to Luiz was ambushed in downtown Veracruz this morning," Lupe said handing his friend another tequila.

"You sure it was Luiz?" Juan interrupted.

"Yes, I think so," Lupe went on.

"But you are not sure…?" Juan said, wondering why he can't confirm it was him.

"I don't know yet… The federales have the body," Lupe said.

"Federales…why?"

"I don't know for sure yet… I believe that Luiz's Mercedes was shot up with over three hundred bullets. Most of them at point blank, making it impossible to make an accurate identification."

Lupe lowered his head.

"The Mercedes looked familiar, so I ran the plates. They came back to Luiz," Lupe paused. "Who else would be driving his car?" Lupe asked.

"I don't know." Juan started crying.

"Do you know what he was doing this morning?" Lupe asked.

"Inventory, I think?" Juan struggled to remember. "How do you know it was Luiz?" Juan asked again.

"There was a schedule and a briefcase with JML Corporation letterhead in the car," Lupe told him. "I'll let you know more when I can, my friend." Lupe poured another tequila, and the two sat in silence for several hours.

The next day, Lupe headed to the federal building to see what he could find out.

"Sergeant, I would like the file on the incident that happened in Veracruz yesterday morning?" Captain Benitez asked the desk sergeant.

"Sorry, sir, that case is off limits," the sergeant answered.

"Off limits to whom?" Lupe pointed at his captain's bars. "Not to me… That was not a request, Sergeant, but an order," Lupe demanded.

"The first sergeant gave strict orders that the file and the case were off limits, sir" the desk sergeant said.

"Who's that?" Lupe barked.

"First Sergeant Roberto Costas," the sergeant explained.

Down the hall, they could hear two men arguing with each other, one was a lab tech, and the other Sergeant Costas. Lupe stepped back from the desk and peeked around the corner to get a better look. Lupe was familiar with the building layout. He had been there on many occasions over the past fifteen years.

Costas and the lab tech were walking out of the autopsy heading down the hall, arguing about something. Lupe snuck down the hall and looked in the autopsy room. Lupe hated autopsy, seeing friends get cut up, but he knew the importance of getting to the truth.

Inside was a body covered with a white sheet. Lupe walked over and read the autopsy notes and looked at a sketch of the body, covered with red Xs mostly around the head and shoulders area. At the bottom of the page was the "cause of death." "Death by multiple gunshots, automatic weapons, 5.56 mm projectiles."

"What?" Lupe stopped and reread the statement. "Multiple gunshots, automatic weapons, 5.56 mm projectiles." *What? That's a US military ballistic round*, Lupe thought as he read further in disbelief. "A US military weapon, possibly the M-4 assault rifle."

"What were US military assault weapons being used on a local hit?"

Lupe knew the casing he picked up were unmarked and looked a little different, but never figured them to be 5.56 mm or from the US military. Lupe walked over to the long table where there was a blood-covered briefcase, JML Corporation folder, schedules, invoices, and a wallet laid out on this table. Lupe opened the wallet and read the ID. "Luiz Fernando De La Cruz."

Could this really be his friend Luiz? Lupe thought in a constant state of denial. *Could this really be his friend that got shot down on the streets of Veracruz? But why*? That is what Lupe wanted to know. *Why and what do the federales want with his body and the investigation*? Lupe wondered as he pulled back the plastic sheet, revealing the body. Lupe nearly fainted at the sight of the remains. The face was gone, mutilated. Lupe heard voices approaching and quickly covered the body, then ran to the long table and took several files, slid them into his waistband, and disappeared out the back door.

Costas and the lab technician still arguing, returned to the autopsy room. The lab technician stopped suddenly, realizing something was wrong, and slammed his fist on the table.

"Where are the files?" he yelled at Costas. "Did you take the files?" he yelled again.

"What files?" Costas asked looking around the room.

"Right here. There were some files sitting right here on this table," the lab tech yelled loudly.

Costas looked around the room, then out into the hallway.

"Sergeant, has anyone been in here in the last thirty minutes?" Costas barked running toward the desk sergeant.

"Yes, Captain Benitez," the sergeant responded.

"Capitan Benitez...what did he want?" Costas asked heading for the door to look around.

"He wanted a update on the case...wanted to look at the files. The shooting, the one in Veracruz," the sergeant said.

"Where is he now?" Costas asked angrily.

"He left, I think," the sergeant said, wondering if he actually did or not.

Costas picked up the phone and called someone, spoke for a few minutes then hung up.

Later that night, Juan got a personal call from Lupe Benitez.

"Juan, are you alone?" Lupe asked.

"Who is this?" Juan asked squinting, trying to hear the voice on the phone.

"It's Lupe...we have to meet right away," Lupe said with a crackle of fear in his voice. In all these years, he had never known Lupe to be afraid of anything or anyone. "Juan, meet me behind the old school house, by the swings at ten thirty...park down the road and walk in." Lupe abruptly hung up the phone.

Juan drove to the old schoolyard and parked a few blocks away, walking the rest of the way as Lupe requested. The old schoolhouse brought back memories for Juan as Gabriella and Lupe's two sons all went to the same little school, playing on the swings and football field. Juan waited for Lupe in the back of the schoolyard where the swings once stood, now it was just an overgrown area where the locals dump trash and other unwanted items.

"Juan," Lupe whispered from the tree line.

Juan turned toward the woods as he spotted Lupe wearing all black leather jacket, hat, and sunglasses that blended in well with the darkness of the night. Lupe pulled Juan into the nearby bushes, then handed him a plastic bag.

"Here, take it..." Lupe whispered. "It's about your brother's murder," Lupe said looking around cautiously.

"Murder? What? Who?" Juan asked surprised.

"Don't trust Costas and the Feder—" The swoosh startled Juan as Lupe's head snapped back from the impact of the high-powered bullet.

Juan took off running through the woods then dived head first into a nearby drainage ditch. Juan's head was spinning, heart racing, probably from the sudden surge of adrenaline. *What just happened?* he thought to himself as he crawled deeply into a nearby culvert. His best friend for over a decade just got his head blown off. *By whom? What's going on?* Juan asked himself as he heard voices and footsteps nearby as he moved deeper into the drainage pipe. *What did Lupe say?* Juan's heart was beating over two hundred beats a minute and could hardly remember who he was, let alone what Lupe just told him. "Why can't I remember what Lupe said?" Juan cried out in frustration.

Juan spent the rest of the night and better part of the next day up in that culvert trying to remember what happened to Lupe and what he told him. Juan returned to the schoolyard, but there was no body. Lupe was gone. Juan made his way back to the truck and later to his home in Veracruz. Maria was worried because Juan never made it home last night.

"What's going on?" Maria asked as she comforted her husband. "I don't know… Luiz is dead, and now so is Lupe."

"Luiz and Lupe… Oh my god." She quickly crossed herself. "What happened?"

Juan pulled out the plastic bag that Lupe handed to him just before he was killed and laid it out on the table.

Inside the plastic bag were invoices, transportation logs from JML Corporation, nothing unusual or out of order for Luiz who was the transportation officer after all. There was also a microdrive, a piece of paper with a number scribbled on it—2156—and a bullet casing with no serial numbers.

What was Luiz involved with? Juan wondered. *Why was his brother and now best friend murdered?* Juan had no answers and was afraid to go to the authorities. The local police captain was dead, and the federales were not talking. Then he remembered… "Don't trust Costas or the federales."

CHAPTER 5

Present day

Luiz De La Cruz was buried three days later in the small village
of Santa Anna where the boys grew up. Family and friends came
from all over. It was the largest gathering of any kind for the small
farming community. After the funeral, several close friends gathered at the house for a meal in honor of Luiz. One friend was Frank
Griffin III was an original board member of JML Corporation, and
the other was a great friend Texas Senator Bradley K. Stevens.

Juan pulled Frank aside and told him what happened the night
Lupe was killed and about the bag he gave him. "Could it have been
the cartels?" Juan asked looking at his friend for any help.

"I don't know maybe," Frank said quietly.

"What about the federales?" Frank asked. "No... Lupe said
don't trust the federales or their First Sergeant Roberto Costas."

"Isn't, your son...hmmm, 'Frankie' involved in the military and
the US government?" Juan asked, remembering the time the boy's
helped to rebuild the community after the flood.

"Yes, he is... Why?" Frank asked.

"I would like his help... I can't trust the federales and this
Costas." Juan hung his head down in despair. "Do you know where
he is?"

"He's on assignment somewhere in the world," Frank explained.

"Please leave him a message for me. Tell him what happened,
and that I could use his help," Juan asked.

"Okay. I'll reach out to him and pass the message on," Frank said.

Frank Griffin III, one of the original board members of JML Corporation, had two sons Benjamin and Frank "Frankie" Griffin IV. The boys grew up on the homestead just west of Houston, Texas. Benjamin, the oldest son, was the all-star quarterback for the high school football team. Frankie was two years behind him and was an outstanding wide receiver. For two years in a row, the brothers were the best one-two combinations in the whole state of Texas and won two state championships.

After high school, Ben joined the Marine Corps and later served with the US Border Patrol, working closely with the ATF. Frankie went on to Georgetown University, and in his second year was appointed to the US Naval Academy in Maryland. After graduation, Frankie was recruited into the NAVY SEALS and later into the CIA as an operative. Frank "Frankie" Griffin IV would later change his name to Rex Nelson mainly to hide his identity and protect his family and close friends; to the outside world, Frank Griffin IV did not exist.

CHAPTER 6

Present day

That next summer, the torrential rains throughout the region caused the worst flooding in Santa Anna history. The De La Cruz farm and all their crops were destroyed, the topsoil had all but washed away. The De La Cruz boys had several warehouses but just enough inventory for about two weeks at the most. Juan, Luiz, and Maria were devastated. Their company had grown to be the largest distributor of fresh fruits and vegetables in the area, but now it was all gone, except the four main warehouses.

Despite the tragedy, they opened all their warehouses and fed the local communities affected by the floods. They went as far as taking out additional mortgages on their business and personal homes to pay dedicated and loyal employees.

A local news agency from Veracruz covered the disaster and interviewed Juan and Maria one wet cold night.

"I understand that you are opening up all your warehouses to anyone in the community, is that right?" the reporter asked Juan.

"Si, yes, it is correct. We have four big warehouses of fresh fruit, vegetables, meats, and cheeses. We will do whatever we can to help the families affected by the tragedy," Juan told the reporter.

"What about your family? I understand that you have a new baby," the reporter asked. "Yes, we do. This is my wife, Maria, and our daughter Gabriella… We all are affected by this flood. This community is my second family," Juan said.

*****

The news feed was broadcast on local and international evening news stations.

Thousand miles away, Frank Griffin III, a wealthy cattle rancher from West Texas, sat in a padded leather recliner watching the evening news, sipping on an eighteen-year-old Glenlivet scotch when he caught the interview with Juan and Maria.

Frank closed his eyes and remembered the devastating dust storms that swept through West Texas area a decade ago. It was the worst storm in over one hundred years. It killed all his cattle and his lovely wife, Elizabeth, of thirty years.

With plenty of time on his hands and resources at his fingertips, he made a call to his old friend Senator Bradley K. Stevens, a man who had helped him recover from the devastating dust storm a decade ago. "Bradley ole boy… I hope I didn't catch you at a bad time?" Frank asked pouring himself another scotch.

"Never a bad time for an old friend. What can I do for you, Frank?" the senator asked.

"Did you happen to catch the evening news tonight about the flood victims in Mexico?" Frank asked.

"No, can't say, I have…been really busy with these Senate appropriation bills that are due on Monday morning," the senator replied, shuffling through some papers.

"About these flood victims in Mexico…years ago, I got some help from total strangers at a time when I needed it the most. I'm well off now. I would like to help. Any chance you can help me get something started?" Frank paused and got to his feet. He always said his best ideas came to him standing up.

"Gee, sorry, Frank…just a little busy at the moment. It is Mexico. I am not sure if I can even help you."

"Look, all I need is a way in…and with the elections coming up, the extra PR would not hurt your reelection campaign at all. Let me give you the rundown. 'The two brothers run this fruits and veg-etable business that got wiped out… They really seem like nice folks giving away all of that is left of their business to the community and families," Frank went on. "I heard one of the owner took out a loan on his house to pay his employees for a few months." "That says a lot…don't you think, Bradley?"

"Okay, Frank… You drive a hard bargain. How can I help?" the senator asked.

"We can go to Mexico and do something like a charity or some-thing," Frank paused. "I have the money. I'll call in a few personal favors of my own. Do you have any ideas on how we can help them, get involved maybe?" Frank asked. "They seem like a nice couple. The family that lost everything and is trying to help the community, can't we?" Frank stood up again. He always thought better standing up.

Frank's next phone call was to his rancher friend in Oklahoma Tom Fitzgerald.

"Hey, Tom, this is Frank. I need two of your best bulls and sev-eral dozen of your best cows," Frank said with authority.?

"What are you doing, Frank? Starting another farm?" Tom said.

"Something like that. It's for a Mexican family and their com-munity that was devastated by the floods," Frank told him.

"I'll arrange for someone to pick them up in the morning."

"No need. I will drive them down myself. Anything else I can do to help out an old friend?" Tom smiled.

"Yes, come to Mexico. I could use a hand. I'll see you in a few days."

Tom hung up the phone.

Frank called his banker and set up a disaster relief fund that could be used in a foreign country.

Frank flew his Citation II aircraft to Bergstrom AFB, just south of Austin, Texas, and met the senator who said he had a little surprise for him and his trip.

"Hey, Frank, I managed to round up a few supplies. They are being loaded over there," the senator pointed at a C-130 Hercules.

"Wow, how kind of you… How did you manage that?" Frank asked.

"Don't ask."

Frank thanked him.

Early the next morning, Frank and the senator took off from Bergstrom AFB in Frank's private Citation II jet heading for Veracruz, Mexico.

"I think I can get used to this," the senator joked.

"Well, don't get any ideas… I already contributed to your campaign once this year."

"Do you serve alcohol on this flight?" the senator asked.

"Why, of course… What would you like?" Frank offered.

"How about some rum?" the senator asked.

"I have a nice bottle of Cajun Spiced Rum from New Orleans." Frank opened the bottle and poured two glasses.

It was a short flight to Veracruz from Austin. The C-130 would be a couple hours behind. The two men jumped on a helicopter and toured the disaster area and the hardest hit areas. Veracruz was a disaster. Everywhere you looked was covered with water, some places the water so high it crested the rooftops of some homes. With the help of a few local fishermen, they made their way through flooded streets to where Juan, Maria, and Luiz were sheltered, along with several hundred other locals. A very large Catholic church on the mountaintop, it could be seen for miles in all directions.

Frank recognized Juan and Maria from the news broadcast when he walked through the door, but there was no sign of Luiz anywhere.

"Juan y Maria De La Cruz?" Frank introduced himself in the best Spanish he could muster. "I am Frank Griffin III, and this is Senator Bradley Stevens from Houston, Texas," Frank said politely struggling with his Spanish.

"Cómo puedo ayudar le… Necesitas algo?" Juan said too quickly for Frank to understand.

Frank pulled out an English to Spanish dictionary "We saw the devastation that the flood had in your area"—Frank pointed at the book and made a lot of hand gestures—"and what you are trying to do is good." Frank went on and on, but Juan and Maria did not understand.

"Tengo amigos, that would like to help you rebuild, ajudar le," Frank continued. "Bradley, do we have a translator anywhere around?" Frank asked.

Juan was busy handing out care packages to some of the villagers and did not understand what Frank was trying to say.

"Does anyone speak English?" the senator called out.

A young lady walked up. "I am a teacher at the university. I speak English," the young lady said politely.

"Great," the Senator said, walking back over to Frank who was a little frustrated. "Tell Juan that I would like to help him and Maria." Frank looked at Juan when she translated.

Juan put down the bags and walked over to Frank and the senator. Frank explained through the translator that he was willing to help Juan and Maria rebuild their business, that he thought it was a wonderful thing he and his family were doing for their community.

One of the local farmers interrupted and said something quietly to Maria. Maria immediately fell to her knees crying out.

"Papa...my papa esta Muerto," she cried out.

"What happened?" Frank asked with concern.

The farmer told her that Señor Fernandez (her dad) had a bad accident on the farm trying to save one of the cows that got stuck in a drainage ditch, that when the lightning struck, the cow spooked and trampled Señor Fernandez.

The sun finally came out the next day, and over the next week, the floodwaters slowly receded. The spirits were high once again all over town, except at the Fernandez family where they were making arrangements to bury Maria's papa, their head of household.

Tom Fitzgerald arrived that week with several heads of cattle, bulls, and a few pigs. The senator contacted the 4H club of Texas and arranged for a group of students and their teachers to help plant and harvest for the next several years. Juan Maria and Luiz, along with Frank and the senator help from other prominent businessmen, purchased the Fernandez and the De La Cruz farms as part of a farmers co-op. Over the next several months, they built a modern and more efficient processing center, one that included a packaging department for a majority of the goods and services. The new company would be called the JML Corporation with its first three board members, Frank G. Griffin III, Senator Bradley K. Stevens, and Tom Fitzgerald.

CHAPTER 7

Present day

Rex got the message from his father and returned to Santa Anna to help Juan with the investigation. Pulling up to the ultramodern JML Corporation was almost unrecognizable till he spotted the old tractor and plow from the old farm. Rex remembered the days, weeks, and sometimes months he and his brother spent working on the farm, plowing, milking cows, and feeding animals.

Rex never seemed to change much, except for the few extra pounds of muscle that he added to his frame. Rex looked over and almost didn't recognize the little girl, at least that is what she was when he last saw her ten years ago. Gabriella had grown up to be a very lovely woman.

Rex apologized for not making it to Luiz's funeral but promised that he would find out what happened and who killed his brother. Juan took out the package that Lupe gave him before he was murdered and spread it out across the table. The flight logs showed regular flights, along established routes into Central and South America with several of them circled throughout the month. Flight no. GC-2156 a daily flight out of Mexico City, Mexico, to Bogotá, Colombia. There were standard invoices and custom forms, nothing unusual for Luiz, he was after all one of the CEOs and the head of the transportation department. What was unusual was the 5.56 mm shell casings found near the body, the piece of paper with a bunch of roman numerals across it (III I-III-II IIIII-II), and the microchip.

Rex thought back to his CIA days, the agency, and the resources he had at his disposal. This crime could have been solved in no time, but with the way the federales and the local law enforcement agencies were treating this, Rex would have to do this on his own or off the books as the agency would say.

Rex, at five feet eleven tall, 195 pounds, former Navy SEAL and Delta Force team member, later recruited into the CIA. With proficiency in the martial arts—jujitsu, kempō, krav maga—had a very special set of fighting skills that you would rarely find in any one individual. But investigating crimes and playing with computers were not among them. Rex knew he needed the help of some old associates from his CIA days with the investigative skills he lacked.

The next morning, Rex headed out to the last known location of his old buddy, the northern shores of Scotland near Aberdeen, took some poking around, but he eventually found him, some twenty miles out on the North Sea, aboard an old fishing boat. Milton "Milty" Bishop, a decorated RAF pilot (Ret), Scotland Yard Chief Inspector (Ret), CEO of a private security firm (Ret), fluent in three languages—Spanish, French, and German—a bit of a recluse if you ask me…no phone, TV, or even a radio. Milton, a Brit by birth, but you would never know it by the way he sounded. Scottish, definitely Scottish. Milton was a graying old man in his late sixties, tall and lanky at six feet seven tall, 180 pounds.

Rex had no easy or direct way of reaching him, accept to go out, and physically get him.

Rex called on an old buddy that flew helicopters for Her Majesty's Royal Coast Guard Sir. William "Billy" Buchanan, stationed at Aberdeen station.

"Billy, this is Rex," the phone crackled a bit.

"What can I do for you, Rex?" Billy responded.

"I have to find the old man. Do you know where he is?" Rex asked.

"Well, sure I do… I wouldn't be doing my job if I didn't. I always know where he is…even if he doesn't want me to," Billy responded. "The old man's fishing. You know he hates visitors when he's fishing," Billy cautioned him.

"I have to get him. Can you give me a lift?" Rex asked.

"Suit up. I will see you on the pad in ten minutes."

Rex arrived a little passed one in the afternoon at Her Majesty's Royal Coast Guard Station at Aberdeen, where Billy flew the AW139 search-and-rescue helicopter. Rex jumped into an all-blue jumpsuit and waited for Billy to arrive.

Rex hopped on board the red-and-white Helo and plugged into the headset.

"Welcome aboard, Rex. This is Marie Masterson, medic and gunner."

Billy said, "She will be joining us on this op."

"Hi, what do you do? Shoot them first and then patch them up?" Rex laughed as Marie manned the .50 caliber machine gun hanging out the side door.

Milton's fishing boat was about ten nautical miles northeast of their location.

"I see you had no trouble finding him," Rex said over the intercom.

"We have been keeping an eye on him the whole time," Billy responded.

"Don't let the old man find out, he might hunt you down," Rex said laughing.

Billy did a quick flyby and spotted the old man sleeping in the rooster's nest. When he came around, the second time a little slower, a shot went off hitting the side of the Helo.

"Damn," Billy called out pulling away from the vessel in an evasive maneuver.

Marie immediately jumped on the .50 caliber standard procedure for any weapons fire.

The second pass was a little slower as they approached. "Milton, it's Rex," blared out over the helicopters loud speaker.

Another shot was fired just missing the Helo.

"Milton, knock it off. It's Rex," Rex yelled over the loudspeaker, waving his hands frantically at his friend. "May we aboard?" Rex asked.

"I told you this was not a good idea," Billy said circling the craft.

"Just hover above the deck, I'll jump," Rex called out to Billy, pointing at the tiny deck.

"Thanks for the ride." Rex slapped Marie on the back then jumped to the tiny deck below.

"Crazy American," Marie said giving him the thumbs up as the Helo pulled away.

"Rex, ole boy, how have ya been?" Milton asked in a half Scottish and English accent. He just loved the sound of that Scottish accent, didn't always understand it but loved it anyways.

"Just great. Now lower that gun before you shoot someone's eye out and give me a hug," Rex opened his arms wide.

"So how's the agency been treating ya?" Milty asked.

"I left a year ago, all freelance now. I see you finally retired," Rex said looking around the boat and the open sea.

"Not my doing, lad. They trying to get rid of us old ones, ya see," Milton gruffled loudly.

Milton, a retired RAF combat pilot and former Scotland yard inspector before joining the CIA as an operative, was forced to retire due to cutbacks.

"I have a job for you if you are not too busy, playing with the fishies." Rex laughed.

"Let me check." Milton looked at the boat and then back at Rex. "I am freeee," Milton said. "This retirement gig is not for me. What ya have in mind, laddie?"

"I need a chief inspector," Rex said. "Look into a murder possible conspiracy case. You up for it?"

"A CIA gig?" Milton asked.

"No, off the books…and doesn't pay as well could get a little dicey," Rex told him.

"I love it. Wouldn't have it any other way," Milton agreed. "And I won't be need'n the money," Milton responded looking around the boat.

"I'll book you the next flight to Veracruz," Rex told him.

"Veracruz, Mexico? Nice and hot. I'll bring my beachwear and tanning lotion," Milton said sarcastically. "Hey, will the lassie be joining us?" Milton perked up.

"What would a black op be without her?" Rex said punching him in the arm hoping she would agree since he hadn't asked her yet.

"Good lad. Now go on, raise the anchor," the ship captain commanded.

Rex landed at Fort Bragg, North Carolina, that next morning and headed for the special operations department. Rex thought about calling her about this mission but figured "she could not hang up on him if he was standing in her office." Rex walked through the main lobby and registered as a special guest. "Special guest always got the VIP treatment," Rex told himself smiling hoping for the best.

It had been a few years since Rex had actually seen this particular fiery redhead, standing at five feet two, and about all of 105 pounds, the guys at the CIA called her the "fireplug." A wiz kid when it came to computers, a graduate at MIT with a major in computer science she could crack any code imaginable, everyone except one, the uncrackable code at the CIA HQ in Virginia. Trust me, if anyone could do it, she could.

Capt. Jennifer "Fireplug" Campbell reviewed the visitors and special guest list for that day's tours and stopped suddenly at a familiar name, Rex Nelson. Immediately, her blood pressure shot up. Let's just say the two have not had a great history. Out in the lobby, all the VIPs or other special guest enjoyed a light snack of doughnuts, bagels, and coffee before their tour.

Rex was approached by two armed Marines. "Put down your bagel and coffee, sir, and come with us," the Marine Sergeant ordered.

"Is there a problem?" a high-ranking VIP asked.

"Sure it's just a misunderstanding," Rex said as he was dragged away.

"We have it all under control, sir. Enjoy your visit," the Marine Sergeant said, escorting Rex down the hall to a unmarked elevator.

"Get in, sir," the sergeant ordered.

"I'm sure there must be an explanation for all this," Rex offered.

The three of them got in the elevator and proceeded to the sub-basement of the building, two stories down.

The doors opened, on the wall was a big sign that read, training center, and men's locker room. Rex was pushed down the hall to the men's locker room.

"Get dressed, sir, then report to the main gymnasium," the sergeant stood guard just outside the door. Rex was handed a gray T-shirt with the army logo written in black across the chest, white gym shorts, tennis shoes, white socks, and most importantly an "athletic supporter," then told to report to the main gymnasium ASAP and wait for further instructions. Rex stepped out into the hallway, started walking toward the elevators when a Marine called out, "This way sir."

The Marine escorted Rex to the gymnasium where he was joined by four other Marines, similarly dressed standing at attention around a large mat.

Captain Jillian "Fireball" Campbell walked in flanked by two armed Marines at her side. The captain was wearing a pair of black pants, green T-shirt tied at the back, white socks, and white sneakers. She stepped in to the middle of the mat and looked at Rex.

"So, Rex, what brings you to Fort Bragg, North Carolina?" she asked pointing at the first Marine, who attacked with a right cross. She, blocked with a left forearm, stepped passed him on the left swept his leg, grabbed him by the throat, and slammed him to the ground.

"What's with the heavy security?" Rex asked, admiring her very nice technique. "That's a base regulation. It states that the commanding officer will have an armed security detail present at all times." Like if that was ever necessary, Jillian was very capable of taking care of herself. Would not be surprised if she trained them herself. She pointed at the second and third Marines who attacked her from two different directions.

She stepped toward the closest Marine, closing the gap, who was charging fast, then stepped out of the way at the last second, grabbing him by the wrist as he flew by. With a quick change of direction, she flipped the Marine into the other as he approached. With a firm wrist lock, she controlled the Marine's direction using him as a human shield, winging him back and forth. The second Marine, a little frustrated, walked straight into a full front kick, doubling him over. Jillian, pointed at the last Marine who was a little confused about how to attack, hesitated and never saw the round house followed by a spinning back kick.

"Well, Rex, you never answered me. What brings you to Fort Bragg?" she asked hooking her leg around the Marine's arm twisting it like a pretzel.

"I need a favor?" Rex asked quietly.

"What was that? I did not hear you right. You need a favor!" Jillian said as she paired up the Marines to work on their fighting skills. "Why would I do you a favor, Rex?" Jillian asked.

"Well, because you are my friend, my buddy, my pal," Rex said with a half grin.

"Really? I haven't spoken with you in over three years. Why should I be your pal now?" Jillian said pointing at him to engage.

"What is this?" Rex asked trotting around the mat.

"My disciplinary method for dealing with misbehaving young men," she said shadowing his every move.

"So what did they do?" Rex asked juking in and out.

"Two were smoking in the head…the other two were late for chow," she said moving back and forth.

"I take it. This is my disciplinary session?" Rex asked as she advanced, quickly kicking him in the groin. Rex grunted and fell to one knee.

"Yup, I see you are not wearing your recommended safety gear as instructed," Jillian said grinning slightly.

"I didn't think I needed it."

"Now that's what you were supposed to do three years ago with a ring in your hand," Jillian said attempting a spinning heel kick to his head.

Rex ducked and rolled back to his feet.

"But you chose to walk out in the middle of the night like a coward," Jillian said moving in with several rapid hand strikes that Rex expertly blocked.

"You know why I left," Rex countered with a front kick and a step behind side kick, knocking Jillian back off the mat. "I had a mission…an undercover mission," Rex said as the petite redhead ran straight ahead with two crescent kicks and a spinning back kick, knocking Rex off his feet.

"You certainly were undercover, Rex. Did you have to get her pregnant?" she said with a devastating stomp that just missed Rex's head.

"That was unexpected," Rex said sweeping her leg out from under her, mounting and pinning her to the mat.

"So what happened to her, Rex? Did she have your baby?" She kicked Rex in the hip, flipping him over reversing the position.

"No, she was killed in a freak car accident. They both died," Jack mumbled and remembered the accident like it was yesterday. "The undercover mission was over. I was pronounced dead and had to go dark and into hiding," Rex said quietly as his eyes drifted away.

Jillian just sat there for a few minutes.

"So, Rex, why are you here?" Jillian asked getting to her feet.

"I need your help. I need to get the old team back together," Rex said standing up.

"What team? The CIA covert team?" she said looking at him strangely, wondering if he was serious.

"Yes, that one. The only team that I trust," Rex said wondering if it was even possible.

"So what's the mission…and why that team?" she asked.

"My father asked me if I could look into the mysterious death of an old friend of the family in Mexico," Rex explained. "Remember when we were kids, I told you about the trip my brother and I took to Mexico. When we helped that family during the floods. Luiz, Juan's brother, was killed. I believe he was murdered," Rex explained. "The Mexican federales are not investigating the case and are covering something up. I need your help and can't do it without you," Rex went on.

"So let me get this straight. After all these years, you want to get the old CIA/covert ops team together to investigate the case?" Jillian said enthusiastically. "And you need my help…and can't do it without me?" Jillian smiled. "I'm in."

"Okay, hold on…it's not sanctioned by the agency," Rex said cautiously. "Totally off the books and could get a little hairy…"

"Yup, I got that… I'm still in," she said.

"The pay is not that great either, like nothing," Rex said as they headed for the door.

"Well, Rex, what can I say…you were always a cheapskate," Jillian said punching him in the gut. "I have some leave time built up on the books. It will be fun," Jillian said.

"What about the rest of the team… Have you told them yet? Milty, Specks, and Buster?" Jillian asked enthusiastically.

"Milty, yes…but I haven't found the rest," Rex said.

"When do we leave?" Jillian asked as they headed for the showers. "Milton is on his way to Veracruz, Mexico, and should be there in the morning… I could use your help finding the others," Jack said with a perplexed look on his face. "Does this mean I don't get my guided tour?" Rex said with a sigh.

"You just got it. Dismissed…" she yelled back to the four Marines.

CHAPTER 8

Past

Over the next several years after the floods, JML Corporation grew by leaps and bounds. With its new headquarters located in Veracruz and the new modernized agriculture and livestock processing center in Santa Anna, JML Corporation was able to open larger warehouses and distribution centers in the larger cities like Monterrey and border towns of Nuevo Laredo and Reynosa. JML Corporation with the large warehouses, trucks, and well-established routes were prime targets for the small Mexican gangs and drug smugglers looking to move drugs and contraband across the border into the USA from Colombia and Central America. Luiz would get regular phone calls from his drivers being harassed or delayed by these thugs. One night, he got a phone call from Pepe.

"Luiz, it's Pepe. Are you there?" Pepe sounded horrified.

"Yes, Pepe, I am here," Luiz responded.

"Luiz, they went to my house and threatened to kill my wife and kids if I didn't drive the drugs across the border," Pepe cried on the phone in fear for his life.

Northern Mexico especially Nuevo Laredo was the focal point for all of Latin America for drugs and other contraband to be smuggled across the border into the USA. Luiz spent a lot of time and money protecting his drivers against these gangs, but every day, he would get calls from his drivers.

"Pepe, who threatened you?" Luiz asked in a pissed-off tone of voice.

"Rico and one of his men here in Nuevo Laredo," Pepe said. "I can't keep driving. My family is too important to me," Pepe continued.

"Pepe, calm down. I will take care of this," Luiz assured him.

Mexican gangs would transport heroin from Colombian drug cartels across the border into the USA and got paid 30 to 50 percent profit on any and all the merchandise that got sold across the border by any means possible, busses, trains, cars, and even human mules.

The trucks from the JML Corporation were large and could carry bigger loads, making them prime targets. Over the years, Luiz has had many encounters with these gangs, usually a fight would break out, and the two parties would go their own ways, but in recent years, the gangs have become bolder, resorting to extreme violence, robbery, hijacking, and even kidnapping of family members for ransom and other favors. With Pepe and his family, it was the last straw for Luiz, he'd had enough.

Luiz and Pepe walked into a small bar on border town of Nuevo Laredo.

"Where is the man named *Rico*?" Luiz asked the bartender.

"Over there," the bartender pointed as several men at the bar started to stir.

Luiz walked over to the man's table, plopped his beer on the table. "Are you *Rico*?" Luiz asked.

"Who wants to know?" the man looked at Luiz and grinned.

"Luiz De La Cruz," Luiz said as he pushed the table against the man pinning him to the wall. "Are you *Rico*?" Luiz repeated the question a little louder.

"Yes, the name's Rico," the man said gasping for breath.

"I own the trucks that you and your men keep on stopping and harassing. Who do you work for?" Luiz demanded as he shoved the table harder against the man. "Who do you work for?" Luiz asked a little louder.

The man grunted and finally broke. "Rodrigo Campos," he mumbled.

"Where is this Rodrigo Campos?" Luiz kept the pressure on the table. "Where does he live?" Luiz shouted.

"The hacienda on Second Avenue," Rico said as Luiz smashed the half-empty mug of beer over the man's head, knocking him out.

Rodrigo Campos was a local drug lord that lived in a modest home a few blocks from the bar with a perimeter fence and two security guards at the front gate. Luiz pulled up to the gate and demanded to see Rodrigo Campos.

"Donde esta Rodrigo Campos," Luiz yelled at the guard.

"Vaya se…" the guard said pushing Luiz away.

Luiz stepped back and bull rushed the guard, tackling him to the ground.

The other guard noticed the commotion and rushed over, gun drawn, about to shoot.

"Para," the man yelled from the porch. "Stop right now," Señor Campos repeated as he approached the fighting men. "Holla, Luiz," Campos said extending his hand as if he knew him.

Luiz shook the man's hand and wondered how he knew his name. Señor Campos invited Pepe and Luiz into the house, offered them a drink, and led them to his office.

"What can I do for you, Luiz?" the man asked as they sat comfortably in a fancy leather chair.

"How do you know my name?" Luiz asked.

"I know everything about you, your brother Juan, and his lovely wife, Maria, the new baby Gabriella, the corporation, everything," Rodrigo said handing Luiz a hand rolled Cuban cigar.

Luiz was not a refined man. The cigar, the fancy drinks meant nothing to him. Luiz looked at the cigar and left it on the table.

"So what brings you so far north, my friend?" Rodrigo asked.

"I got a call from the US Border Patrol about one of my trucks transporting illegal contraband across the border, and it cost me a lot of money to get it back," Luiz explained.

"I don't understand what that has to do with me, Luiz," Campos said leaning back into his chair.

"Well, it was Pepe's truck that was hijacked and forced to drive across the border, transporting your drugs," Luiz said angrily. "And… when he refused, his family was threatened by your men…threatened to kill his wife and kids," Luiz said leaning in over the table.

"Some of my men you say…a misunderstanding, I assure you" Rodrigo said. "Who threatened you?" he asked.

"A man named Rico and his men," Pepe said. "He's at the bar now."

"I asked him who he worked for. He told me you…Señor Campos," Luiz said raising his voice.

"Aah…Rico…ehh?" Campos turned, picked up the phone, and made a call.

"Rico does not work for me, you understand?" Campos said as the gate guard called.

"Señor Campos…it's Rico."

"Let him in," Señor Campos said, sitting comfortably at his desk. "Rico, come in," Campos invited him to have a seat directly in front of him next to Luiz and Pepe.

"So tell me, Rico. Do you know these men?" Campos asked.

"No, Señor," Rico said as his voice trembled as the sweat beaded up on his forehead.

"They just told me a very interesting story. Sure you don't know them?" Campos asked looking directly at him.

"No, sir. I don't know them, Señor." Rico squirmed in his seat.

"Luiz here said that you threatened Pepe, his wife, and kids." Señor Campos waited for an answer.

"No, Señor Campos…not me," Rico said.

"So you did not hijack Pepe's truck and force him across the US border to sell illegal drugs?" Señor Campos said.

"No, Señor…not me…you told us to stay away," Rico told him shaking his head back and forth.

"Exactly," Campos said. "Pepe said that it was you…and you even threatened his wife and kids." Campos stopped and looked at Rico then back at Pepe.

"No, Señor, that was not me," Rico repeated it several times.

Campos reached over and picked up the phone.

"Si, gracias," Campos said.

Suddenly, Luiz pulled out his .45 and shot Rico in the head.

The security guards came rushing in, and Señor Campos quickly called them off, then sat back in his leather chair and laughed out loud. Luiz looked at him then back at Rico with a hole in his head and started laughing.

"Why did you do that?" Campos asked.

"Too many lies," Luiz said, lowering his gun.

"I know, but I was going to do it," Campos said putting the gun on the table. "Why exactly?" Campos asked.

"He was weak and a liar. Just kept lying to your face," Luiz said.

"Who was on the phone?" Luiz asked.

"My friend at the US Border," Campos said. "It was Rico." Campos sat back and laughed louder than before it could be heard throughout the whole house. Pepe just sat there staring at Rico in the chair.

"You knew all along?" Luiz said.

"I told you… We know everything about you. We have been keeping an eye on you for some time now," Campos explained.

"Who is we?" Luiz said as he got up and started to walk away.

"Hold on, Luiz…the syndicate…could use a guy like you. Someone not afraid to make a decision and take chances," Campos continued.

"The syndicate… What is the syndicate?" Luiz asked.

"This is…this is a small part of the syndicate… Do you like this house?" Campos asked.

"Yes, very nice," Luiz said.

"This could be your house, the servants, the guards," Campos told him.

"This house? I could never afford it," Luiz said turning away.

"You could have it…working for me…" Campos said. "I see how they treat you at the corporation. Sometimes it's like your opinions don't matter." Campos turned and looked at Luiz.

"How do you know these things…how I've been treated?" Luiz asked.

"The syndicate knows everything," Campos said.

"It's yours."

"What?" Luiz said.

"This house… I know that when Juan and Maria got married, Juan bought that nice house for himself. You were left in the mini apartment at the warehouse. Of course, we can have it cleaned up, but everything here is yours," Campos told him.

"What would I have to do?" Luiz asked looking around the lovely home.

"Keep the trucks moving, making your regular deliveries."

"What about Pepe?" Luiz interrupted.

"Keep driving without any harassment from any gangs," Campos continued.

"We will add other routes…and as the corporation grows, we will expand internationally. I'll take care of the rest."

Several days later in a small cantina on the US-Mexico border, near the town of Nuevo Laredo, the cantina was a split right down the middle, half on the US side and half in Mexico. You could literally have tacos in Mexico, then walk across the room and have a banana split in the USA. It was the only bar with a bartender that doubled as a border agent. Luiz and Señor Campos sat at a table on the Mexican side. From the far side of the room, a tall lanky man walked in with several armed security guards.

"Rodrigo, quien es este hombre, un hombre muy importante." Luiz laughed a little but stopped when he recognized the man. "El Senator," Luiz told Campos. "This was the man that came to Mexico several years ago and helped us rebuild the corporation… A board member at JML Corporation."

"So you remember me?" the senator said to Luiz.

"Si, Señor Bradley K. Stevens, senator from Texas," Luiz said.

"Rodrigo told me that you are not happy with the way things are being run in Mexico, too many delays and threats from the Mexican gangs, your drivers, and their families are being harassed," the senator said "Hopefully, Rodrigo told you that I can make things better for you and the corporation," the senator said. "Do you like the house? the senator asked Luiz.

"Yes, of course," Luiz told him.

"It's yours, with all the cars and the servants too. Rodrigo will help you get settled in," the senator said.

"But, Señor…like I told Rodrigo…I am not sure what you want me to do?" Luiz looked at him.

"Ha, ha, ha, ha, ha. Well, Rico is dead. You will take over for him as one of my guys," the senator laughed.

"He was weak and a liar," Luiz said pounding on the table.

"Then he deserved what he got," the senator agreed.

Luiz gladly shook his hand.

Rodrigo and the senator did as they promised. With their contacts and influences in several countries, JML Corporation expanded into the international market, opening routes into several nearby countries like Colombia, Venezuela, and the United States of America. Juan was excited about the expansion of the corporation but also a little cautious, a little too cautious for Luiz. The two brothers fought and had several heated arguments about how fast the corporation was growing. Juan was all about wanting to save money, but Luiz was excited about the growth, moving lots of merchandise to the new international market. Luiz assured him that he had it all under control, with the help of Rodrigo and Senator Stevens. Several months later, they acquired a small airline cargo company—General Cargo Direct that flew out of the airport in Mexico City. With the new airline, they were able to set up distribution warehouses in Medellin, Colombia, and Caracas, Venezuela. Luiz was on top of the world over the next couple of years. Luiz was having regular meetings at the house with visitors from several countries, powerful and important people in the import and export business. Luiz was not happy when the JML Corporation got involved with more contraband merchandise than agricultural products.

One summer, during a very large gun-walking probe, the ATF along with the US Border Patrol monitored a large cache of weapons firearms these included AK-47 variants, Barrett .50 caliber sniper rifles, .38 caliber revolvers, the FN Five-sevens, antiaircraft machine gun, grenade launchers, and military-grade weapons difficult to obtain legally in the United States.

The ATF and the US government spearheaded several sting operations into the trafficking of weapons to high-level traffickers, a project intended to stem the flow of firearms into Mexico. The stated goal of allowing these purchases was to track the firearms as they were transferred to higher-level traffickers and key figures in the Mexican cartels. US Border Patrol agents were paid off by the senator, and elaborate schedules were set up for them to look the other way.

Luiz was saddened to hear of the death of Rex's brother, United States Border Patrol Agent Ben Griffin, who questioned the tactics during the operation, where the guns were tracked by the ATF had been found at crime scenes on both sides of Mexico-United States border estimated that more than two hundred Mexicans were killed by guns linked to the botched operation was shot and killed. The ensuing investigation got swept under the rug. As a result of the dispute over the release of the justice department documents related to the scandal, members of the cabinet were held in contempt. The sitting president invoked executive privilege in order to withhold documents relating to the incident. Most of the weapons were never recovered, and Ben's murder went unsolved.

CHAPTER 9

Present day

Rex and Jillian met up with Milton in Veracruz at the corporate headquarters for the JML Corporation. Juan gave them the plastic bag that Lupe handed to him just before he was killed. Inside the plastic bag were standard invoices, custom forms, transportation logs from JML Corporation with the flight no. CD-2156, a daily flight out of Mexico City, Mexico, to Bogotá, Colombia, circled on it, nothing unusual for Luiz, he was after all one of the CEOs and the head of the transportation department officer after all. What was unusual was the 5.56 mm shell casings found near the body with no markings on them, the piece of paper with a bunch of roman numerals across it (III I-III-II IIIII-II IIII-I II II-II-III), and the microchip.

Rex, Milton, and Jillian headed to Mexico City where they met JML's Corporation logistics officer Pedro Garcia at the main warehouse, a small skinny man with tiny thick-rimmed glasses that perched off the end of his nose.

"Holla, me Llamo Jillian Campbell. Soy empleada...shit," she said in frustration. "Do you hablo ingles?" she asked reaching out to shake his hand.

"Why yes, English, Spanish, French, German, and several African dialects," he said smugly waving off the hand shake with a wave of his hand. Pedro studied English at the University of Texas in Austin, Texas.

"How can I help you?" he asked impatiently looking over the end of his clipboard. "What can you tell about this number 2156?" Jillian asked.

"Nothing," Pedro answered pushing his glasses up the bridge of his nose.

Jillian looked at him, wanting to slap the smugness off his face. "2156," Jillian repeated pointing at it on the schedule.

"What is this?" Pedro snapped. "What do you have there?" Pedro reached over to grab the paper from Jillian's hand. She slapped his hand away and repointed at the number.

"It does not exist," Pedro said without looking. Pedro kept meticulous records for a warehouse of over a million square feet, and with a photographic memory, he knew when and where every shipment came in or out of the warehouse.

"Why are you asking about that number?" Pedro asked.

"It was circled on a bloodstained piece of paper we found on Luiz De La Cruz's body when he was murdered," Jillian told him.

"Señor Luiz estas muerto." Pedro's face turned ashen. "Muerto Señor Luiz," Pedro repeated it over and over again.

"So why was that number circled?" Milton asked. "Did it get shipped to Colombia?"

"No, no, no, that number does not exist," Pedro insisted shaking his head back and forth, looking at the number carefully.

"We show that it was received in Colombia a few days ago," Jillian told him, pointing at the flight.

"No, no, no…" Pedro shook his head back and forth. "That is the flight number. Invoice GCI-2256…right here in the computer and all the merchandise and invoices accounted for shipped to Colombia," Pedro insisted.

"I need a full print out of the file?" Milton said.

"I gave it to Señor Luiz last week," Pedro said.

"What did you give to Luiz?" Jillian asked.

"A microdrive," Pedro said.

"What was on it?" Milton asked.

"I don't know… Señor Luiz moved some files. I loaded it and then erased it," Pedro said.

47

"What computer did you use?" Jillian asked.

Pedro pointed at the computer station. Jillian jumped on the computer and tapped a few keys. "I told you. I erased the file," Pedro smirked.

"Password protected. What is your password?" Jillian asked staring at him.

"Don't worry she will find it...give her the password," Milton ordered.

Jillian pulled out a small thumb drive and plugged it in. "Let this run... I'll be back to get it," Jillian told him.

"How did Señor Luiz die?" Pedro asked.

"He was ambushed in his car, murdered in Veracruz," Milton said.

"The cartel. It was the cartel," Pedro repeated several times.

"No, he was shot up...not the regular MO for a cartel hit," Milton told him.

"Jillian...how long for the file?" Milton asked.

"Not sure, it's in there somewhere," Jillian said running a few more programs.

"Señor Luiz murdered by the cartel...for the microdrive?" Pedro mumbled to himself. "Señor Luiz dead...the Cartel." Pedro threw his hands up in the air. Pedro was terrified of the cartel and all the bad things they do to people. "No, no, no. The cartel will kill me, torture me, and cut my throat," Pedro said truly terrified of the cartels.

"Pedro, listen... I need a copy of that file," Jillian said again.

"One hour." Pedro walked away mumbling.

"Keep this running. I'll be back in an hour to get it," Jillian said. Jillian and Milton returned to the car.

"What did you find out?" Rex asked.

"Pedro gave Luiz the microdrive last week and a copy of some files, but he's terrified that the cartel is going to kill him."

"The cartel," Rex said.

"He's convinced that the cartel killed Luiz and will kill him for saying anything."

Milton jumped into the car. "We can come back later after he's had time to calm down. I have an inquiry program running to locate the lost file," Jillian said.

They headed to the nearby airport terminal used by JML Corporation for all of their cargo needs. They spoke with the tower and some of the ground crew, and they all confirmed that flight CD-2156 was the regular flight to Bogotá, Colombia, from Mexico City.

A nearby flight crew member who was close enough to hear the conversation gave Jillian a strange look, then walked away quickly. Jillian looked up at Milton; without a single word, Milton knew what she was thinking. Milton followed the pilot down the hall to a steel door a sign that read, "Restricted Area." Milton quickly looked around the terminal where there was a couple of pilots chatting up a few ladies at the bar.

"A pint of Guinness," Milton called out as he strutted up to the bar, then casually bumped the pilot next to him. Jillian looked over at him strangely.

Fine time for a pint, Jillian thought wondering why he did not follow the pilot.

"Sorry, mate," Milton apologized for his clumsiness.

Jillian casually walked by wondering what he was up to till she spotted the slide of hand.

Milton quickly downed his beer and headed to the steel door, flashed the badge, and entered. A quick look around, there was no sign of the pilot. Milton walked through the mini-lounge with a TV, couple of small offices with computer terminals, still no pilot. At the far end was a double glass door leading into the next room. Milton pushed the door open and peeked inside. There were shower stalls and several rows of lockers. The pilot was showering but left his locker open and unlocked.

Trusting fellow, Milton thought to himself as he sat down in front of it.

The door opened and closed behind him. Two pilots walked in. One sat down a couple of lockers down from him, the other headed for the head. Milton nodded his head and slowly fumbled through the locker. There was a change of clothes, shirts, shoes, and a flight bag.

"Are you a pilot with General Cargo Direct?" the pilot next to him asked.

"Why, yes," Milton said as he casually looked over the schedule book and slipped it into his jacket pocket. "Just came in this morning heading to Colombia later tonight," Milton said casually.

The pilot looked at him strangely, got up, and headed quickly for the door.

Must have been something I said, Milton thought as he reached in his pocket and pulled out a small rubber mallet used by every British bobby for over hundred years, then thumped him on the back of the head. Milton sat him in a lounge chair in front of the tele with a newspaper in his lap. Milton returned just in time as the showering pilot returned to his locker. Milton quickly grabbed his credentials, logbook, and flight bag of the sleeping pilot and exited the secured area. Milton returned to the bar.

"Thought I would have to go in after you," Jillian said giggling at how short his trousers were.

"Are you planning on flying somewhere?" Rex asked.

Milton smiled then handed the schedule books over to Jillian who compared them to the company schedule. Flight CD-2156 was in both of their flight logs, a flight that the airport said was the regular flight to Bogotá, Colombia. Rex stayed at the airport and searched through the pilot's bags for any clues.

"Why was the pilot so jumpy?" Milton wondered as he and Jillian headed back to the warehouse in Mexico City to get the information from Pedro.

Pulling up to the front entrance of the warehouse, they noticed a considerable police presence and were stopped at the gate.

"Hola, tenemos que hablar con Pedro García," Jillian said very slowly in Spanish but immediately was waved off by the federales. "Hablar con Pedro García," Jillian repeated.

Again, she was waved off by the federales. There were several employees milling around, and Milton tried to speak with a couple of them, but they all were terrified of someone or something and refused to talk. Milton drove around back of the warehouse that was also blocked by the federales.

"I have an idea...pullover," Jillian said.

"That's what I like to hear," Milton said as they parked near the warehouse in an adjacent driveway. "What's the plan?" Milton asked as Jillian got out and popped the trunk, pulled out a blue cap, and a bright yellow vest. "Aha," Milton said, shaking his head in agreement.

From a distance, she looked just like the policia. She walked up to one of the guards on the perimeter.

"Donde esta El Capitan?" she said with authority.

The guard smiled and pointed toward the creek running behind the warehouse. She leaned over the bridge for a closer look—nothing.

"Hey, que paso?" Jillian called out to the lieutenant who appeared to be in charge.

"El gerente está muerto," he said.

She nodded pretending to understand what he had said. She figured somebody was muerto or dead.

"El cuerpo?" Jillian held up both hands, palms up.

"Ambulancia," the lieutenant said, pointing in the opposite direction.

Jillian walked over to the ambulance and knocked on the driver's side window, startling the young ambulance driver.

"Abrir," she barked in her best Spanish.

The ambulance driver, a young man fresh out of medical school, walked behind the bus and opened the doors. Jillian jumped in acting real official like, waved him away, and pulled back the white sheet—Pedro Garcia. Now she understood what a "gerente" was as she looked at the nearly decapitated body of Pedro Garcia, the manager. This did not look like the work of the cartel. They would never use a garrote. Jillian noticed his right two fingers were burned and twisted slightly. *Wonder what would cause that?* she wondered as she looked up and spotted the police lieutenant walking quickly toward the ambulance.

Jillian had to think of something fast. She knocked on the inside window and smiled at the young driver, then whispered something in his ear. Seconds before the lieutenant arrived, he jumped out and asked the lieutenant a bunch of useless questions, giving Jillian time to get away.

"Donde esta la mujer?" the lieutenant barked.

"Mujer, no mujer," the young man said.

The lieutenant opened the back of the ambulance and inspected it for himself. The young man looked off into the distance, spotted Jillian at the edge of the tree line, blowing him a kiss.

Jillian doubled back to Pedro's office. The computer was still on, and her thumb drive was still plugged in. Jillian punched a few keys and pulled up the history—"nothing." The computer was wiped clean. Jillian grabbed the thumb drive and returned to the car.

"So what happened?" Milton asked.

"Somebody killed him with a garrote," she said jumping into the car. "They wiped his computer too," Jillian said putting on her seat belt.

"The cartel?" Milton asked.

"No, this was not a cartel hit," Jillian said as they drove off. "The cartels kill to leave a message, a warning... This is more like a torture than an execution," Jillian paused.

"What? Why would you say that..." Milton punched the accelerator and drove away from the warehouse.

His two fingers on his right hand were twisted and burned, electrical burns I think. Like he was tortured before they killed him, Jillian thought as they headed back to the airport to pick up Rex. Jillian powered up her laptop and popped the thumb drive in. "Damn... it's blank."

A white van pulled up next to them, driving erratically. Jillian turned and made eye contact.

"Milton, I think we are being followed."

Milton punched the accelerator and peeled out, leaving a cloud of burned rubber, changed lanes a couple of times, and turned right down the next intersection.

"I think we lost them," Milton said checking his rear mirrors.

Jillian watched as the white van turned down the road in their direction. "Not yet," Jillian said as Milton punched the accelerator once again.

Two blocks down, Milton turned right, then a quick left down into a residential neighborhood. Two more blocks then another right-hand turn, right again on the next block. When they got back to the main street, the van was only a few cars behind them on a very crowded and busy street.

"Milton, pull up to this restaurant and make a scene," Jillian said. "I'll jump out of the car and double back behind them."

"What kind of scene?" Milton asked.

"I don't know…something to delay them long enough so I can get around the block behind them."

"Got it," Milton said as Jillian got out of the car ran down passed the restaurant to the alleyway. Jillian sprinted down the alley, remembering her college days when she could run the hundred yard dash in eleven seconds flat.

Milton turned the wheel to the right and pulled straight into the parking spot at a ninety-degree angle, then quickly reversed right into oncoming traffic, almost hitting another car. The driver behind him rolled down his window, laid on the horn, and yelled profanities at him. Good thing it was in Spanish because he did not understand a single word he said. Milton turned the wheel back to the left and gunned it, jamming on the breaks a little too late, running into the other parked car in front of him. Milton checked his mirror, and when the man that was shouting profanities tried to pass, Milton gunned it right in front of him, tearing up his radiator.

Milton sat quietly in the car acting all confused as the man approached the car from behind. Milton rolled down his window…

"Oh, my…did I just hit your car?" Milton said whipping the door open, slamming it into the man's knee, then running back to inspect the damage. "Oh my," Milton ran around then speaking loudly in English. The man was outraged, yelling profanities at the old man.

Milton looked up as Jillian had made it around the block, a few cars down from the van. The passenger drew a gun and opened the door. *Thump…thump*…the man disappeared behind the van.

The driver panicked and tried to get out of the blocked right lane and pulled out in front of a minibus that crashed into the driver's side door, blocking it closed. He slid across the seat and opened the passenger door, but Jillian kicked it closed right on his arm, breaking his wrist. Jillian flung the first man on the ground and grabbed the second man by his broken wrist when he fell out of the van.

Milton ran back heroically to help Jillian, followed closely by an obnoxious man yelling obscenities.

"What's with the fan club?" Jillian asked.

"He's mad. He got rear-ended by some old man." Milton smiled sheepishly.

"Hey, knock it off," she yelled at the guy as she walked the other two guys around to the sidewalk. "Milton, you want to give me a hand with these guys?" Jillian asked as she walked them around in a wristlock like a bunch of little kids.

"Oh well, it looks like you got things well in hand. I mean, two hands," Milton said with a grin. They dragged the two men into the nearby alley.

"Why are you following us?" Milton asked the driver.

The driver did not respond but pushed back and attacked Milton. Jillian blocked the strike with her left hand, then hooked his arm with her right arm and hip tossed him to the ground.

"The man asked you a question."

When she turned, the second man was trying to escape. She spun around and kicked the man in the head, knocking him to the ground.

"Wow, where did you learn how to do that?" Milton asked in amazement.

"Detroit," she said smiling.

The two men refused to talk; all they could do was spew profanities. Milton tied the two men to the drain pipe, then gagged them with their own socks.

"Geez, Milton, what did you do to the rental car?" Jillian said as she approached the damaged car. "I hope you have the geriatric parking rider on your insurance policy." Jillian laughed as they drove back to the airport.

CHAPTER 10

Past

Luiz was in his office going over the Northern Mexico routes when his phone rang.

"Señor Luiz...emergencia," Esmeralda yelled frantically into the phone.

"Calma Se... Esmeralda... Que paso?" Luiz asked.

"You have an emergency phone call from Dr. Martin," she said. "Mui importante."

Dr. Ernesto Martin was a local doctor at El Hospital de Santa Maria in Veracruz.

"Gracias, Esmeralda," Luiz said taking the call.

"Dr. Martin...es Luiz."

"Luiz, you need to come to my office at the hospital immediately," the doctor informed him.

"But why? What happened?" Luiz asked.

"Come, come... Better to tell you in person."

Luiz left his office and drove as fast as he could across town to El Hospital. Luiz met Dr. Martin in the lobby.

"Thank you for coming so quickly, Luiz," Dr. Martin said.

"So what's going on?" Luiz asked as the doctor rushed him through the emergency room down the hall to the morgue.

"Luiz, early this morning, a young lady bought in a body, a woman she claimed to be her mother. And with her being a minor, I needed someone to claim the body and confirm her identity."

"Why did you call me?" Luiz looked a little puzzled at the doctor.

"You were named as the next of kin."

"What?"

"Who is this young lady?" Luiz asked.

"Her name is Anna Ramos, and she is sleeping in the next room."

Luiz thought good and hard but had no recollection of any young girl named Anna Ramos.

"Let her sleep for now. Come with me. She doesn't have to be with us for this." Dr. Martin waved his hand.

Who is Anna Ramos? Luiz wondered as they walked down the hallway. Thinking back to all the people he had met over the years, nothing came to mind.

"What was the name on the body?" Luiz asked.

"Natalia Ramos," the doctor told him.

"Natalia?" He reached inside his breast pocket and pulled out his wallet, inside was a small piece of paper with the word "Natalia" written on it and a heart drawn on it.

Could this be the Natalia of his dreams, the one from the barrio? Luiz thought. The vision of her lovely face flashed in his mind.

The doctor led him down a long hallway to a stainless steel elevator, two floors down was the county morgue, the place sent chills down his spine. The double stainless steel doors opened into a very large white sterile room, lined with stainless steel wall lockers. Dr. Martin checked the chart and walked over to no. 5, unlocked it, and rolled out the steel bed. The body was covered from head to toe with a bright white sheet. Luiz could hardly imagine that this could be the woman he met briefly years ago, the woman of his dreams.

"Natalia Ramos," the doctor announced, pulling back the sheet.

Luiz stared at her face, but nothing seemed familiar. She seemed much older looking and heavier, but the spark of his Natalia was not there.

"Can you do me a favor, doctor?" Luiz asked quietly.

"Yes, of course."

"Turn her over on her left side?"

Dr. Martin slowly turned her over on her side.

There it was. Luiz's heart sank as he spotted the little angel on her right shoulder blade. It was Natalia. This was his love of his life… Natalia.

"How did she die?" Luiz asked as a tear ran down his cheek.

"Hit-and-run according to the federales," the doctor said.

"Any eyewitnesses?" Luiz asked.

"Just one, the young lady sleeping upstairs." The doctor covered up Natalia and closed the steel coffin. "When she came in, she was hysterical we had to give her a mild tranquilizer to help her sleep," Dr. Martin said.

Luiz and the doctor returned to the room upstairs where the young lady was sleeping but now awake.

"Hi, my name is Luiz Fernando De La Cruz," Luiz said holding out his hand.

"I know who you are," Anna said shaking his hand lightly. "My mom told me that if anything should happen to her that I should find you," Anna said.

"Your mom?" Luiz said turning toward the morgue then back toward the doctor.

"Yes, my mom…Nathalia Ramos."

Luiz looked at the young lady standing across from him. "Oh… so you are my daughter? I never knew, I never knew. She never told me," he said reaching out to give her a hug.

"She did not want you to know," Anna said quietly. "My mom talked about you all the time and was really sorry for running away that night. But she was afraid of what her father would say about her being in the barrio bar at her age.

"Later, when she found out she was pregnant, she ran away from home and raised me on her own, serving drinks as a waitress nights at the barrio bar. Sometimes she woke up in the middle of the night crying, calling out your name, hoping things could have turned out differently, better perhaps. After she died, the policia went through her things. They found a hotel receipt with a note that read, 'Luiz, mi amor,' but the note was blank after that. I returned to the barrio bar looking for the man named Luiz or anyone that knew of him. Nico, a rather large Chicano, that lived and worked nearby overheard me asking about you. He was sad to hear about Natalia's death and that he knew the little guy named Luiz, that same little guy that knocked him out cold…that day many years ago. Nico also told me that you were one of the CEOs of the JML Corporation in Veracruz a few miles away. Luiz and his brother Juan came in regularly looking for extra help to work at the warehouse. That is how I found you."

Luiz took Anna home that evening where they spent the rest of the night getting to know each other for the first time.

CHAPTER 11

Present

Rex met Milton and Jillian when they returned to the car rental counter at the airport.

"What happened to the car?" Rex asked admiring the handywork.

"Senior citizen," Jillian said pointing at Milton as she passed by.

"What was on the drive?" Rex asked as Milton went over to explain what happened to the rental car.

"When we got back to the warehouse, the policia and federales had the place surrounded… Pedro was murdered with a garrote," Jillian said.

"Dosen't sound like the cartel," Rex said thinking it over.

"Something else that did not make sense. His fingers were twisted and burnt at the fingertips. Looks more like a torture than an execution," Jillian said as Milton pulled up in a new Nissan Altima.

"Did you get the extra insurance rider on that one?" Jillian asked looking back at the bashed-up sedan.

"Oh, dear," Milton walked up slowly. "We were followed by a white van shortly after leaving the airport. I tried to give them the slip," Milton said.

"Yes, I see," Rex nodded.

"You said you wanted a diversion, you got one." Milton smiled at Jillian.

"I managed to retrieve the thumb drive, but unfortunately, it was erased. His computer was wiped too."

Rex decided to take a more direct approach. Flight CD-2156 originated from Mexico City and was on a regularly scheduled flight to Bogotá, Colombia, that left later that night. Now the flight logs Milton lifted from the two pilots showed the same flight number but at different times. "I'll check out the flight… You check with the tower on why the flights would be different." Rex turned and headed to the airport employee parking garage and jumped on the express bus to the terminal.

The bus was packed with pilots, stewardesses, grounds crews, food service, and even executives heading into work that night. The bus stopped in front of the security checkpoint, a steel reinforced double door with an electronic card scanner. Rex had to think fast. Everyone scanned the reader as they passed. Rex reached in his pocket, pulled out his gym membership card and quickly scanned it, and then moved quickly through the door. The alarm blared as security personnel came from all over, stopping and detaining everybody near the entrance, but by this time, Rex was one hundred feet away moving in the opposite direction.

Getting in the main terminal was the easy part, getting past security and access to the rest of the airport, that might be another problem. Rex had one of the credentials from one of the pilots from earlier today. Rex headed to the security door and flashed the badge, nothing happened. "Maybe they cut off his access… Maybe that card only worked in pilots only rooms." Rex shook his head, disappointed. He needed a way inside, a distraction, real distraction to get past the guards and into the secure area. Rex recalled a movie where they used a cigarette in the men's room to set off a fire alarm. Well, why not give it a shot? He bummed a cigarette from an employee and headed for the closest bathroom then into one of the stalls.

I could actually get arrested for doing this in a public bathroom. Maybe that's only on the planes, Rex pondered as he lit up the cigarette and placed on top of a toilet paper roll. Rex checked his watch… "Hmmm, ten minutes." Rex locked the stall behind him and headed into the terminal near the security door entrance. Rex checked his watch. "Wait for it, wait for it." Rex checked his watch again… *Fifteen minutes had passed… Maybe someone found it and put it out…*

Rex thought about heading back into the bathroom when…*waaaaa, waaaaa, waaaaa.* The fire alarm sounded all over the terminal. An employee came running out of the security door.

"El Fuego, El Fuego," Rex yelled in Spanish, quickly sticking his foot out in time to stop the door from shutting all the way. "El Fuego, El Fuego," Rex yelled pointing down the hallway toward the closest exit.

A few minutes later, the fire alarms shut off, and everything went back to normal.

The terminal had several bays assigned to JML Corporation, but only one that was scheduled for Colombia. Rex checked the flight number CD-2156 and manifest GCI-2256 clothing, electronics, food. Rex looked out onto the tarmac and spotted the cargo plane being loaded. Rex walked out to the tarmac, put on a safety vest, earplugs, then pretended to know what to do next.

"Señor, Aye hombre," a flight line supervisor yelled out. Rex turned. "Yo, Soy Nuevo."

The noise of the flight line muffled Rex's lousy Spanish accent. The man pointed at the cargo then the plane. Rex hopped on the closest forklift and helped several other employees load the rest of the cargo. *Wonder how much these guys get paid around here to load this stuff,* Rex wondered, maybe considering a second career.

The pilots had just finished their final walk-around. When the line supervisor looked away, Rex slipped into the back of the cargo compartment just as the last remaining ground crew member closed and buttoned up the cargo bay door. The engines fired up a few minutes later. The smell of burning jet fuel filled the compartment, making Rex sick to his stomach. Rex looked around for something to hold onto as the plane taxied down the runway. "This was definitely a no-frills flight." Rex chuckled to himself as the plane rumbled down the runway for what seemed like forever before the nose rotated back, pinning him against one of the cargo boxes as it gained altitude, a couple of shallow turns the plane leveled off and settled on course to its final destination.

Rex looked over some of the cargo boxes and compared them to the manifest that Jillian printed up from corporate HQ. Fruits, vegetables, electronics, nothing unusual for the JML Corporation, things seem to check out. Rex pried open one the crates marked as fresh fruit.

"What is this? It was supposed to be fresh fruit." Rex looked at the description on the box then compared it to the invoice. Not fruit…but a large steel lock box, something you'd see in a bank. Rex pulled out his trusty lockpick kit he picked up online and went to work on the tiny lock. Fifteen minutes later, the lock tumbler finally turned. Inside were smaller drawers like a safe deposit vault at a bank. Rex opened one of the drawers. It was packed with one-hundred-dollar bills, all newer bills all recently printed. Rex pried open several other drawers, same thing all one-hundred-dollar bills.

Rex felt the power drop as the plane decelerated and dropped slightly. *Could they be landing?* Rex wondered as he check his watch… way too early for a flight to Colombia. Rex quickly sealed up the crate and wondered if there was some sort of in flight emergency. *The regular flight to Colombia should take about three hours. We were only about an hour into the flight.* A couple of shallow descending turns later, the plane slowed and touched down, then taxied to a full stop. Rex slipped back into the shadows between two shipping crates and waited.

Voices could be heard from outside the plane, too low to make out over the engine noise. The cargo door opened, three men jumped on board all speaking in Spanish. Rex pulled his six-inch ceramic KA-BAR knife strapped to his leg and waited in the shadows as the three men scanned some of the cargo crates, picked out several of them, and transported them to a smaller private plane. Rex peeked out and read the tail number, Spart or Spartan 215; it was dark out and hard to see clearly. The cargo bay closed, and soon the cargo plane took off and continued on its way to Bogotá, Colombia.

The following day, Rex called Jillian.

"What can you tell me about Sparta airlines?" Rex asked.

"Okay, give me a few minutes," Jillian said. "How was your flight?" she asked.

"Very interesting," Rex said.

"How interesting?" Jillian asked.

"After takeoff, I checked a couple of crates, the manifest paper-work, and invoice numbers matched, but the cargo was all wrong," Rex hesitated.

"What did ya find, lad?" Milton asked.

"Money, lots of money, one-hundred-dollar bills in a cabinet like a bank deposit boxes. The plane made an unauthorized stop in Panama near the Panama Canal. I think it was France Field," Rex said. "Made some sort of transfer of cargo from the cargo plane to this smaller private jet...tail number Sparta 215," Rex explained.

"Well, there's a Sparta Air Conditioning Company, probably not what you were looking for," Jillian continued. "Okay, looks like we have a Spartan Aircraft Co. out of Bogotá, Colombia. Send me the address," Rex said.

It's actually Spartan Airlines, a small private jet company that operated out of a nearby airport about forty kilometers from Bogotá, Colombia.

Rex flagged down a local cabbie. "Aeropuerto," Rex said in per-fect Spanish.

"Aeropuerto?" Manuel asked shaking his head back and forth wondering what the destination was.

"Estamos aquí en el Aeropuerto," Manuel said thinking the American was confused.

"No, aeropuerto de Spartan," Rex repeated in perfect Spanish pointing at the address scribbled on the piece of paper.

"No, Señor. No permiso," Manuel said almost immediately.

Rex watched as the sweat beaded up on Manuel's forehead for just mentioning airport Spartan.

Rex pulled out a very crisp one-hundred-dollar bill from his pocket.

"Take me to aeropuerto Spartan... Si..." Rex said holding the bill out in front of his face.

The one hundred US dollars was a lot of money in Colombia, especially for a cabbie. You could see the fear in Manuel's eyes as he considered the offer.

"No, Señor," Manuel said nervously.

Rex pulled out a second one-hundred-dollar bill. "I give you one now and one when you drop me off at the airport Spartan," Rex said handing Manuel the first bill.

"Okay, I take you, Señor," Manuel said as he took the first one-hundred-dollar bill, then headed south out of town. The one-hour trip was eerily quiet as Manuel did not want to talk about this place.

"I drop you off here, Señor," Manuel said, pulling the cab over a mile or so short of the destination. "It's too dangerous for me to go any further," Manuel said looking around nervously. "If I get caught, Señor, I could lose my license, maybe my life," Manuel said.

Rex handed him the other one-hundred-dollar bill as promised.

"Good luck, Señor," the cabbie said as he sped off, leaving a cloud of dust behind.

Aeropuerto Spartan was as secluded private airport with a fifteen-foot perimeter fence, couple of cameras, but no guards or alarms. *Why was Manuel so scared of this place?* Rex wondered as he surveyed the fifteen-foot single-strand barbed-wire fence. Rex had seen worst in his day. Rex worked his way around the side away from the cameras, backed up a few feet, and ran toward the wall, planted his foot halfway up the wall, and caught the top just short of the barbed wire. Now a simple scissors kick, throwing his right leg over the barbed wire, and then with the left leg. Seemed so easy in gymnastics class till he snagged the inside of his pant leg on the barbed wire, tearing out the whole inseam. Rex landed on the other side unscathed except for his pride. "Built-in air-conditioning I guess," Rex said with a sigh.

Rex made his way to the main entrance where a small group of pilots stood outside on a break all having a quick smoke. Rex walked up to one of the younger pilots, put two fingers to his mouth, mimicking a cigarette. The young man pulled out a pack of Marlboros, handed it to Rex with a lighter, then waved his hand.

"Keep it. I get them for free. Are you new around here?" the kid asked in broken English, looking strangely at Rex's attire.

"Yup, just transferred in this morning," Rex responded leaning up against the nearby wall, hiding the large gaping hole in his pants.

Rex took a couple of long drags from the cigarette. Rex hated smoking but needed a way into the building.

"When do you fly out?" Rex asked, casually flicking his cigarette butt across the patio.

"Later tonight," the kid said.

Rex thanked him for the cigarettes and walked on down the pathway toward the entrance. Rex passed by a few bags leaning up against the brick wall, grabbed the last one, and casually walked into the airport terminal.

CHAPTER 12

Present

Juan feared for his life and that of his family. With the murder of his brother, best friend Lupe, and now Pedro, the warehouse manager, in Mexico City, Juan hired two friends of the family, personal security guards Victor and Gustavo Herrera. The brothers had worked for Juan on many occasions, mostly making bank runs in town. But this was a special occasion and a very important assignment as Juan and his families personal bodyguards. Victor was at one time a personal guard to the presidente.

At around seven in the evening, Juan was enjoying a nice family dinner with his daughter Gabriella and Anna Ramos. Juan sat the girls down and explained what happened last week. "How Luiz was involved in some really bad things with some really bad people." Juan sighed still bitter for his best friend getting killed. "My dear friend and brother were killed for what is in this package," Juan explained pulling out the plastic bag Lupe handed him, laying the contents out on the table in front of them. Inside the plastic bag were standard invoices, custom forms, transportation logs from JML Corporation with the flight no. CD-2156, a daily flight out of Mexico City, Mexico, to Bogotá, Colombia, circled on it, nothing unusual for Luiz. He was one of the CEOs and the head of the transportation department officer after all. What was unusual was the 5.56 mm shell casings found near the body with no markings on them, the piece of paper with a bunch of roman numerals handwritten across it (III I-III-II IIIII-II IIII-I II II-II-III), and the microchip.

Victor suddenly raised his hand interrupting Juan after hearing a strange noise coming from the backyard. Victor held a finger to his lips.

"Stay here. Gustavo…? Donde estas?" Victor called out to his brother as he opened the back door.

It was a dark overcast night out with very little light from the porch. Victor spotted something lying in the backyard.

"Gustavo, is that you?" Victor called out. It was his brother. He had been shot twice in the chest.

Victor rushed back inside the kitchen door just as a bright flash and a loud explosion went off in the room, temporarily blinding him. Four men rushed through the door. Victor pushed Juan and the girls to the floor, leveled his gun and shot blindly getting off three shots, hitting one man center mass and the other in the arm. Victor dove on top of Juan and the girls as several bullets ripped through Victor's back. One bullet went through Victor's shoulder and into Juan's upper thigh. One man kicked the table away and shot Victor in the head, exploding it like a ripe watermelon. Victor's body was slumped on top of Juan. The microchip and papers were scattered all over the floor, just out of Juan's reach. Anna reached over and picked up the microchip, knowing how important it was to her father, looked directly at Juan, and swallowed it. The fourth man through the door kicked Victor's body to the side and grabbed Juan, and the girls off the floor loaded them into a white minivan and drove off.

The short flight to Panama only lasted a few hours, but for Juan, it was forever. The gunshot wound to Juan's leg was not bleeding but had shattered ricocheted off the bone, making it extremely painful. The captors didn't say much, except for an occasional word in Spanish among themselves. The plane took off and landed several hours later where they transferred to a van and driven several hours to an unknown location deep into the Panamanian forest.

The hoods were pulled off. Juan, Anna, and Gabriella were tied to metal chairs facing a long metal table, something you might see in coroner's office or slaughterhouse. Several armed men walked in along with a small semibalding man wearing a white lab coat and thick-rimmed glasses. They called him El Doctor. The doctor was accompanied by a giant of a man, at least eight feet tall and well over 400 pounds. El Doctor walked around the room staring eerily at each of them as he passed. Without saying a word, he stopped at the end of the table, unzipped a large black bag, and pulled out a funny-looking wooden box with a hand crank and long electrical leads hanging out of it. El Doctor secured the base to the end of the metal table. With a quick nod of his head, the giant pulled Juan's chair up to the table, untied his right hand, and placed it inside the box. When the cover was closed and locked, Juan's entire hand was inside, except for his fingers that poked out the front of the box. El Doctor attached the two electrical leads to Juan's first and second fingers.

"I am going to ask you a very simple question," El Doctor said in a high-pitched German accent. "You give me the right answers, I promise not to make it hurt, for long. But a wrong answer." El Doctor slowly cranked the handle, sending an electrical charge up Juan's arm into his chest then down to his feet. Juan gritted his teeth but yelled out in pain as the electricity ran through his body. "Now where is the microdrive?" the doctor asked in his high-pitched voice. Juan said nothing. The doctor slowly cranked the handle several times. The voltage increased and surged up though Juan's fingers, up through Juan's arm.

"Ahhhhhhh," Juan cried out.

"Sooner or later, you will tell me what I want," he said cranking the handle once more. "Where is the thumb drive?" the little man yelled again in a high-pitched German accent.

"Аннннни!" Juan yelled as the smell of burning flesh filled the room. Juan's heart fluttered as his blood pressure went through the roof, popping small blood vessels in his eyes. Juan looked back briefly at Anna and whispered something.

"What was that?" El Doctor looked at Anna then back at Juan. "What did he say to you?" El Doctor snickered. "Did you have something to say, little lady?" El Doctor said.

The doctor reached inside his bag and pulled out a leather pouch, folded in on the ends, and tied in the middle. El Doctor rolled open the pouch, the shiny knives glittered in the dimly lit room. He grabbed a long single-bladed spike and rolled the metal tip across the other blades, letting out an eerie tune that filled the room. "Where's the microdrive?" the doctor repeated, shoving the tip of the spike deep into the bullet wound of Juan's right thigh.

The tip of the dagger hit the femur bone and made a sickening crunching noise as El Doctor twisted it round and round.

"Ahhhhh," Juan yelled as his pulse rate increased, shooting his blood pressure through the roof. "Where is the microdrive?" The doctor looked at Juan then back at Anna and noticed that he kept whispering something to her. "What did he say? What are you trying to hide?" El Doctor asked angrily walking over to her, pointing at the giant.

The giant walked over to Anna, cutting her loose from the chair laying her out on the table, securely tying her down. "What are you hiding?" the doctor said in a sickening voice.

Anna's eyes were red and swollen from crying as she watched her uncle, nearly tortured to death. "No, Tio...no," she whispered softly, knowing he was about to tell him what he wanted. El Doctor walked over to his quiver of knives, rolled his fingers across several till he had the right one, a two-sided bladed knife with a slight curve. The razor-sharp knife blade slid across her body slowly cutting open her blouse one button at a time.

"The radio crackled," the doctor spoke quietly, then a little louder, "Si." The doctor stopped and told his guards to stand guard that he would be back. El Doctor and his giant bodyguard walked out into the hallway. The door closed, the one guard looked at the other then at Anna's partially exposed body lying on the table.

"Hey, hombre, Vamanos....Vai..." the guard said motioning toward Anna.

The one guard watched the door as the other took off his gun belt, then his pants, and headed toward Anna. "Hey, baby, want to party?" he said as he fondled her body.

The second guard joined in later as they repeatedly raped her one at a time.

CHAPTER 13

Present day

Rex slipped into the closest restroom for a quick change of clothes. He opened the flight bag, inside was a flight jacket, toiletries, toothbrush, razor. Rex tried on the jacket. It was a little tight in the shoulders, but if he left it unbuttoned, he could get away with it. The slacks were a different story, short and a bit wide in the hips. "Lucky me, I must have grabbed a bag from a short chubby guy." Rex sighed as he synced up the belt. Rex zipped up the bag and headed back into the main terminal.

The little airport was not that busy, so Rex headed to the lounge for a bite to eat, and after a quick sandwich and a beer, he opened the bag and took a closer look inside. *Two passports, one for official business, the other for personal use,* Rex thought, *but they had two different names Antonio Franco and Antonio Borges both official passports, one Colombian, the other Mexican. Wonder what's up with the two passports,* Rex wondered as he reached into the next pocket. A flight schedule, calendar, and a small black notebook with several flights written in it. Rex looked at the flights. They seemed to be the same as the schedule Milton lifted from the other pilot in Mexico City. Rex reached into the larger deeper pocket and felt the steel of a handgun.

"Hi, may I help you?" a lovely voice asked.

As Rex slowly turned his head toward the lovely lady, keeping a tight grip on the weapon in the flight bag. Rex read the name tag Elsa, a tall blond waitress just stood there smiling. Rex relaxed his hand and remembered that he was in an airport lounge.

"Aah, yes," he said pulling his hand slowly from the flight bag. "I'll have a double Glenlivet on the rock, that's one rock please," Rex said holding up one finger. "Anything to eat this evening? We have a couple of sandwich specials or perhaps something more traditional like a tortilla?" Elsa offered. Rex was famished after all that walking around and jumping walls. "Ham sandwich on rye bread would be fine."

Rex thought about that unusual stop on yesterday's flight, wondering where the boxes were headed and what was in them. Rex finished his drink. "Time to go to work, Rex," he said walking up to the computer terminal. Rex typed in the information into the computer. "CD-2156...ENTER."

"Restricted access. Enter your password."

"Damn," he said punching a few more buttons.

"Damn, damn." He slammed his fist on the counter in frustration. "I wish Jillian was here right now... She could get in," Rex said mumbling to himself.

"Hi, can I help you?" a soft sexy but familiar voice asked him.

Rex looked up at her and read the name tag "Elsa."

"Wait, aren't you the waitress at the lounge?" Rex asked looking at her strangely, then quickly toward the lounge.

"Yes, I pretty much do everything around here... Who's Jillian?" she asked casually rubbing up against him.

"My dispatcher. She called me and asked me to cover for Antonio Franco...but I don't know what flight he was on tonight," Rex lied convincingly.

"Is that so?" Elsa said pulling the keyboard toward her.

"So what's your name, dear?" she asked sweetly.

"Charles, Charles Whitmore," he said shaking her hand.

Elsa punched in her password, pretending to shield it from his eyes as he peered over her shoulder. "Lisa0682." "So what happened to Antonio Franco, the regular crew member?" Elsa asked.

"I am not sure, just subbing in at the last minute," Rex said.

Elsa knew he was lying because she would have been the one making the call, but she didn't.

"Hmmm...that flight isn't till 0700 tomorrow morning," Elsa told him.

"Tomorrow morning?" Rex said looking at his watch. It was a little passed eight in the evening.

"Thank you," Rex said heading back to the lounge followed closely by Elsa who wondered who he was and what he was doing here.

Rex scanned his badge at the pilot's lounge and went in. There was a scuffle going on just outside the window in front of the airport.

"What's going on out there?" Rex asked sitting near the window.

"Looks like the policia was called, must be a security breach," Elsa said as she poured Rex a fresh Glenlivet with one rock. The policia handcuffed the man and shoved him into the back of the squad car.

"Wonder what he did?" Rex asked curiously.

"Probably got caught impersonating a pilot or something," Elsa said as the policia removed the man from the premises.

Rex took a deep breath and finished off his scotch. "Can I have another?" Rex held up his hand.

Rex sat in the booth and looked over the schedule Elsa gave him…and compared it to the pilots logbook. The times were off slightly twenty minutes here, thirty minutes there…but they all seem to mirror the cargo flights of the JML Corporation, very strange.

Rex sat back and watched as the pilots and other employees gathered around the TV to watch the football game, Mexico versus Colombia. Things got a little tense as the two groups of fans cheered for their teams. With less than a minute of regulation time, game tied 2 to 2. Mexico pushed the whole team forward of midfield, putting tremendous pressure on the Colombian defense. The goalie kicked the ball passed midfield, picked up by center midfielder who passed it quickly to the right forward into the corner. The ball was crossed twenty yards in front of the goal, both offense and defensive players jump for control of the ball. The ball was headed toward the corner of the goal by the Mexican forward. The Colombian goalkeeper made a diving save, deflecting off his fingertips toward the sideline. Two players fight for the ball, deflecting it in front of the goal. With only seconds left on the clock, the Colombian defensive player attempted to clear the ball, but it caromed off the foot of a charging Mexican midfielder, sliding toward the goal. The whole crowd stopped and went totally silent as the ball slowly rolled across the line. The crowd erupted, and the announcer howled over the TV loudspeakers.

"Gggggggoooooooooalllllll!" the announcer howled again over the TV's loudspeakers, this time twice as long, "Gggggoooooooooalllllll," as the Mexican team piled on each other in the corner of the field, celebrating their tremendous victory.

"Hi, I see you are still with us, Mr. Whitmore," Elsa said walking up to the table. "Would you like to join me?"

"*Lisa*," Rex said pointing at the seat across from him.

She looked at him for a second then around the room. "*Shush*," she said, slipping in next to him in the booth. "Why did you call me Lisa?" she whispered.

"That is your name, right? *Lisa*, born June 1982," Rex said.

"You saw that?" she said acting surprised.

"Easier to remember your password using your real name and birthday." Rex smiled, thinking he had outsmarted her.

"Why are you using an alias?" Rex asked.

"Well, I should ask you the same thing… Mr. Whitmore, is it?" Lisa paused and cocked her head to the side.

"Rex, Rex Nelson," Rex said wondering how she knew. "How did you know?" Rex asked.

"I make all the calls when pilots can't make their scheduled flight times." Lisa grinned. "Not only that I had you when you walked in the lounge with those baggy trousers, all scrunched up under that beltline." Lisa laughed out loud.

"So why didn't you call the policia?" Rex asked.

"I had to check you out, find out what you were really doing here," Lisa said.

"So what have you found out? What am I doing here?" Rex asked loudly.

"Shushhhh, not here," Lisa whispered.

"Will you be spending the night with us, Mr. Whitmore?" Elsa asked loudly so other patrons and employees clearly heard the conversation.

"Well, since my flight does not leave till 0700, I could use a good night sleep." Rex looked up and smiled as Lisa nodded her head up and down.

"Okay, follow me," she said waving her hand.

They headed out the back door, across the tarmac to a second two-story building.

"What is this place?" Rex asked looking around half expecting an ambush.

"Relax, silly. It's my apartment, best food, drink, and accommodations at the airport," she said with a grin.

Lisa pulled out her keys, then clumsily dropped them.

"Oops," she said, apologizing as she bent over to pick them up.

Could this be a trap? Rex wondered as he cautiously followed her into her apartment.

She knew he wasn't who he said he was. *Maybe she had a partner...a partner waiting to attack. I don't even know her or why she has an alias*, Rex thought.

"Damn, Rex, you are just being paranoid. Would you like something to drink?" she asked heading for the kitchen for a tumbler and a bottle.

"Glenlivet, right? One rock..." She smiled holding up one finger.

Lisa pushed a button near the couch, soft jazz piano started playing. "Do you like it?" she asked slowly dancing to the beat.

Rex wasn't sure what to say. "Very nice," Rex said taking a long swallow of his scotch. *Was she referring to the drink or to her sexy dance moves? Maybe she was just being friendly, or maybe he was being setup.*

"So why are you here?" Lisa asked pouring Rex another drink.

"You first...why the alias?" Rex asked. "You only have an alias if you are trying to hide something."

"What? Me? You think I am trying to hide something..." she said innocently.

"Yes, I do think you are trying to hide something," Rex said waiting for an answer.

"My real name is Lisa Monroe...but you figured that out already."

"So what about you?" she asked nudging him in the arm.

"What about me? Rex Nelson…but you knew that because I told you." Rex smiled and was enjoying this little game. *Don't let the cat out of the bag too early,* Rex thought to himself. "Who do you work for?" Rex asked.

Lisa hesitated but figured Rex had to be involved in law enforcement of some kind.

"I'm undercover," she said scooting up next to him.

"Who do you work for…Rex?" She smiled pecking him on the cheek.

"Myself," Rex said, wondering if this was some new form of interrogation. "What are you looking for?" Rex asked.

"Information and the whereabouts of two people of interest," she said kissing the other cheek.

"What are their names? The guys you are looking for?" Rex asked carefully.

"Who said they are guys?" Lisa got up to change the radio station to a more upbeat song.

"So tell me who they are." Rex got up and walked toward her.

"I can't tell you that," she said, shaking her hips back and forth to the beat of an old-time rock and roll song.

"Why not?" Rex asked.

"I don't know you…yet," she said grinning.

"Well, I just told you. It's Rex Nelson," he said.

"I know that…but I haven't vetted you yet…" she said finishing off her drink.

"So is this part of your vetting process?" Rex asked reaching for the bottle of scotch, pouring her another drink.

"Yup, you could say that," Lisa said pushing him back into a plush leather couch, nearly spilling his drink. Lisa moved toward him, sliding her hips around and around to tropical rhythmic beat of the steel drums playing on the radio. Rex reached out to touch her, but she slapped his hand away. "The song's not over yet, silly," she said softly, slowly straddling him as the music faded away.

Later that night while relaxing in bed, "So why are you here, Rex?" Lisa asked.

"I am helping a friend, find those responsible for murdering his brother."

"Here at the airport?" Lisa asked surprised to hear of the murder.

"No, last week in the streets of Veracruz."

"Where did you say?" Lisa interrupted.

"Veracruz, Mexico…shot to pieces in broad daylight…on his way to work," Rex repeated.

"What's his name? Can you tell me his name?" Lisa asked.

"Luiz," Rex said.

"Oh my god… Luiz De La Cruz. Your friend's name is Luiz De La Cruz," she said frantically.

"Yes, it is," Rex said turning toward her.

"Luiz is dead?" Lisa sprang up from the bed crying.

"You knew Luiz?" Rex asked.

"He was my friend and confidential informant," Lisa explained.

"Luiz, a confidential informant?" Rex paused trying to put all the pieces together.

"Luiz was working with this Mexican gang leader by the name of Rodrigo Campos, a lieutenant of the La Rosa Negra Cartel up north near Monterrey. We had some intel a few years ago of a gun sale of illegal guns being smuggled across the border, but it was never verified. Then we got a lead from an executive that worked directly with Rodrigo Campos and had concrete evidence that linked Campos with the guns, but one step closer to 'El Jefe.' Luiz, my confidential informant, was bringing me that information. When he failed to deliver the intel, I lost track of him. Are you telling me the reason he failed to contact me…was because he was murdered?" Lisa started crying.

"The ATF has been trying to tie this underground weapons syndicate to the powerful cartel for years. We had a good lead a few years back with the straw buyers, but that got all messed up, and we lost our informant then too."

"Ben Griffith," Rex said.

"What… How did you know?" Lisa asked.

"Ben was my brother… I was never happy with the explanation the government gave me for the way he was killed." Rex hung his head for a moment.

"This Campos was the best lead we had to the El Jefe and the Rosa Negra Cartel. No one really knows what he looks like. The deals are all secretive and hushed. He never handles the cash himself and is very careful about his identity," Lisa stopped talking for a minute or two. "Do you know how he died?" Lisa asked.

"It was an ambush on his way to the office… The body was so badly mutilated it could barely be identified," Rex told her. "So what is your plan?"

"I don't know… Without Luiz, we no longer have a credible CI on the inside."

"What about me?" Rex said.

"I can go in and get the info you are looking for… It's the same thing we are looking for…the same man that killed Luiz and my brother Ben."

"I will have to clear it with my superiors," Lisa said heading back to bed.

Rex woke up early the next morning. There was no sign of Lisa anywhere. Rex checked his watch. There was plenty of time to get a bite to eat and a coffee before his scheduled flight at 0700. Maybe Lisa had to go to work early and was somewhere in the terminal. Rex returned to the lounge and sat in the same booth where he first met Lisa.

"How can I help you this morning?" the lovely older woman asked.

Rex looked up and read the name tag "Elsa."

With a lost expression on his face, half expecting to see someone else. "The special and a cup of coffee, black no sugar."

Rex spent the next several hours walking around the small airport looking for Lisa but never saw her again.

CHAPTER 14

Present day

Rex's flight was out of gate B2 where the pilot was finishing up his preflight walk-around, a standard procedure for the industry where you walk around and visually check the aircraft for any abnormalities. Rex stowed his gear in the cockpit, then headed outside. The pilot was a little surprised to see Rex, a new man on the job. Rex reached out his hand.

"Charles, Charles Whitmore," Rex said in a subtle British accent.

The man hesitated, then responded, "Leonardo Vega."

"Vamanos, El Jefe is waiting," Rex whispered heading for the cockpit.

Obviously, Rex was on the right track, and Lisa's intel was right on. Rex was familiar with the Lear 35; it was basically the same aircraft that the US Air Force used but called it the C-21A.

Rex wondered if this flight was going to deviate from the scheduled route; by his calculations, that would take place somewhere near Panama. Two hours into the flight, the pilot started a preset checklist for landing. Rex knew the procedure and followed along. *We were nowhere near Mexico City, our final destination.* The pilot descended from a cruising altitude of forty-five thousand feet to the air over five thousand feet, stayed on the direct heading for the Panama Canal. This was very unusual for a commercial air traffic. It was almost like he was intentionally trying to avoid the air traffic control radar. Captain Vega adjusted his course and speed, then made a few low-level passes over what looked like an old airfield. The Lear jet landed miles from a main airport in a small seldom used airfield, France Field. France Field that was once occupied by the US military back in the mid-1950s, but to the best of Rex's knowledge, it had been abandoned and closed down for many years.

The Lear taxied to the end of the runway and stopped. Captain Vega ran through the shutdown procedures, checked his watch, then waited.

"Must be running a little late," Rex said checking the time himself. Rex just agreed and went along with it because honestly, he had no idea what Captain Vega was waiting for. A cargo plane broke through the clouds and made several low-level passes. Rex recognized the cargo plane; it was one from the JML Corporation. The plane touched down and headed to the end of the runway. Several men jumped out of the plane, opened the cargo door, and proceeded to unload several large crates. Captain Vega supervised the transfer. A total of six pallets were unloaded off the cargo plane, one pallet with three smaller crates was loaded into the Lear jet. The other five pallets were moved to a small hangar off the end of the runway.

Rex slipped around behind of the hangar and hid.

"Captain Whitmore…donde estas?" Captain Vega called out looking around, tapping at his watch.

The men locked down the cargo bay doors and took off, about a half hour from start to finish.

"Captain Whitmore," Vega called out a few profanities then boarded the Lear and took off. Rex picked the lock on the hangar door in record time. Jillian would be proud of him, he thought to himself. Rex inspected the two crates. From the outside, they had all the right tags, JML Corporation logo, inventory, and customs stickers.

Why would they drop off crates of vegetables in a hangar? Rex wondered. Rex pried open the first crate.

"What?" Rex was surprised to see the inventory. "Automatic weapons. M-4 assault rifles." Rex quickly wrote down the serial numbers then sealed up the crate. A quick look around. *What was this place?* Rex wondered as he ran toward the big warehouse structure.

There were old aircraft bunkers, refueling pumps. France Field was supposed to be abandoned, shutdown. *Maybe this wasn't France Field*, Rex thought.

Rex checked the outer doors on the warehouse; it was unlocked. Inside was a kitchen, showers, game room, cots all lined up from the looks of it all recently used. This seemed more like a summer camp than an abandoned airfield. Rex heard voices coming from the back of the warehouse as a sixteen-foot box truck pulled up to the storage hangar. Several armed guards ran out and stood guard as the weapons were being loaded. The guards stepped away from the truck to have a smoke, leaving it unattended for a few seconds. Rex walked over to the truck and slipped in between the cab and the cargo box a space just barely big enough for a stowaway.

The trip seemed to take forever, but it was only about thirty minutes down the road. The truck slowed and turned into a long winding drive up the side of a small mountain. As the truck turned, Rex spotted the main hacienda with guards and automatic weapons.

"Time to get off this ride," Rex said as he jumped into a grove of trees. Rex watched as the truck pulled up to a small garage. A man on a mini forklift came out of the garage and took the crates into the garage. Rex moved closer and peeked in the back window of the garage. *What?* Rex thought. *Where did the mini-forklift and the crates go?* Rex wondered as he moved around to the side of the garage and tried to open the door. *Darn it.* It was locked. Rex reached in his pocket and pulled out his brand-new shiny lock-picking tool that he bought online. "You can pick any lock in under a minute" was the guarantee.

Rex started working on the lock. Several minutes went by, and Rex was still working on the lock. *I probably should have kept the instructions*, he thought to himself as he fought with the lock. "Damn, Jillian makes it look so easy," he said grumbling a little. Rex turned back toward the hacienda, six guards with automatic weapons, two inside and four on the perimeter. Rex went in for a closer look. The security was pretty heavy for a building that size. "What could they be hiding?"

Rex watched as the time interval increased when the guard moved to the back of the building. Rex waited in the shadows and counted as the sentry made his rounds back to the front and figured he had about five minutes before he headed back. Rex skipped across the courtyard to a nearby bush, then hugged the wall all the way down to the side of the building. Up ahead, there was a light on in the window. Rex peeked inside—it was the kitchen. Rex thought, *Great place to gather info. Everybody talks around the kitchen table.* Rex reached inside his pocket and pulled out a small electronic bug, stuck it to the outside of the window.

A second light further down. Rex peeked in…it was an office. Rex planted that bug on the window and headed back to the garage area before the sentry finished making his rounds. Rex wasn't ready to give up on this garage door and tried to pick the lock once again. *Click*, the lock finally opened. Rex turned on the receiver and listened to the first bug that was on the kitchen window. Not much going on, a lot of laughter and joking around. They were playing some card game that involved a lot of betting. The second bug was more interesting. The man on the phone mentioned that somebody was visiting, then hung up the phone. The reception was muffled and only able to pick up bits and pieces of the conversation. A second man walked in the room.

"Did you find it?" There was a slight pause.

"No," the man said clearly. "So what are you going to tell him?" Another pause. "I don't know…nothing I guess. I don't have it." You could see the headlights heading up the winding driveway, leading up to the main house. Three cars pulled up in front of the house, a sedan and two SUVs. Several armed guards got out of the SUVs and escorted the passenger of the sedan into the house.

Rex listened carefully to the conversation.

"Well?" the man asked as he walked through the door.

"The old man is dead," the man responded.

"Do you have it?" the man asked.

"No, I don't have it. It wasn't in the car," the man said.

"What do you mean it wasn't in the car?" the man barked back.

"We know he had the microdrive in his briefcase. Our informant told us it was in the car when he left the corporation."

"The local police captain was looking through the car when I got there. He was also at the precinct when the folders went missing," the man continued.

"What folders?" the man gasped.

"The autopsy notes…and the bag," the man whispered.

"Go talk to this captain, bribe him. I don't care what you have to do…but get me that microdrive," the man yelled.

"Can't, sir, he's dead," the man said.

"What? What happened?" he asked pounding on the desk.

Rex's signal suddenly went dead, quickly tuning to the other bug.

"He was getting too close. We had to neutralize him," the man said.

"What? Neutralize him? You killed the captain of the policia?"

"But, sir, he was getting too close."

"But you still don't have the microdrive?" Slight pause. *Pop, pop, pop.* "Clean this up… I want that microdrive." There was a long pause. The voices faded out again.

"Damn," Rex said as he switched frequencies once again.

"Roberto, I don't care about your men… Just have Niklas get you more," the man said.

"We should know more tonight," the man said.

"Why's that?"

"We have them," the man said.

"*Niklas*…get more men," the man said angrily as the signal faded out.

Niklas—there was that name again… It was several years ago when Rex heard the name for the first time. Niklas Muller was Ben's squad leader in Mexico when he was killed on a joint ATF/FBI raid. Even though Niklas was exonerated by the military trial, Rex's mind flashed back to the military inquiry into Ben's death. During that retreat, Ben was shot in the back.

When the team was finally debriefed, there was conflicting evidence on how Ben died and who shot and killed him. The autopsy showed that he was killed by a .45 caliber round, shot in the back. Rex knew that Niklas carried a .45 as his backup sidearm. Rex always wondered what really happened. But it could not be him. Niklas was dead.

Rex pulled out his satellite phone and called Milton. There was an eerie silence in Milton's voice, something that Rex had never experienced before.

"What is it, Milty?" Rex asked, knowing something was really wrong.

"It's the De La Cruz's. They have been kidnapped, and their security guards were both killed," Milton told him.

"Who was kidnapped?" Rex asked.

"Juan and both girls Anna and Gabriella," Milton told him.

"Were there any demands, phone calls, anything?" Rex asked.

"No. Not at all. Jillian and I just got here—"

"Rex," Jillian interrupted. "There was a gunfight, and they must have been in a hurry," Jillian said.

"Why do you say that?" Rex asked.

"Well, Rex, they left two of their men behind…both dead," Milton said from the background.

"There is something else, and I don't like it," Jillian said looking over the bodies.

"What is it?" Rex asked.

"They are both American… Merc's, I think?…Green Berets… with Special Forces tattoos."

"Damn," Rex said.

The last thing you want to hear, being a patriot, is that it's one of your own guys.

"Jillian, what time was the kidnapping?" Rex asked.

"At 7:00 p.m. or 8:00 p.m. last night. They were sitting down for dinner," Jillian said.

"Damn, that's what they were talking about," Rex whispered loud enough for Milton could pick it up.

"What did ya say, boy?" Milton asked.

"I said that is what they were talking about," Rex repeated.

"Do you have a lead?" Milton asked.

"I am following the money and the guns that led me to a hacienda in the middle of the Panamanian jungle," Rex continued. "I believe these guys are the ones responsible for kidnapping of Juan and the girls," Rex said. "I need the two of you down here right away…" Rex said.

"Okay, we'll get on the first available flight. See you soon."

"Milton, check your contacts in the ATF and see what you can find out about some high-powered weapons I found down here in Panama."

"Weapons? How is Luiz involved in that?" Milton asked.

"Not sure he is… Just see what you can come up with. Here are their serial numbers. I'll see you in a few hours." Rex hung up the phone.

Rex heard a noise coming from the main house. Three men walked across the driveway toward the little garage and spoke loudly in Spanish, boasting about who was going to get some from the chichitas. Rex strained to hear, but his Spanish was not that great and only picked up a little if anything of value from the conversation. Rex was curious as the three men opened the garage door and headed inside.

Rex followed as close as possible but not close enough to be detected. Rex dropped to the ground and rolled under the garage door just as it was about to close. The door suddenly stopped and started up again.

"Hey, is someone there?" the guard called out, wondering why it had started up again.

Rex quickly rolled under a large steel rack as the guard walked nearby to investigate but found nothing.

"Vamanos," the other two guards yelled out.

The guard closed the garage door and hit another button. The floor shook and dropped away below them. Rex watched as the three men headed down the ramp. Rex rolled onto the ramp and into the tunnel below. *What is this place?* he thought, remembering the disappearing miniloader from the night before. *It probably headed underground.*

Rex followed the men down a long twelve-by-twelve-foot all-concrete tunnel dimly lit by a loose string of tiny yellow bulbs. The conversations faded as they moved around the far corner. Rex peeked around the corner, but they were gone. *Where did they go?* Rex wondered, and he continued down the long path. Up ahead was a small wooden ladder heading up to a small trapdoor. Rex climbed up the ladder and stopped shortly, listening for any conversations when the lights went out. He figured the coast was clear. Rex waited a few extra minutes then slowly opened the trapdoor, peeking through the opening. The room was pretty dark, all-concrete walls, small rectangular windows all around.

Rex heard voices down the hall. There was an armed guard standing outside the last room on the right.

"Ahhhhhhhh," a loud shriek came from inside the room.

Rex moved in a little closer, and then he heard another yell from inside the room.

"Ahhhhhhhh."

Rex banged loudly on a metal electrical box and mumbled something in Spanish.

"Quien, paso ai" the guard yelled down the hall.

Rex grabbed a small metal object and threw it down the hall it made a loud clanking sound when it hit the floor.

"Que paso," the guard called out again, walking down the hall to investigate.

Rex waited till he walked passed, then *thud*, Rex chopped him on the back of the neck, knocking him out, dragging him into a nearby closet.

Rex looked down the hallway as two men walked out of one of the rooms. Rex looked again. A small balding man with tiny spectacles wearing a white doctor's coat followed by a *giant*, standing what had to be eight feet tall, weighing at least four hundred plus pounds. *What was that anyway…a man?* Rex wondered as they headed in the opposite direction. Rex heard chants in Spanish coming from the other room.

"Vamanos Muchacho…Vai…"

Rex peeked through the little window in the door. There was a man tied to a metal chair with his right hand inside a small wooden box. Rex looked around for the *giant* and the doctor as the jeering continued with chants, "Vamanos hombre."

Jillian and Milton said the De La Cruz's were kidnapped last night. *The kidnapping*, Rex thought. *Could this be Juan and the girls?* He could only see into one side of the room but figured the room couldn't be more than fifteen feet long, and if he went in fast, he could cover that ground no problem. *What would he be facing? Armed men with automatic weapons.* Rex stepped back and readied himself, not knowing what to expect on the other side of the door. Rex looked both ways for the doctor and his large friend, then crashed through the door. Rex spotted three guards in the back of the room. With a running start, Rex leaped across the metal table and side kicked the guard that was raping a young woman on the table, slamming him into the back wall. Rex turned to the second guard who had his pants around his ankles, grabbed him by the head, pulling down as he threw a devastating knee to his jaw, knocking his head back. The last guard had no time to react as Rex pulled his KA-BAR, flipped it in his hand, and flung it toward the man, striking him in the side of the neck.

It was Anna, totally exposed on the table, her hands and feet tied to the leg post. Rex quickly cut her loose when the door opened. The doctor and the *giant* returned. The giant lumbered his way across the room, grabbed Juan who was tied to the chair, and flung him to the floor, ripping his fingers from the wooden box. Rex threw a devastating front kick and followed it with a spinning side kick. The blows just bounced off the big man. Laughing, the giant picked Rex up, pinning him against the wall with hands the size of a baseball mitts. Rex grabbed the man by the hands, curled up, and kicked him in the jaw with both feet, knocking him back a little. The giant just grinned, picked Rex up over his head and body, slammed him hard onto the concrete floor.

Rex rolled over on to his knees with both hands on the floor, trying to catch his breath. The giant approached, reaching down for another round, but Rex threw two devastating blows to the inside of both of his knees, then one straight up the groin. The giant grunted then smiled but kept moving forward. When he reached for him the second time, Rex grabbed his hand, pulled him toward him, and threw the giant off balance, stumbling to his knees. Rex quickly jumped on the man's back, wrapped an arm around his neck in a rear naked choke, and wrapped both feet around his torso.

The big man wrestled to his feet and backed up as fast as he could, slamming Rex against the wall. Rex held on for dear life, slowly squeezing and applying more and more pressure to the carotid artery finally slowing the man as he fell to one knee. Rex let go and grabbed him by the neck, pulling his chin back and to the right as hard as he could. The crack was loud and could be heard across the room. Rex looked around the room, but the doctor had escaped out the back door. Juan was barely alive. His leg was torn up with the gunshot wound, and his first two fingers on his right hand torn off, thanks to our good friend.

"Where is Gabriella?" Juan whispered softly.

Rex moved in closer. "What was that my friend?" He put his ear closer to his lips.

"Where is Gabriella?" Juan said a little louder. "She was with us. She was just here," Juan continued fighting through the pain.

Rex ran out the door, looked around but was too late as a dark sedan with two to three passengers drove down the long winding road.

"The sedan. They must have her in the sedan," Rex said.

Rex only had a few minutes and one shot of getting a bug on the car. He ran down the hill through the woods to the gated entrance. When the car slowed as it approached the gate, Rex rolled under the car, slapping a bug on the back bumper. The car rolled away. Rex noticed an US embassy sticker on the back window. *What did the US embassy have to do with any of this*? Rex wondered.

Rex ran back to the bunker and helped Anna get dressed. She was in shock. Her eyes were glassy and stared into the distance.

"Gabriella?" Juan whispered.

Rex just shook his head.

"I didn't tell them anything."

"I know you didn't, my friend," Rex said helping him to his feet.

"Trust me… We will find her… I will find her," Rex said with conviction. "Now let's get you to a hospital," Rex said stepping outside the bunker, looking around for any means of transportation.

They were out in the middle of nowhere. The only thing he could see was a war relic. An old jeep parked next to the bunker, a very reliable and robust vehicle in World War II. But no telling what kind of shape she was in now, Rex looked her over.

"Amazing! No rust. Looks like someone was taking care of her over the years." Rex popped the hood. The engine was still there. He checked the oil and took one big whiff. She had gas too. Rex jumped in the driver's seat. *Where are the keys?* Rex thought, checking under the seat, then under the floor mat. No luck. One more spot, the visor. Rex pulled down on the visor, and the familiar sound of the jingling keys fell out. Rex caught them in midair on the way down.

"All right," he said as he turned her over. "Oh yeah." She started on the first try.

Rex loaded up Juan and Anna and headed down the mountain road. He has no idea where he was but figured that he just followed the tracks of the Sedan till he came across a familiar sight—Highway 3. Highway 3 was one of the main roads in Panama. Rex knew if he headed south, that would lead him to Panama City and the Gorgas Military Hospital.

Rex called Milton and Jillian who were working on the microchip and any other clues they could find from the kidnapping scene.

"I found them," Rex said exhausted from all of the day's activities.

"Are they okay?" Jillian asked.

"Yes. Anna was raped but right now resting comfortably. Juan, on the other hand, went in for emergency surgery for a gunshot wound to the leg."

"Glad they are okay," Jillian said.

"Oh, and by the way, I am okay too," Rex added sarcastically.

"Of course you are, dear, you are still talking," Jillian snipped back.

"I need the two of you down here right away," Rex said as he hung up the phone.

CHAPTER 15

Later that day

Milton and Jillian landed in Panama to rendezvous with Rex after hitting a dead-end with Pedro and the JML warehouse in Mexico City, Mexico.

"Where's the car, Rex?" Jillian asked as they moved through the parking lot.

Rex pointed at the jeep from hundred feet away.

"Really, Rex, that is the best you can do?" Jillian said tossing her bag into the back.

"I think she's a beaut," Milton said. "A bit of a classic," Milton said giving Rex the thumbs up.

They headed for the Gorgas Medical Hospital where Juan and Anna were recovering from their injuries after the kidnapping.

"What about Gabriella?" Jillian asked as they headed for the emergency room.

"I don't know," Rex said. "She was picked up by this doctor and got away…drove off in this dark sedan," Rex paused. "Something else… It had a US embassy sticker on the back windshield."

"US embassy… What do they have to do with it?" Milton asked.

"Not sure, but I managed to get a bug on the sedan before it got away," Rex said as they entered Anna's room.

Anna lay comatose and unresponsive after the attack. Her injuries were more psychological than physical. Juan, on the other hand, had a really bad infection, requiring the amputation of his right leg right below the hip. Juan had a more serious problem. The infection was spreading fast to all the major organs of the body, and the prognosis was not that great.

Rex Milton and Jillian returned to the hacienda later that night, hoping to get a lead on where the doctor took Gabriella. Rex turned on the bugs he had planted a few days ago, hoping they were still active—all seemed pretty quiet at the main house. Rex headed for the garage where he watched them unload the cargo from the truck into the garage. Rex watched as Jillian quickly picked the lock on the back door.

"What?" She looked at Rex strangely.

"Never mind," he said popping into the garage.

Inside, there was no sign of the miniloader or the cargo boxes from the other day.

"Maybe they moved them," Milton said looking around.

There was a noise. The ground shook, and the floor opened up. They all scrambled as the garage door suddenly opened, and a man driving a miniloader pulled in and went down the ramp.

Rex hit the floor and rolled into the opening. Jillian and Milton followed close behind as the door shut quickly behind them.

"Wow, an underground tunnel," Milton said staring at a twelve-by-twelve-foot concrete tunnel running under the house, dimly lit by a single strand of yellow lights.

"I think it went this way," Rex said pointing down the long tunnel.

They made their way down the tunnel to a solid steel door with an electronic keypad. Rex pointed at the electronic keypad. "What do you make of that?" Challenging Jillian to open it. *Even Jillian would have a hard time with this door*, Rex thought as he casually knocked on the door three times.

The door clicked then opened. Rex looked at Jillian and at Milton then laughed loudly as they heard a noise coming up behind them. It was the miniloader headed back to the garage. With no place to hide, Rex ran directly at him. The driver spotted Rex in his headlights, panicked, turning the wheel sharply to the right, smashing it into the side of the tunnel wall. Rex jumped up, caught the cage rail, swung his leg around, kicking him in the head, knocking him clean out. Rex grabbed the man's key card and headed back to the steel door.

Inside was a hub of tunnels leading in six to eight different directions from under the house. Rex scanned the next door. It was a huge warehouse lined with cubbies of all sizes. Milton and Jillian fanned out and looked around the room. It looked like a storage facility for a doomsday shelter. There were separate rooms for electronic equipment, dried and canned food.

"Hey, Rex, check this out," Milton called out from across the room, a weapons locker with thousands of guns of all types—handguns, automatic rifles, shotguns, bazookas, grenade launchers, even small handheld missiles.

Rex turned on the receiver then hit it a few times.

"What's the matter, Rex?" Jillian asked as they continued looking through the inventory.

"I can't get a signal from the bugs I planted," Rex said in disgust.

"Hold on," Jillian said as she scampered off. Jillian returned with several pieces of electronic equipment. "Let me have it," Jillian said holding out her hand. Rex handed over the receiver. "Your cell phone too," she said impatiently waiting, wiggling her fingers.

"Really? Will I get it back?" he asked as she smashed it on the side of a crate.

Jillian wired the cell phone to the receiver, then hooked it up to an amplifier, and a small monitor.

"Now try it," Jillian said, handing it back to Rex who turned it on.

"Wow, now I can see inside the house and hear what they are saying," Rex said as he moved through the frequencies.

Milton and Rex shuffled through some of the weapons, but one thing was abundantly clear to Milton, all the weapons were old and mostly discontinued, obsolete inventory from US military surplus.

Jillian called her old friend Captain Bruce Buxton in the State Department as it turns out they are very good friends. Apparently, they were lovers when they were stationed together in Washington, DC.

"Hi, Bruce," Jillian said in a low sexy voice.

"Jillian, is that you?" Bruce responded. "Nice to hear from you, Jillian. I really missed you?" he said sheepishly.

"Is that right, Bruce? You really missed me? So why haven't you called me?" Jillian asked.

"I don't know… I didn't want to seem too pushy…" Bruce said.

"Now why would you say that, Bruce? You know I have a thing for you…right?" Jillian said suggestively.

"Well, you sure didn't show it when you and I—"

"BRUCE!" Jillian interrupted. "Never mind that. I still have a thing for you. Bruce, I need a favor. It's very important," she said softly.

"Oh okay… It's important to you…but when it comes to me… well, that's a different story," Bruce rambled on and on.

"BRUCE!" Jillian interrupted again. "I will make it up to you when I get back…I promise…muaaa," Jillian said, blowing him a kiss into the phone.

"Oh okay… You promise?" he groveled.

"Yes, of course," she said softly.

"So what is the favor?" Bruce asked with a smile on his face.

"Do you still have your old contacts in the ATF?" Jillian asked. "I need you to check out some serial numbers we found down here in Panama," Jillian said.

"Yes, I do… Jillian, who's *we*?" Bruce asked.

"What?" Jillian was suddenly distracted.

"Is it that cowboy you hung out with in the CIA?" Bruce asked.

"Bruce, stay on point," Jillian said.

"What does he have you mixed up with now?" Bruce wondered.

"Don't fuss about that now… I'll send you the serial numbers in an encrypted message," Jillian said.

"When are you coming back?" Bruce asked, sounding a little desperate. "I really do miss you."

"All good things come to those who wait…patiently," Jillian said hanging up the phone.

"Wow, what was that all that about?" Milton asked.

"Unfinished business." She grinned.

"Any word on the weapons serial numbers I sent you?" Rex asked.

"I reached out to my friend Bruce in the State Department who can get the classified info from the ATF...but nothing yet," Jillian said with a slight sigh.

"What's going on?" Rex asked.

"Nothing... Nothing I can't handle."

"Is it Bruce?" Rex asked.

"What?" Jillian looked at Rex with a blank expression. "Yes, it's Bruce. I left him in the middle of the night...with no explanation," Jillian said.

"Hmmm, sounds familiar," Rex said.

"That's not the same," Jillian tried to defend her position. "It's complicated."

"Sure was," Rex said.

"Who are we talking about here?" Jillian said as her SAT phone rang.

"Captain Campbell," Jillian answered.

"It's Bruce," he whispered. "Are we on a secure line?"

"Yes, we are. My SAT phone is encrypted. What's the matter, Bruce?" Jillian asked.

"What are you mixed up with?" Bruce yelled into the phone, breathing heavily looking for a secluded place to talk.

"Calm down. What are you talking about?" Jillian asked.

"I ran those serial numbers you sent me," he said still whispering. "They brought up a whole lot of red flags," Bruce said breathing hard.

"What red flags?" Jillian asked.

"Several years ago, the government came up with a plan to flush out the major gun smugglers." Bruce took a deep breath. "They tagged a few most popular guns and gave them to straw buyers, then traced them back to the source intending to catch the big fish." Bruce breathed a little harder. "But something went wrong. The Mexican government was supposed to keep track of the serial numbers. Someone tipped off the buyers, and the guns disappeared...thousands of them." Bruce was almost hyperventilating. "Later, the ATF was aware of two hundred of the weapons that were found at various crime scenes in Mexico and several US cities along the border. The serial numbers you gave me were part of that ATF/FBI raid to smoke out gun traffickers and straw buyers in Mexico," Bruce added. "There were several ATF/FBI agents that got killed during that raid… It was a huge failure for the department and the administration."

"When an unnamed intelligence agent and unidentified confidential informant came forward with information on the leak," Bruce stopped suddenly.

"What was that?" Jillian asked.

"I heard something," Bruce whispered. "Jillian, the lead intelligence officers name was Benjamin Griffin…Rex's brother, and the confidential informant was Luiz De La Cruz…" Bruce still breathing hard. "Okay, listen…the investigation was botched before it started… The bureau of Political-Military Affairs Office and Public Affairs Department paid a huge price to cover it up, the attorney general and as high up as the presidency were embarrassed by the loss and huge mistakes," Bruce said sputtering. "The investigation went on for over a year, but eventually, it was buried and sealed. Till last week, when it all resurfaced again…when a confidential file was accessed and downloaded," Bruce paused so he could catch his breath.

"I pushed a little further. Those weapons you found were all supposed to be collected from the buyers and the gun runners and destroyed," Bruce hesitated then took a drink of water. "The Senate passed a bill WR-1584, a weapons reduction bill that would take the guns off the streets and out of the hands of the thugs." Bruce could barely breath. "After the weapons were collected, cataloged by the ATF and FBI, then verified by a congressional subcommittee to be destroyed," Bruce started whispering again. "However, other accounts of the operation insist that ATF agents were prevented from intervening, not by ATF officials but rather by federal prosecutors with the attorney general's office who were unsure of whether the agents had sufficient evidence to arrest suspected straw buyers."

"Hold on… I think someone is here," Bruce said quietly.

"Where are you?" Jillian asked.

"In my office…in the State Department. Okay, listen, the contracts were given to a company that specialized in weapons disposal,

DDR, Demobilization, Disarmament, and Reintegration Co. Jillian, the DDR Co. is a bogus company. A shell corporation set up in Panama." Bruce took a deep breath. "Every year, an appropriations committee votes on and approves millions of dollars toward the program," Bruce said. "But the money was paid to the DDR Co.," Bruce said breathing hard. "There is no trace of the weapons that left the defense department, heading to the DDR Co. I'm still trying to dig further into it, but it's kinda scary. The subcommittee was led by a powerful senator from Texas, Bradley Stevens. When I tried digging further, my computer was infiltrated and taken over. The firewall was breached…" Bruce said panicking "They are going to come after me…I know it," Bruce said whimpering.

"Did you download anything?" Jillian asked.

"No."

"Bruce, stay off the computer. I will see you in a couple of days. Love you…muahhh."

Jillian hung up the phone.

"What was that all about?" Rex asked.

"Bruce stumbled across some very sensitive information on those serial numbers you gave him," Jillian explained. "Apparently, they don't exist, at least that is what the State Department, the ATF, and even a subcommittee in Congress said," Jillian stopped.

"So what are they doing down here?" Milton asked.

"What exactly was Luiz into…and what is on that microdrive?" Rex asked. "Any luck on breaking the code?"

"Not yet, got some pretty heavy inscription, something close to what we used in the CIA," Jillian said.

"We can get Specks to help you," Milton said.

"Who? Robert?" Jillian said raising her eyebrows. "He's in custody," Jillian said.

"Well, not exactly…kinda on furlough with the government," Milton said. "I'll ring him in the morning," Milton said.

"See what else you can find out about the guns and the micro drive…. I am going to follow up on a lead at the embassy," Rex said.

"Rex?" Jillian said softly, wanting to tell him what Bruce said about his brother. "Never mind. It can wait. Good luck." She smiled.

CHAPTER 16

Rex headed to the US embassy hoping to get a lead the on the sedan with the sticker in the back window. The US embassy was located at Fort Clayton, just outside of Panama City. Rex pulled up outside the main gate and turned on the receiver.

"Darn, nothing," Rex said. "Probably too far away to get a signal." Rex needed a way into the embassy. *How do you get inside a US embassy?* Rex thought for a few minutes. One way, wait till nightfall and sneak under the wire like he did at the airport and hope not to get caught and thrown in the brig. Two, he could storm the gate probably get shot, not a very good option. This is after all a US embassy, guarded by some of the best and most dedicated guards you could ever ask for in the US Marines. *I would definitely get killed, also not a very good option. Wait a minute*, Rex thought. *This is a US embassy...in a foreign country.* A US citizen can seek refuge in a US embassy on foreign soil, so can a US military man on liberty especially, if that military man is in trouble with the locals. But Rex needed a good cover.

"I got it!" Rex shouted. Rex waited until nightfall and pulled the jeep around the back alley, stashed his wallet and ID under the seat. Now all he needed to do is make it look convincing.

Think, Rex. He looked around the alley. *Hmmm, a robbery. That's it.* Rex grabbed a piece of wood from the ground, held it firmly with both hands, then slammed it into the side of his head. The blood trickled down his cheek on to his favorite Hawaiian shirt. *Gotta make it look like I put up a fight*, Rex thought. He walked up to the brick wall, punched it, and slammed the wall with his elbow, hard enough to leave a nice bruise. *Can't have these Marines thinking the Navy man was a wimp for not putting up a fight.*" Rex wobbled up to the front of the embassy gates, fell to his knees.

"Help, I need help," Rex yelled.

Two Marines ran up to investigate.

"American, US Navy," Rex uttered then pretended to pass out.

The Marines followed protocol, signaled for the gate to be opened, and called for a medic. The Marines took Rex to a secure location inside the embassy, tended to his wounds, and waited to be debriefed by the security officer.

"Name, rank, and serial number?" the Marine captain asked.

"Rex Nelson, US Navy, 367-56-3467," Rex spouted off.

"So what happened?" the Marine Captain asked.

"Rex Nelson, US Navy, 367-56-3467," Rex said deliriously. "I was attacked by five locals. They beat me up and stole my wallet and tags, sir," Rex winced as the medic sewed up the gash above his left eye. "Have to get back to the ship, sir, can't be late," Rex yelled deliriously. "Gotta get back to the ship, sir. Rex Nelson, US Navy, 367-56-3467…can't be late, sir," Rex kept repeating.

"We will keep you for observation and contact your CO and let him know you are here," the Marine captain said. "Who's your CO?" the captain asked.

"I don't know… Rex Nelson, US Navy, 367-56-3467, gotta get back to my ship…can't be late, sir," Rex repeated deliriously again.

"What is the matter with him, corpsman? He keeps repeating himself," the Marine captain asked.

"I think it's the head wound, sir… He's been repeating the same thing since we brought him in," the corpsman said.

"Keep him confined till we can confirm his story," the Marine captain told the corpsman who was bandaging up his wounds.

"We will get you back to your ship soon enough," the Marine captain told him as he walked into the next room.

"Rex Nelson, US Navy, 367-56-3467, get back to my ship… can't be late, sir," Rex repeated deliriously again. "Where's the head?" Rex asked the posted Marine guard, wiggling like a five-year-old about to pee his pants. The Marine Corporal escorted Rex to the head and waited outside the door. Rex jumped up on the sink and removed a ceiling tile then pulled himself up into the attic space above, then walked across the rafters like a tightrope performer in the Barnum and Bailey's circus. Rex hid in an isolated corner of the attic.

Waaaaaaa, waaaaa, waaaaaa, the alarms immediately sounded, and floodlights came on all over the embassy to search for the man and possible intruder. After an hour, the all-clear signal was given, and the alarm turned off, and the embassy resumed normal operations. Rex activated the receiver and picked up a very weak signal, coming from his right and below him. Rex looked around the attic space then through a small window. There was nothing there, except a solid concrete wall and another concrete structure next door. *How do I get down there without going back into the building?* Rex thought, looking around.

Next to him was a service door for the elevator shaft. Rex pried the door open and looked down. *Hmmm…had to be six stories, the building isn't that tall.* Rex figured the reason for the weak signal. The sedan had to be somewhere in an underground parking structure.

Rex looked down the shaft again. He's seen it in the movies a dozen times, jump out, grab the cable, and slide down. *How hard could that be? Piece of cake. No problem.* Rex reached out, grabbed the cable, wrapped his legs around it, and slid halfway down. The elevator made a funny noise. The cables shifted in his hands, one going up, and the other down. Rex lost his grip when the elevator suddenly stopped and changed directions. Now in a free fall with an elevator car racing toward him from below. "This is gonna hurt," he said as he sprawled out like a cat getting tossed out of a second story window. Fortunately, the elevator was moving up as Rex landed hard on top of the cage. Rex could hear several voices as the elevator headed in the wrong direction…straight up.

Rex looked at the top of the elevator shaft quickly approaching. With absolutely no time to get off, he braced himself, hoping not to get squished like a bug when it reached the top floor. The elevator stopped just in time, then reversed heading back down.

"Oh boy, here we go again," Rex said hoping this wild ride would end soon. When the elevator finally stopped, the signal was much stronger and directly ahead of him. The garage was full of dark blue sedans all lined up in the lower parking garage, but as the signal got stronger, Rex found the one he was looking for. He jimmied the lock in record time and jumped in, probably too long if you ask Jillian, but he did have the record at the CIA Academy, an amazing twelve seconds flat.

Rex checked all the usual spots for anything that would give him a clue as to whom the sedan belonged to or who had it last. There were candy wrappers, cigarette butts, and a chewed pieces of gum in the ashtray. The glove box was clean, just a manual on how to change a tire.

"Ya, that was really useful…as if that's ever going to happen." Rex giggled to himself. "Bingo," Rex said after he pulled down the visor. A small piece of paper fluttered down in front of him. It read: "Senator Stevens. Aeropuerto Internacional de Tocumen 3pm, yesterday."

Senator Stevens? Rex thought. *Could that be the same Senator Bradley Stevens from Houston, Texas, a member of the board of directors at the JML Corporation, Senator Stevens? What was he doing down here? Could he somehow be involved in all this?"* Rex's mind went in ten different directions.

Rex remembered a formal ceremony when Senator Bradley Stevens endorsed his appointment into the US Naval Academy. Rex reached into his pocket and pulled out a small bug and planted it under the ashtray, then moved to the back seat, and planted one between the two seats.

Bleep, bleep…the door locks popped open. They couldn't be too far away.

"Come on, Rex, think." Rex ducked out the back door, onto the ground, and under the car next to him. Rex listened carefully as all four doors opened then closed. Rex plugged in the remote earpiece but could barely make out the voices from the front seat and made it impossible with the radio playing.

Rex adjusted the frequency and picked up the conversation in the back seat.

"What the hell happened last night?" the man asked angrily.

"There was a breach of security," the man told him.

"You call that a breach of security? More like an all-out war.

"How many men attacked?" the man asked.

"I spoke with the doctor, and he said there was only one man."

"WHAT?" the man yelled from the back seat. "Are you trying to tell me that *one* man killed…what *five* of your men…and he took two of the hostages?" the man continued yelling.

"And one of the twins too," the second man added. The doctor was pretty upset about that."

"I don't care about the doctor or his dead twin."

"What about the microdrive?" he asked.

The sedan moved slowly through the garage.

"Nothing yet, sir… We can't find it."

Rex rolled out from under the car and ran to the edge of the parking structure.

"What about the other—" The signal broke up and faded away.

Rex went to the jeep parked in the alley across the street. Rex belly rolled off the top of the parking structure, then dropped down to the next level, barely grabbing the last rail.

"Wow, just four more to go," Rex said as he dropped to the next level then the next. Finally, dropping the last twenty feet, tucking and rolling when he hit the ground. Rex listened again to the signal as he ran across the street to the back alley.

"Who was the man?"

"We don't know, but he's well-trained, probably ex-military."

"Obviously—" The signal broke up and faded.

Rex ran for the jeep, started it up, and headed toward the front of the parking garage, looking around for the sedan. The last thing Rex heard was "the airfield" as the signal faded away.

Rex pictured Panama in his mind. The man mentioned that he would see them at the "airfield." *What airfield could he be talking about?* Rex thought for a minute. The airfield he mentioned could be the one Rex flew into a few days ago—the so-called abandoned France Field where they dropped off the weapons. On a hunch, Rex headed north about two hours to France Field in Colon on the north coast of Panama, bordering the Atlantic Ocean.

France Field was the first military airfield established in Panama to protect the Panama Canal. In the mid-1950s, it became a civilian airport with the USAF, maintaining jurisdiction till 1973…but now it's seldom used and occasionally used as a satellite field of Albrook AFB. Rex parked the jeep in a cluster of trees and headed in on foot. It seemed abandoned except for the lights in one of the big hangars. Rex peeked inside the door. This place was set up like a huge summer camp. Small rooms lined the main hallway, an open area with several couches, chairs all arranged in little groups. The long hallway led to a cafeteria of sorts with about fifty girls lined up eating dinner.

Rex watched as several girls got up and headed down the hallway and into one of the small rooms. *What was this place?* Rex wondered. *Some sort of camp for girls?* Rex slipped down the hallway and into one of small rooms. Two young ladies walked in a few minutes later, chatting loudly with each other in what sounded like Spanish, but it was broken and sounded different.

"Holla," Rex said as the girls stared at him, startled to see a man standing there. "Yo soy el conserje y barre los pasillos todos los dias." Rex smiled then grabbed a trash can and proceeded to change the bag. "Que paso aqui?" Rex asked one of the young girls in really bad Spanish.

The one girl looked at him strangely as she tried to understand what he was saying, chitchatting with her friend again, "Must not be Spanish," as he tried to explain.

"You speak English?" she asked quietly.

"Yes, of course," Rex continued in English. "What's going on here?" Rex asked.

"We are going to America," the young lady shouted from across the small room.

"Where are your parents? Are your parents not with you?" Rex asked.

"My sister and I are going to school in America. Student exchange program," the girl said. "My father paid three hundred thousand pesos for each of us. We are meeting our foster families in the USA," the other sister said.

"Silencio." There was a loud knock at the door. "Silencio," the voice shouted, then a big woman entered the room. "Who were you talking to?" she blurted out.

"The janitor," they both said in unison.

"What janitor?" she barked.

"He was changing the trash bags," the young lady said pointing toward the trash can.

"Shushhhh now," the big lady said looking around the room. "We don't have a janitor," she mumbled to herself as she walked out the door.

It was one in the morning when the lights came on all over the warehouse.

"Despierta se, Despierta se," the burley woman yelled out, knocking on all the doors.

The girls came out of their rooms wandering aimlessly wondering what was going on, wearing nothing but their pajamas. Armed guards gathered up the girls and led them to a large school bus parked out front. Rex watched as the bus full of young girls pulled away. *Where were they going at this time of night?* Rex wondered, heading back to the warehouse where the girls were held. There was one guard left on duty making his rounds. Rex snuck in the small room at the end of the hallway that looked like an office, papers and files were scattered all over the small desk along with a couple of metal chairs and a pot of coffee still on the burner. "A sight for sore eyes," as he could barely resist the aroma. "Not the best cup of coffee, but it hit the spot."

On the desk was a memo DOC-32 at 3:00 a.m. Rex checked his watch…close to 2:00 a.m. *Must be why they left in such a hurry,* Rex thought as he looked over at the large map of Panama hanging on the wall. Rex picked up the phone on the desk and dialed Jillian. The phone buzzed a couple of times, then Jillian picked up.

"Jillian?" Rex said.

"Wow, you are on a landline?" Jillian said wondering why he was doing that.

"Why, yes, I am…for a very good reason," he said. "I want you to trace this number and let me know what you can find out about it?" Rex asked.

"Anything in particular I should be looking for?" Jillian asked cautiously.

"Oh, anything unusual… One more thing, can you tell me where I am?" Rex asked.

"What? Now that is unusual. You okay?" Jillian busted out laughing.

"What happened?" Milton asked.

"You forget where you are?" Jillian continued laughing.

"He's lost. He doesn't know where he is," she whispered to Milton who was listening in.

"How'd he managed that?" Milton let out a howl.

"France Field," Jillian told him.

That's it, Rex thought for a minute.

"France Field was used by the US military in the mid- to late-50s, but it was decommissioned and closed years ago," Jillian said.

"Why are they here?" Rex thought out loud.

"What was that, Rex?" Jillian asked confirming it was France Field.

"Who are they, Rex?" Milton asked.

"France Field, that is where we are," Rex mumbled.

"Yes, Rex, France Field," Jillian confirmed.

"DOC-32 must be a dock or marina near the ocean." Rex slid his finger across the map, the international port in Colon, Panama. "That must be where they have gone."

"Where did who go?" Jillian asked looking a little confused.

"The girls."

"Girls…what girls?" Jillian asked.

"One more thing… What can you tell me about a DOC-32 in and or around Colon and the Panama Canal?" Rex asked.

"What are you planning a cruise or something? Can I come along?" Jillian asked playfully.

"We can talk about vacations once we solve this murder/mystery," Rex answered. "I am at a warehouse at an abandoned airfield that used to be used by the US government in the fifties. I spotted thirty girls being loaded onto a bus. I think they were headed to DOC-32 in Colon headed to America," Rex paused.

"What did you say?" Jillian interrupted. "They might be headed to America?"

"Yes, I was following up on a lead from last night. I managed to get a bug on the sedan that took Gabriella, the one with the US embassy tag on the back window. When I followed them this morning, they led me here. An abandoned airfield."

"Rex, not much on DOC-32 in the port of Colon," Jillian said after researching it on the computer. It's been shut down for over three years since the major fire. Since then, it's been under construction."

"The little girl in the room said they were headed to America."

"Why were they headed for America?" Rex wondered.

"I think we may have stumbled across a smuggling operation. One that involves girls heading to America," Rex said. "Okay, thanks, Jillian. I'll see you tomorrow." Rex hung up the phone and finished off the coffee.

Rex headed for the port city of Colon, a thriving town of over two hundred thousand people. It was nearly three o'clock in the morning when Rex pulled up to the *dock* off Avenida Randolph in Colon. The southern tip of Manzanillo island was designated as the Colon Free Trade Zone, a large entity near the Atlantic entrance to the Panama Canal, dedicated to exporting a wide variety of merchandise to Latin America and the Caribbean. It was a perfect choke point for drugs and other contraband coming up from Central and South America, heading north to the United States of America.

Jillian forwarded Rex a map and location of the so-called DOC-32. As Rex headed down Avenida Randolph, he spotted the sedan from the other night parked next to the school bus and assumed that Gabriella was nearby. Rex parked the jeep in a wooded area just off the main road and headed in on foot. This part of the port was surrounded by a fifteen-foot barbed-wire fence with a row of concertina wire across the top, security post with armed guards. Rex recalled his last encounter with a barbed wire fence, and it did not go so well.

Rex walked up to the main fence to get a closer look when he heard a rustling behind him. It was a port security patrol, making its rounds, one guard and a large dog. Rex hid in the bushes nearby and watched as they made a security sweep of the area around the jeep, but he knew he could not stay there much longer before the dog picked up his scent. Rex made his way straight down the fence line for one hundred fifty feet, then doubled back passed the jeep in a big semicircle back around to where the jeep was. Rex's plan worked as the dog picked up on the scent and made its way down the fence line one hundred and fifty feet then stopped. By the time the dog and the security guard doubled back and followed the sent around the circle, Rex had plenty of time to get into the jeep and down the road.

Rex drove down, and after making the final turn onto Avenida Randolph, he encountered a security checkpoint. The guards were on alert and appeared to be actively looking for someone. Rex drove slowly passed the security post, trying not to raise too much suspicion, but it was too late. The guard recognized the jeep and set off the alarm. Rex considered his options carefully. Pull over and talk his way out of it, but without papers, passports, or reason for being in the country at that time of night, that might not go over so well. The second option of casually making a U-turn and heading in the opposite direction, when he realized that the SUV was heading directly toward him and gaining speed. Rex punched the accelerator of the old jeep to the floor. It lurched then belted out a cloud of black smoke as it accelerated, but not fast enough as the security force wasted no time catching up. Outrunning two high-power SUVs in a 1945 relic of a jeep was not a viable option.

Rex had to think of a plan and fast. Up ahead was a sharp left hand turn, and from the looks of it, a steep embankment on the other side, his plan was a risky one, but it was a plan, nonetheless. Rex took the turn at around forty miles per hour. Once he cleared the corner and out of sight of the fast approaching SUVs, Rex straightened the wheel then jumped out, tumbling down a small hill, colliding with the base of a large tree. The jeep ran straight and true for about one hundred feet before plunging over the side down the hill into a ravine. The fast moving SUV swung around the corner just as the jeep made its final plunge over the cliff.

Rex figured if he ran straight down the hill in the same direction of the SUVs, when they realized that he was no longer in the jeep, they would double back to search for him; by that time, he would be in front of them. Rex jumped up, took two steps, and fell flat on his stomach, feeling a sharp pain in his lower back, radiating down his left leg. With all the adrenaline pumping through his veins, he never realized he was hurt, impaled by a small branch. Rex doubled back through the woods to the perimeter fence around the port facility. It was about 2:50 a.m., and the doctor's sedan was still at the DOC, but the ship *Le Saint Vincent* flying the French flag had already left port.

This time when Rex heard rustling behind him, he faced two very hungry and angry dogs; apparently, they tracked him through the woods. The guards shoved him up against the chain-link fence and pulled the ten-inch piece of wood out of his back, then punched him in the lower back. Normally a blow like that only tickled, but when you have been thrown from a moving jeep at forty miles an hour and had a ten-inch tree limb sticking out of you, it hurt a little.

Rex was blindfolded and taken to an undisclosed location. Chained and bound by his hands and feet hanging from the rafters, like a piece of meat waiting to be butchered. The door creaked open, and a very large man walked in, wearing an oversized camo shirt with an ammo belt slung across one shoulder, followed by a little man wearing a white doctor's smock.

"Do you know who I am?" the doctor asked.

"A little man that enjoys hurting old men and raping young girls," Rex said grinning.

"My friend over there wants to tear you to pieces," the doctor whispered in a low-guttural German accent. "Do you know why?"

"Damn, I thought I killed him yesterday," Rex sneered.

"You killed his twin brother. I told him that after I got some answers from you, he could have you all to himself."

The doctor laid the small leather satchel on the table and unrolled it slowly, the glitter of the knives reminded Rex of the time he was imprisoned and tortured by the Somali pirates. They liked to play with knives too. The large man ripped Rex's shirt off, then leaned back and laughed, for he knew what was about to happen.

"No mata el hombre," the big man told the doctor as he stepped back from Rex.

The doctor walked over to the table, picked out a long curved blade and slowly rolled the tip across the other blades, making a loud tingling noise like musical notes of an eerie song. The doctor walked up behind Rex and looked at the scars.

"I see you have been here before," the doctor said, tracing some of the old scars with the tip of the knife.

"They regretted it too," Rex said grinning.

"So who are you?" he asked leaning in, expecting a quick answer.

Rex just looked him and said nothing.

"We can do this the easy way or the hard way, your choice," the doctor said jabbing the tip of the knife into Rex's right shoulder socket.

"Who are you?" as he twisted it slowly from side to side.

"Hey, little man…maybe the big man can make it hurt this time," Rex joked as the knife tip scrapped across the bone, shooting a sharp pain up his arm to the side of his neck.

"Let me…let me…I'll make him talk," the big man told the doctor.

"Soon," the doctor said clearly pissed that he was not getting the results he had planned, stepped out of the room, closely followed by the big man begging to take care of him.

When the door closed, Rex knew he had only a few minutes to figure out a way to get loose. Rex had very loose joints, great for getting out of tough spots, and a unique ability to dislocate his thumbs, making it a sure way of getting out of handcuffs or manacles. Rex rotated his thumb till they popped, then slipped out of the restraints.

Now as far as his ankle restraints are concerned, that was a different story. He had never been able to dislocate his ankles like his thumbs. Rex looked at the shackles. They were bolted to the ground with a single bolt. Rex wrapped the chains around his wrists, crouched down, and pulled. The muscles in his upper back tensed up as the bolt moved slightly, but the strain on his right shoulder was too much to bear. Rex reached down to the chains around his ankles, wrapped them tightly around his thighs to take up the slack, then reached up with his left arm to the chain on the rafter above. Rex pulled with his left arm and pushed with his powerful legs. The bolt wiggled them, finally broke loose. Rex thought about running but decided to end the reign of the doctor once and for all.

The doctor returned a few minutes later with a small wooden box as Rex hung motionless, almost lifeless from the beam. The doctor poked at him a few times, but Rex did not respond. When the big man passed within striking distance, Rex reared up and kicked him in the jaw with both feet, snapping his head back violently. The doctor turned to see what was happening but was too late. Rex kicked him, throwing him up against the wall, momentarily knocking him out. The big man dropped to the floor, woozy from the blow. Rex wrapped the chains from his feet around his neck and curled up his legs, cutting off the circulation to his head.

When the doctor finally woke up, he was hanging from the rafters. Rex wanted to just kill him for all the things that he had done, but that would have been too easy. He wanted to teach him a lesson and make him suffer at least a little anyway.

"Wake up, doctor." Rex slapped him across the face several times.

The doctor woke, then pushed down on the ropes to alleviate the stress on his arms; at the same time, the rope slowly moved around tightening the noose around his neck.

"I wouldn't do that if I were you," Rex cautioned the good doctor, "might be bad for your health."

His hands were tied behind his back with one loop down around his feet, and the other wrapped around his neck from behind, then into a one-way slipknot. The Spanish called it "strappado," a very uncomfortable position to be in.

"So, doctor, you like playing with knives...ehhh?" Rex walked around the doctor the same way he had with Rex.

"Well I like playing with ropes. Several years ago in the CIA, I met this magician friend that taught me a few rope tricks," Rex paused. "This one is a self-induced sentencing rope trick... You see, with a judge, jury, and executioner all built into one... You like it? The more you struggle the faster the sentence. Who do you work for?"

Rex listened carefully, but there was no response.

"Where is Gabriella?" Rex asked.

The doctor's legs grew tired of supporting his weight, so he pushed down with his legs, in turn pulling up on his arms, slowly tightening the noose around his neck.

"It is truly a self-fulfilling prophecy," Rex said. "One more thing…there is no escape, and the end result is always the same… justice. Now, where is Gabriella?" Rex asked for the final time.

"El Jefe," the doctor whispered, pushing down with his legs as the noose tightened around his neck. It is truly a self-fulfilling prophecy as the doctor slowly suffocated and died.

CHAPTER 17

ㅡㅡㅡ◈◈◈ㅡㅡㅡ

Rex returned to Gorgas Medical Hospital in Panama.
"What happened to you?" Jillian asked as Rex hobbled into
the emergency room.

"The name El Jefe mean anything to you?" Rex asked Jillian as
several nurses tended to his wounds.

"Ah iiii… Que passo," the head nurse said as she examined Rex's
wounds.

"No, why?"

"It's the last thing the doctor uttered before he died…he whispered El Jefe."

The nurse took Rex into a treatment room and laid him down
on a gurney. Jillian and Milton followed close behind.

"Maybe that is why Luiz was murdered…because he found out
something about this El Jefe guy," Rex continued. *What is El Jefe?*
Rex wondered.

"The boss, the boss," the pretty nurse said as she made Rex take
off his clothes and get into a hospital gown.

Rex's wounds were pretty severe, puncture wounds to the right
shoulder and lower back, lacerations to the arms, severe bruising to
the thighs and forearms.

"Just patch me up, doc," Rex said as he lay on the treatment
table.

"I have to give you a shot, Señor," the nurse said, holding a
syringe in her hand.

"Is it going to hurt?" Rex asked the nurse.

"Turn over please."

"Just turn over, you big baby." Jillian laughed as she grabbed a pinch of flesh and jabbed Rex in the buttock. "Ouch," Rex cried out when the needle went in. He hated shots; they always hurt.

"Where is Anna?" Rex asked. "Is she okay?"

Anna's injuries were mainly superficial. The minor scrapes and bruises would heal over time, but the psychological trauma of her being brutally raped and watching her uncle being tortured and nearly killed would take much longer.

Rex walked into Juan's room. Juan's leg wound was more serious. The treatment wasn't working, and the right leg had to be amputated above the right knee.

"Jillian, where's Milton?" Rex asked.

Jillian pointed over her shoulder.

"Is he okay?"

Milton was in a wheelchair surrounded by several lovely Latin nurses, listening intently to him going on about his missions and acts of bravery.

"Yup, just fine for a sixty-five-year-old," Jillian snickered.

Rex walked up to the nurses station. "He's a little crazy," he said whirling his finger around his ear in a circular motion. "Time to go old timer," Rex said, pushing him out of the wheelchair.

The nurses laughed as he tried to get all their phone numbers.

"We have a new mission," Rex said walking back to Juan's room.

"Where are we with the guns?" Rex asked.

"I reached out to my friend Bruce in the State Department. The guns were supposed to be destroyed by DDR Inc...part of a arms reduction initiative run by the US Senate. As far as we can tell, the job was cancelled, funds diverted to an offshore account in the Cayman Islands, and the guns to France Field. That is all we have right now. Bruce was getting back to me about the accounts in Panama," Jillian explained.

"I followed the sedan to the airfield...where I ran across several young girls all heading for America. Some kind of exchange program...tied in with churches." Rex pulled out one of the flyers from the small office.

"Sounds like a smuggling ring…transporting girls from Central and South America to the USA," Milton said looking over the flyer.

"I got picked up by the security patrol at the port of Colon, DOC-32. They were loading a cargo ship, the *Saint Vincent*, flying a French flag."

"I tracked Gabriella to the warehouse facility at the abandoned airport, then on to the ship. The *Saint Vincent's* that left port from Panama at three o'clock this morning. I think it was headed to the United States."

"Do you think Gabriella was on board that ship?" Jillian asked.

"Possibly, but I never saw her."

"There was somebody else in that sedan, giving all the orders," Rex said, "somebody tied to the embassy."

"What's our next move?" Milton asked.

"Gotta find out how all these pieces fit together," Rex said.

"How are we going to do that?" Milton asked.

"I have an idea," Jillian said dancing around. "I can go undercover."

"What? I don't get it." Rex looked at Milton and wondered what she was up to. "Milton, do you know what she's talking about?"

"With the girls?" Jillian said prancing around.

"I will go undercover with the girls and find out where they are being taken. Maybe even get a lead on where Gabriella is being held."

"Not sure if I like this plan," Rex said.

"I'll be fine. You said it was like summer camp."

"Rex, I need to make a stop," Jillian whispered as they headed for France Field.

"Where?" Rex asked.

"The mall, got to pick up a few things for the trip," Jillian said grinning.

"You go on. I'll wait for you in the car," Rex said pulling up to the mall entrance.

"Oh no, come on, I need your help. Besides, you are paying for the bill. Park over there," she said pointing at an open parking spot.

Jillian headed right to the teen boutique store. "Perfect," Jillian said, pulling Rex into the store against his will. Jillian ran over to the preteen section and picked out several cute outfits.

"Why am I here?" Rex asked as Jillian handed him several pieces of clothing for him hold. "You are buying them for me, silly…hold this." She took his hand playfully and headed for the changing rooms.

Rex followed cautiously as to not attract too much attention, but he stuck out like a sore thumb.

"Hey, baby, can you get that miniskirt I showed you and bring it to me?" Jillian yelled out from inside the dressing room.

Rex walked over to the rack and picked out two colors, a plain and a multicolored, then returned to the dressing room.

"Thanks, dear," she yelled loud enough to be heard across the whole department.

Jillian came out of the dressing room wearing a short multicolored miniskirt and a white short-sleeve top. "What do you think, Daddy?" she asked, running up to Rex kicking up her leg as she pecked him on the cheek. Not far away, an older woman shook her head back and forth in disgust as she looked on.

At the register, Jillian turned to the older lady.

"My daddy is buying it for me. What do you think?" She smiled and pecked him on the cheek.

Later that night, Rex and Jillian arrived at the warehouse at France Field where Gabriella and the other girls were last seen. It was late at night when a school bus pulled up with twenty or so young girls on board. Jillian watched as they got off the bus one or two at a time heading into the warehouse. Jillian looked at Rex.

"Time to go," she said. "How do I look?" she asked spinning around like a ballerina.

"Lovely, like a daughter I never had," Rex said. "Listen, you will need this," Rex pulled back the slide then handed her a compact Sig Sauer P938 with a concealment holster and extra magazine.

Jillian took the Sig, slipped the elastic strap up around her leg, and pulled it up and under her miniskirt.

"Thanks, babe," she said, giving him a quick kiss as she hurried down the hill toward the bus. Jillian loved going on undercover covert missions it made her feel alive.

Some of the girls were giggling and fumbling with their bags as they got off the bus. Jillian slipped in line.

"Here, let me help you with that." She reached down and grabbed the suitcase of one of the girls and helped her along. Rex watched as she sauntered her way to the back of the warehouse.

*****

Inside, the girls were paired off into separate rooms. Jillian threw her stuff on the bed, then jumped on it a few times. Jillian greeted her roommate with a big hug who started jabbering something in Spanish. Jillian looked at her strangely.

"Do you speak English?"

"Yes, a little," she said smiling.

"What is your name?" Jillian asked.

"Antonia Rodrigues, you?"

"Jillian Campus," she said slapping her hand the way two girls would at that age.

"So you going in America?" Jillian asked, hoping to get more information.

"Yes, New Orleans. Then my sponsor family will take me to Boston," Antonia said.

"You not get a paper?" Antonia handed Jillian a flyer.

"Oh yes." Jillian scanned it quickly and came up with a story.

"My sponsor family will meet me in New Orleans and go to Houston, Texas," Jillian said. "My mom and dad in Quito, Ecuador… I go to America, go to school, get job, visa live free in America." She handed Jillian the flyer.

> Go to America
> Fulfill your dreams, FREE education,
> Green card and work visas offered for FREE
> Stay with foster families

Jillian looked it over. Wow, there was no mention of who she was meeting, just a foster family in New Orleans. *New Orleans?* Jillian thought. *That had to be the destination. By boat from Panama through the Panama Canal across the Gulf of Mexico to the port of New Orleans had, in a cargo ship averaging fifteen knots, 1,800 nautical miles. That should take about a week to ten days.*

"Gotta get a message to Rex and Milton," she said.

Later that night, the girls headed to the main dining area for a supper of tortillas, beans, rice, and potato salad. This was pretty nice for some illegal trafficking ring. Jillian waited till well past midnight, making sure everyone was asleep. She got into her cute little red PJs with little white hearts all over them and headed down the hall to the restroom. The chaperone or part-time guard was on the far side of the warehouse talking with another man.

Jillian slipped into the bathroom stall, a quick look around then jumped up on the sink, removed one of the ceiling tiles and in one acrobatic move, kicked into the attic space above. This was a huge warehouse with plenty of room in the attic. Jillian looked around and got her bearings.

Jillian looked around for Rex's care package; it was above the men's bathroom, wrapped in a black trash bag. "Got it." She opened the bag and looked through it. SAT phone, couple of electronic bugs, lock-picking kit with the directions. Jillian laughed then headed for the lighted area, a small office with one man sleeping inside. Jillian quietly removed the ceiling tile and dropped in behind him. With catlike reflexes, she got him in a reverse headlock, squeezed slowly, putting him to sleep.

Jillian pulled out one of the bugs Rex left her and placed it under the desk, quick check of the computer. It was off and password protected. No time to break into it right now.

She ruffled through the file cabinet nearby when she heard a knock at the door.

"Miguel...oh, Miguel," the woman called out.

Jillian ran behind the man and slapped him really hard on the back of the neck, his eyes fluttered, and arms twitched. Jillian heard the jingle of several keys, unlocking the door and barely had enough time to slip back up into the attic space.

A large woman walked through the door. "Miguel," the woman yelled, slapping him on the side of the head knocking him on to the floor.

"Estas borracho, Miguel?" she asked kicking him and the other guard out of the room. "Llamame, en la manana," she said slamming the door.

Jillian headed back to her room, needing desperately to get a message to Rex and Milton. She pulled out the SAT phone Rex left her and turned it on.

Dead battery, light flashes briefly then went out. *Are you kidding me, Rex? How many times do I have to tell you to charge your phone?* Jillian thought to herself, trying to figure out another way to get a message out. The SAT phone was basically useless without power and a charger, which she had neither. All she needed was a little juice. This place was old, and they had the older phone jacks in all the rooms. Jillian pulled the wires from the wall. All telephone wires had a low voltage/current running through it for the dial tone.

She pulled the back off the SAT phone and plugged in a phone wire combination. *Bingo, a slow trickle charge.* Jillian hid the phone and would have to get back to it later after a good charge.

The next morning, all the girls were asked to tell their story, a short bio on camera. Antonia was fourteen years old from a small farming community near Colombia. She was the oldest of four girls. She liked playing games and going to school. Antonia's parents were forced to give up their farm to the government that made it impossible for them to make any money. When Antonia came home from school one afternoon, she had a flyer from a local church, offering opportunities for young girls to go to America. Enroll in school, live with foster families in America, and get a green card, bring your families, all are welcome in America. Antonia's family was desperate to get out of Colombia. With government corruption, things were bad. Antonia's parents took their life's savings—five hundred thousand pesos or twenty thousand US dollars and gave it to the church for the safe passage for their daughter.

Later that night, the girls were dressed in very nice clothes, their hair made up and makeup. Jillian had an idea of what was happening but went along with it to get to the end user. The girls were taken individually to a small separate room. They were told to pose both playfully and erotically for the camera. Jillian returned to the room.

The battery had charged enough to get a message to Rex and Milton. Jillian dialed the phone.

"Hello," Rex answered.

"It's Jillian."

"I see you got my care package," Rex said smiling.

"Yes, but you forgot one very important thing."

"What's that?"

"The charger, Rex…and you forgot to fully charge the phone," Jillian said with a little hostility.

"I see you came up with something…you always do," Rex said like a proud parent. "So what's going on? How's summer camp?" Rex asked.

"Well, it looks like they are recruiting the girls through the local churches, promising them work visas and citizenship," Jillian stopped. "But something else… I think it's part of a human trafficking ring, transporting them…to the USA via New Orleans."

The following night around 8:00 p.m., the guards showed up with automatic weapons, forcing them to board buses. Some of the girls cried out, but Jillian knew where they were headed. The bus route to the *docks*, took them through the worst part of town. Jillian recalled that DOC-32 was shut down because of the fire three years ago; apparently, it had reopened for business.

Twenty-five girls were taken off the bus and jammed into a thirty-by-ten cargo container with the small wooden bench all the way around. Each girl wore a padlocked leather strap around their waist with a small hoop on the back to feed the chains through.

Halfway back was a false wall, a separate room for the two guards and the big woman.

Jillian kept thinking to herself if they were headed to the United States with an intended destination of New Orleans, that's 1,900 miles across the Gulf of Mexico, and at the average speed of ten knots that of a cargo vessel, it would take about a week to ten days to get to New Orleans. The conditions were horrible. There was no place to sleep and without running water, no toilets, just a small bucket and rags were passed around as needed. After the second day at sea, the stench was unbearable.

Once or twice a day, the guards would bring around meat tacos, beans, rice, and water.

"It's not what they promised, not what they promised," Antonia cried out repeatedly, over and over again.

"Who promised you?" Jillian asked softly.

"The school, the school at the church" she cried out.

On the third day, two of the guards came out in the middle of the night, at least that is what it seemed like. Without a clock, it was impossible to know the actual time. They flashed the lights into some of the girls' faces.

The guards were dirty and stink of alcohol. "Esta." The one guard pointed at one young girl.

"Si, bueno, tambien esta." The other guard pointed and grinned as they untied the two girls and took them into the back room. Jillian had a feeling that she knew what they were up to, but being chained to the wall, she had no way of stopping them. Besides, at this point in the mission, it was more important to find the leader and take down the organization than stopping these animals. But there will be a time to do that…just not now. Few minutes later, you could hear the muffled screams. Men laughing and grunting as they took turns on the two young girls. An hour or so later, the guards returned the girls to their spots. Their clothes ripped, faces reddened, and bruised from multiple slaps. Jillian was pissed and wanted to break their stinking necks with her bare hands.

The guards returned the next night and walked down the line, flashing lights into their eyes. "Pick me…you bastards…pick me," Jillian said quietly smiling as the guard passed by.

"Hi," Jillian said softly as the guard stopped momentarily, then untied her and dragged her to the back.

It was a small space, gas stove, a small table, and small single spring mattress. There was a curtain strung across the room, probably for privacy since there was no sign of the big lady anywhere.

One man shoved Jillian's head deep into the pillow as the other one started pulling off her clothes. Jillian knew exactly how she was going to do it. She had it all planned out. Jillian had trained for this situation. She volunteered for the Navy SEAL program that included two weeks of survival, evasion, resistance, and escape (SERE) training one of the toughest courses the Navy SEALs had to offer.

First, lure them in, and at exactly the right time, roll over, swing her leg around his neck, arch her back in a nice tight triangle choke, one squeeze, and *crack*, it would be all over.

A loud woman's voice yelled something in Spanish from behind the curtain as it was pulled back quickly. Jillian watched as the woman walked up and slapped the man off Jillian and onto the floor with a thud. Jillian watched in amusement as the woman punched the second man, slammed him to the floor, and beat the tar out of both of them. Cursing at the two of them in Spanish, something about damaging the merchandise. Jillian was actually enjoying the show and wanted more. Maybe she would not have to kill them after all, that the big lady would do it for her. The two men got up and returned Jillian to her spot and chained her up again.

CHAPTER 18

Rex and Milton have been going over the information that Jillian sent to them the night before. The program was part of a network of independent churches all over the country. "But what ones were involved in the child trafficking ring?" Rex asked Milton.

Rex was really good at fighting and killing anything that walked, talked, or even fought back occasionally, but when it came to computers and electronic gizmos, that was Jillian's department, and with her being undercover and unavailable, that left Milton who wasn't much help.

"Milton, we need help," Rex looked over at him.

"Yes, I gathered that," Milton said. "I really never caught on with these things, you?"

"Nope. Who do we know?" Rex asked. "What about that guy on our first mission, the computer geek. What was his name?" Rex tried to remember.

"You mean Specks?" Milton answered.

"Yeah, Specks McGowen, give him a call." Rex looked at Milton with enthusiasm.

"Sorry, old boy, Robert 'Specks' McGowen is with the feds," Milton said.

"Yeah! Good for him...what department does he work for?" Rex asked.

"Corrections," Milton responded. "The feds have him in custody. He's doing thirty years for hacking the Defense Department Computer," Milton told him.

"Now he's working with the federal government on cyberattacks, making computers less vulnerable to hackers like him and his son," Milton stopped suddenly.

"What?" Rex asked.

"You got that... I have a great idea. Look, rumor was that it was his teenaged son Bobby that did the hacking, and his dad took the fall for him," Milton went on.

"Is he any good with computers?" Rex asked.

"Who?" Milton looked at Rex.

"Bobby." Rex's eyes lit up as they were both thinking the same thing.

"A real wiz, writing, rewriting, and deciphering code," Milton recalled.

"MI-6 wanted to hire him. His dad refused to give permission...Bobby being a minor and all. Would have been too big a risk for Her Majesty's Secret Service," Milton continued.

"Think we could recruit him?" Rex suggested.

"Wouldn't be that much of a risk for me... What about you?"

Rex smiled. "Not for me either."

Milton pulled out his phone and made a few calls. Milton called his contacts at MI-6 and located young Bobby "Scooter" McGowen.

Westminster School for boys is an independent day and boarding school one of UK's leading academic schools, and the only ancient London school located within the precincts of Westminster Abbey.

"How can I help you?" the head secretary asked.

"Do you have a Bobby McGowen enrolled at your school?" Milton asked.

"Are you a parent?" she asked quickly.

"Why, no, I am not. I am the local constable. Is there a problem?" Milton asked.

"All students are required to get their parent's permission before speaking with an outside agency, no exceptions," the secretary said.

"Ohh. Very well and thank you," Milton said hanging up the phone. "Rex, it looks like I will have to go fetch him myself," Milton said hanging up the phone.

*****

Milton took the last flight to London and landed at Heathrow International and jumped on the express tube, a forty-minute ride to Westminster Abbey.

"Good morning," Milton said when he arrived at the school. "Good morning, sir. How may I help you?" the head secretary asked.

"Do you have a young Bobby McGowen enrolled at this school?" Milton asked.

"Yes, we do, are you a parent?" she asked sternly.

"No, I am here to get young Bobby McGowan," Milton said as he flashed his chief inspector credentials.

The secretary looked up the record. "Yes, we have a Bobby 'Scooter' McGowan enrolled at the school," she said.

"Right," Milton agreed.

"He is in the headmaster's office, sir," she said.

"Can you direct me to that office?" Milton asked casually.

"Yes, of course," she said politely.

Milton made his way to the headmaster's office.

"Good afternoon, I am Chief Inspector Bishop for Bobby McGowen." Milton flashed his inspector's badge.

"He's is in our detention facility," the headmaster said.

"Is that so...under what charge?" Milton asked.

"Breach of the code of ethics," the headmaster explained. "Young McGowan was adjusting grades and selling academic papers. The schools is all up in arms about the whole situation and even threatened to expel him.

"I'll make a few phone calls and see if there's anything I can do," Milton told the headmaster.

*****

The next day, Bobby "Scooter" McGowan landed in Panama.

"So how good is this kid?" Rex asked Milton.

"Better than his dad," Milton said. "A year or so ago, the US Defense Department had a huge security breach of epic proportions. He did what everyone at the CIA and Defense Department said could not be done. He broke the latest encryption code, the toughest encryption code devised by the CIA," Milton paused.

"Not the infamous one at CIA headquarters," Rex said with a surprised look on his face.

"No, Rex, that one is still safe…and uncrackable," Milton said with a smile.

"Initially, we suspected the father was responsible for the hack, but later, it turned out to be the kid," Milton continued.

"But he's only a kid," Rex said, not quite believing the story.

"Robert took the fall for the kid and made a deal with the Defense Department, CIA, FBI, and even the MI-6 not to reveal who actually made the breach and not prosecute the kid. They relocated the kid to England into the Westminster School for boys where they could keep an eye on him."

Several hours later, Rex heard "Scooter" yelling in the basement.

"Milton, what's going on with Scooter?" Rex asked running down the stairs into the basement.

Scooter had several computers and monitors going at the same time.

"I hope this stuff is on loan," Rex said as he tried to corral the young man.

"What's going on, Scooter?" Milton asked as he ran by, blaring out a bunch of computer mumbo jumbo.

"Hey, slow down," Rex said as he caught him and put him in a chair. "What are you freaking out about?" Rex asked once he got him to sit still long enough.

"Okay, I reached out to Captain Campbell's friend at the CIA, ahhh, Bruce Buxton…right?" Scooter could barely breathe. "Well, he's not there."

"Okay, get back with him when he gets back," Rex said simply.

"No, you don't understand." Scooter was still hyperventilating.

"I think the boy's going to need a doctor," Milton added.

"He's gone, vanished."

"What do you mean he's vanished?" Milton asked.

"Did you try calling the number Jillian gave you?" Rex suggested.

"Yes, of course, several times," Scooter said. "But there is still no answer, disconnected."

"I did a computer search for him Captain Bruce Buxton/CIA. His records have been erased…his history has been erased…his life was erased, he's gone," Scooter said.

"Let me make a few calls and get to the bottom of this," Rex said stepping away.

Rex used a dedicated SAT phone, then dialed a number that only he knew to a man that he himself did not exist. He was part of a shadow company that Rex was associated with, the one that gave him his own new identity. "Colonel Jerry Jedson."

Rex dialed the number. It rang several times. "Beep…Enter Authorization Code." Rex punched in several codes. The phone "bleeped a few times" then connected. Rex said something strange… then a familiar voice came on line.

"Hey, Rex, how are you?" Colonel Jedson asked.

"Very well, sir, and you?"

"Just great… I wasn't expecting your call for another month. Everything okay?"

"Something came up… I was hoping you could look into it for me," Rex hesitated, knowing that this request was very unusual and might be refused.

"Go ahead, Rex" the colonel said.

"Captain Bruce Buxton, CIA at Langley?"

"What are you looking for exactly?" the colonel asked.

"Anything at all you can tell me about him," Rex said then thanked his friend.

"See you in a month." Then hung up the phone.

Rex returned to Scooter and Milton who seemed a bit calmer.

"So what did you find out?" Rex asked sitting next to him.

"I backtracked the church information like you asked," Scooter paused. "And this goes much deeper than a couple of churches ripping off families and making false promises." Scooter started to jabber and breath heavily.

"Just give me the facts, kid," Rex said.

"There he goes again, freaking out about something," Milton said.

"Might even have to get him a tranquilizer or something. Hold on." Rex walked over to the well-stocked bar and grabbed a bottle of good old Kentucky Bourbon. "Here, kid, take a swig of this." Rex poured Scooter a triple shot in a rock glass.

The kid took one little sip then nearly gagged.

"Go on, boy, drink up. We gotta know what ya going on about," Milton said as he helped Bobby finish the drink. The warmth of the bourbon swirled in his stomach. You could see almost immediately the results as his eyes relaxed, and his speech slowed.

"Okay, now tell us what happened, lad?" Milton listened intently at what the boy had to say.

"The churches are a front to get young girls over to the United States for a child trafficking ring."

"Yes, we kind of figured that," Rex said, "and Jillian is undercover working on that right now. What else?"

"Okay, now Jillian gave me the information on the guns, the serial numbers, and the DDR corporation...that led to the shell company and the money trail to a bank account in the Cayman Islands. When I ran an inquiry, I tried to trace the money, but I kept getting stuck behind some nasty firewalls that kept kicking me out."

"Okay, that is what a firewall is supposed to do," Rex said with his limited knowledge of computers.

Scooter took another deep breath.

"Yes, of course, it is...but it's how it did it is the problem."

"Okay, I'm not following. What's go on?" Milton asked, trying to understand why he was getting so irritated.

"It mirrored me and mutated, then predicted my next move, then mutated again." Scooter got a little scared.

"Why is that a problem?" Rex asked.

"This was my program, the one they shut down, the one that got my dad arrested for thirty years."

"What are you saying…that this is your program?" Rex said with a surprised look on his face.

"Yes, it was an interactive program that I designed to play games on the computer, making games more interesting and realistic…virtual intelligence."

"What is the problem exactly?" Rex asked.

"The computer learns too quickly without the proper safeguards, and in the wrong hands, it could go rogue," Scooter explained.

"Stand-alone computers would be fine with a limited network and memory capacity."

"But if you introduced this, to say a defense computer network with a computer farm, it could be a huge disaster. The power and adaptive capabilities would grow exponentially, and if it got loose… it would go rogue."

"The government put me in protective custody to keep this from happening." Scooted exhaled sharply. Two years ago, I was playing a lot of online games and constantly getting really bored at it. So I wrote a hybrid program that when you played the game, the outcome was more fluid and unpredictable, the scenario would constantly change, in real time, made it more interesting and fun. I used it to lock the Defense Department out of their own computer network, and the program adapted and stayed one step ahead of them it was great. When the US government found out, they shut me down and arrested my dad."

"I may have exposed it and put them on to me," Scooter stopped suddenly.

"Who's on to you?" Rex asked.

"The government or whatever organization this is." Scooter sat back in the chair, staring into the black computer screen.

"Where are you going in such a hurry?" Rex asked Milton as he rushed up the stairs.

"Gotta call MI-6 and let them know. This could be a huge breach of security," Milton said.

"Who debriefed you?" Rex asked hoping not to hear the answer.

Rex worked proudly for the US government and swore to protect her from enemies foreign and domestic.

"I was debriefed by the DOD, FBI, even the CIA…along with several prominent members of both the House and the Senate."

"Got to be someone in one of those departments," Rex said with a sigh.

"Give me some time. I will get to bottom of it," Scooter said.

CHAPTER 19

By Jillian's calculations, they had been at sea and inside that cargo box for eight days. Jillian had a remarkable sense of time. She always could tell you the time within a minute but never carried a watch, even on missions. The conditions were horrible, stench even worse. At least the attacks had stopped. No telling how much longer they could have endured if they had.

It was about 10:30 p.m. when the walls shook and shuddered as the container was picked up by a crane. It swung wildly in the air like a carnival ride before it dropped to the concrete with a loud thud. Apparently, they had arrived at their destination wherever that was.

A second gut-wrenching noise could be heard as the container was tilted and raised at a forty-five-degree angle, several sharp right and left turns later the container came to a screeching halt.

"Pickup in three hours," a squawk on the radio could be heard through the tiny vents.

Three hours later, the big lady and the two guards came forward and unchained all the girls. The dead bolt made a loud thud as the large steel doors were unlocked. The doors swung open, and a rush of warm salty sea air filled the container.

"Hmmm," Jillian said as she took a deep breath.

It was hot and smelled like dead fish, but anything was better than what she endured the last eight days, five hours, and fifteen minutes. It was a port somewhere near an ocean. The port of New Orleans from what Antonia had said, then Rex and Milton would be nearby.

They were rushed into a small school bus with all the windows blacked out.

Jillian closed her eyes and listened as they rode across loose gravel for the first one hundred feet to a crossroad. The bus stopped momentarily then moved straight ahead onto a paved road. After a sharp right-hand turn, the bus accelerated quickly, changing lanes as it sped up. *A short highway drive*, Jillian thought as she focused on the engine slowing down and a slow right-hand turn. A long stop, probably a stop light as she heard cars pull up next to the darkened windows of the bus. Sharp right-hand turn, then a muffled sound as if passing under a bridge or overpass. Another long stop followed by a slight bump in the road, then a downhill with another sharp right-hand turn, again it felt like they were heading downhill. The bus stopped with a small hiss as the air brakes were applied. The half doors broke open as the guards yelled for them to get off. The girls were rushed off four at a time through a double glass door to a small elevator. Less than a minute later, the doors opened into an open foyer, marble floors, chandeliers like an old hotel that was in the process of being renovated.

Very elegant. I hope they keep up with the renovations, Jillian thought as she moved through the lobby to the room. Rooms were spacious but stripped of all furniture and beds, probably due to the renovation. Three small cots lined one corner of the room, no TV, microwaves, or running water.

"Wow, a real dive of a hotel." Jillian giggled. There was a slight musty odor throughout, maybe from a flood. Bathrooms and running water were down the hall past the makeshift kitchen.

Later that night, Jillian headed to the bathroom, dressed in her one piece red-and-blue polka-dotted PJs and smiled at the guard as she passed. With the number of girls running around that night, Jillian was one in a hundred and never missed. Inside she spotted a ventilation shaft, barely big enough for any regular sized human being, but at five feet two and 110 pounds with extremely flexible joints, she was far from normal, sometimes even scary some of the places and positions she was able to get into. She slithered her way into a larger duct where she stripped down to her black full-body

Lycra suit and stashed her polka-dotted pajamas inside the vent. Jillian had what you would say an extensive inside knowledge of most AC and vent systems, and in the end, they were all built the same, eventually leading her to an outside exit. With a little squirming and hard work, she was able to find the outside vent, leading to the flat roof.

The air was heavy, and the fog as thick as pea soup. A quick look around, the smell of the ocean air and restaurant signs advertising spiced Cajun shrimp, their special of the day at a local restaurant in the French Quarter made Jillian hungry, and she also knew she was in New Orleans. *Hmmm, spiced Cajun shrimp sounded good right now.*

Jillian had to let Rex and Milton know she had arrived at her destination. With the quick departure, she left her SAT phone and Sig Sauer stashed at the warehouse. All she had was the clothes on her back.

She moved around the corner of the building and was surprised by one of the guards patrolling the grounds.

"What are you doing out here, lil lady?" the man asked in what sounded like a deep French Creole accent.

"Just out for a jog," she said smiling, moving her hands back and forth as his eyes glanced at her tight little body. Jillian struck with the speed of a viper to his throat, shocking his larynx. His mouth opened, lips moved, but nothing came out as he tried to scream. Jillian stepped behind him with a slight pinch behind the ear. The guard passed out within seconds.

She dragged the heavier man into the nearby alleyway, grabbed the automatic rifle, a AK-47 variant, and in less than five seconds, dismantled it, and threw the slide into a nearby dumpster. The two-way radio was set to monitor all the local chatter and guard movement in and around the warehouse.

But Jillian needed a quick way to get a message to Rex and Milton. Without a working telephone, she had to think outside the box. She flipped the radio several times in her hand and then once really high.

"That was it," she said, looking at the telephone pole in the distance. She stopped at the first pole, looked at it briefly. "Nope." Then followed the wire to the next two poles. "There." That's what she was looking for, a service box. It was at the top of a forty-foot pole. Jillian scampered up the pole, popped open the service box. With a scrap piece of wire, she opened the back of the two-way radio and tapped into the main phone line.

Buzzz…buzz. She punched in Rex's number and waited. *Click.* "Rex…Rex," she called out several times. The phone went dead. She tried again. *Ring, ring…click.*

"Rex, Rex, is that you?" Jillian called out on the phone.

"Who's that Rex?" Milton asked.

"I don't know."

Jillian could hear Milton in the background. Rex hung up once again.

"Damn," Jillian said.

"I can hear them. They can't hear me." Jillian was not ready to give up just yet.

Jillian called again.

Ring, ring…click.

Jillian immediately held down several buttons, then transmitted the international distress signal.

*Dot, dot, dot…dash, dash, dash…dot, dot, dot…*repeated it several times. On the third try, she added *Jillian* to the message, then repeated the whole thing again.

"Come on, Rex…didn't they teach you *Morse code*. You were after all in the Navy." Jillian waited patiently.

Rex held the phone away from his ear, then cocked his head to the side.

"What is that? Morse code?" Rex called out to Milton.

"Yup, sure is," Milton assured him.

"On the phone?" Rex said, listening to the message.

"SOS…Jillian. Wow…I think it's Jillian," Rex said half laughing.

"*Yes*, Rex… It's Jillian." The message was tapped out.

"Hold on, I'll get a pen," Milton said popping up from the chair. Milton grabbed a pen and paper and took the message.

"*Jillian*… Stop… New Orleans…stop…Café Du Monde 10:00 p.m."

"Copy."

Out.

Jillian made her way back to the makeshift hotel through the ventilation ducts to the bathroom where she put on her red-and-blue polka-dotted PJs, then stepped out of the bathroom into the hallway…smiled at the guard as she passed by. Back in her room, she turned on the two-way radio…but it was dead.

Without the power cord, she would have to think outside the box again and come up with something. Jillian rolled over on her cot and stared at the wall. The answer was right in front of her. The old building still had the telephone wires, and all the old phone wires had a little voltage running through them. Jillian pulled the bundle from the wall and stripped several wires, twisted them together, and plugged them into the battery charging wires. Jillian would have to wait a while to see if she was successful.

The voltage was low, but by the next morning, the battery was fully charged. Jillian turned on the radio to monitor the conversations. The big talk around the camp was about one of the guards that lost his radio and his weapon on guard duty. The story being told by the guard is that a little girl took him by surprise, knocked him out, and stole his weapons. Jillian listened when she could, but there wasn't much news at all about what they were here for or if they would be going anywhere.

"*They will be here at 10:00 p.m.*"

"*Roger, out,*" the radio crackled.

"Damn," Jillian said, promising to meet Rex and Milton at 10:00 p.m. But Jillian curiosity won out as she wanted to know who was coming in at ten. Lights went out about nine. Jillian slipped out of her bunk and into her red-and-blue polka-dotted PJs and headed down the hall toward the bathroom at the end of the hall. Halfway down the hall, she passed a guard.

"Have you lost a radio or a weapon today?" she said softly as she passed.

The guard stopped abruptly and looked at her, as she smiled broadly heading into the bathroom. The guard shook his head in disbelief. "She probably overheard somebody talking about it. That couldn't be the little girl," he said to himself, trying to convince himself that it wasn't.

Jillian squirmed into the vent and made her way to a major junction of larger vents, heading in several directions. You could see a beam of light shining in the distance. Jillian slowly made her way to the lighted opening for a quick look. She heard muffled voices in the background.

"When is he coming?" the man asked. "I want to get paid."

"He said at ten. He'll will be here soon… Calm down and be patient," the woman said nervously checking her watch.

A blue sedan pulled up outside the double glass door. Two men got out and opened the back door, escorting the man to the small elevator. As the door opened, and two men walked in a short stocky guy and a taller man.

"That's twenty-two this week?" the man said as he pulled out an envelope from his pocket.

"No, twenty three," the big lady said, counting the money.

"Twenty-three, you say?" the man said.

"We did not get paid for the other girl in the last shipment," the lady said.

Jillian squinted to get a get a better look, but she could only see the back of the man's head.

"I have one more in the other room… The doctor brought her back the other night," the big lady said pointing toward the other room.

"What other girl?" he asked curiously. "I don't know. The doctor said that she was important and not to be mixed with the others," the big lady explained.

"Where is the doctor?" the man asked heading across the hall to the other room.

Damn, Jillian thought to herself looking for a quick way to get to the other room. Up ahead of her was a T junction leading to the right and left. She squirmed her way to the T and turned right. Twenty feet away was another vent a little smaller but still big enough for Jillian's slight build.

A light came on ahead of her as she scooted as close as possible, so she could hear the conversation.

"Niklas, how are you?" the tall man reached out and shook his hand.

"What did he just call him? Niklas?" Jillian struggled to hear it clearly. Jillian thought back a few years when she knew a Niklas, a very unusual name.

"Good evening, sir," Niklas responded curtly in that slight Russian accent.

"Where are they?" the tall man asked looking around the room expecting to see a few other people.

"We only have one girl," he said.

"One girl? You are supposed to have the two girls and that old man with the micro drive," the taller man yelled loudly. "What the hell happened?" he said slamming the door behind him. Jillian squirmed her way closer to the vent.

From her angle, she could only see half of the room. The tall man was facing away from her talking to someone in the back of the room.

"Where is the other girl?" the tall man asked.

"I don't have her."

"Niklas, you were supposed to bring me the two girls and the micro drive," the man said angrily.

"We were ambushed in Panama. The other girl was rescued," Niklas said quietly.

"Ambushed? You?" The tall man turned and shook his head.

"I don't know… Dr. Kalb reported that the man killed my men with his bare hands, even one of the Fuchs twins," Niklas said.

"Dammit, Niklas, I thought you were the best." The tall man turned back toward the vent.

That face, where has she seen that face? Jillian closed her eyes and ran the mental picture in her head.

"He had specialized training from what the doctor reported… maybe a Merc," Niklas said. "The doctor was very upset at what happened."

"Where is Dr. Kalb?" the tall man asked.

"I don't know," Niklas responded.

"And the old man?" the man asked.

"Dead," the voice responded.

"And the thumb drive?" the man asked.

"No."

Were they talking about Juan and the girls? Jillian squinted to get a better look. *Where has she seen that face?* Jillian thought hard as the thousands of faces flashed through her mind.

"What do you mean *no?*" he asked surprised by the answer, turning back around toward the vent.

"What am I supposed to tell the Rosa Negra?" the tall man turned away and walked to the other side of the room.

"That bitch, I'll take care of her," said the man in the shadows

"Shut up. You will do nothing but get me that other girl and that microdrive," the tall man said, walking out the door. "The one girl should be enough to get the other old man to give us the microdrive," he said following close behind briefly passing by the vent.

Niklas? Jillian's eyes blinked a few times, trying to remember where she had seen that other face. Then she remembered… For almost a year, it was plastered all over the US TV stations and the newspapers…during his reelection campaign for US Senate in the state of Texas.

Yes, that senator… Oh, what is his name? She closed her eyes as it came to her. *Bradley Stevens the Senator from Texas. What the hell is he doing down here, and is he behind any of this?*

Jillian wiggled her way out of the ventilation shaft and back into the rafters. On the far side of the building was an exhaust fan leading outside. Jillian shimmied down the outside of the building to an alleyway on the ground floor. About a half block away was a F-150 pickup truck, not her favorite mode of transportation, but it would do in a pinch.

She did not have time to pick the lock and grabbed a rock and smashed the passenger side window, then pulled a few wires from under the dashboard, and she was on her way in less than a minute. Jillian drove down the road a few blocks to a corner store to make a call. She dialed Rex's phone.

135

"Hello," Rex answered on the second ring.

"Hi, Rex, did you get my message?" she said quietly.

"Jillian, how are you? No. Coded messages or Morse code?"

"No, not this time. I am calling from a public phone, so the line is not secure," she said, whispering into the phone.

"How was your cruise? Did you bring me any souvenirs?" Rex laughed.

"Knock it off. Let's not talk about that right now. Where are you?" Jillian asked.

"New Orleans in a small hotel near the docks, waiting on your call," Rex said in a more serious manner. "Milton and I flew down after we got your message," Rex told her. "What about you?" Rex asked.

"Somewhere near the docks, corner store near I-10," she said quietly.

"Let's meet at the Café Du Monde on Decatur Street near Rexson Square," Rex said.

"No problem. Be there in thirty," she said hanging up the phone.

Café Du Monde was just a few blocks from her location on the outskirts of the French Quarter in New Orleans. Jillian pulled up in the F-150 a little after 10:30 p.m. and parked in the back alley. Jillian walked casually through the café, when she spotted Milton sitting at a table sipping his tea.

"Milty," she called out from across the room.

Milton turned and greeted her with a huge bear hug.

"Where's the big lug?" she asked looking around the room.

A door opened and closed behind her. "Boo," he said, goosing her in the back.

"You know I could have decked you for that," Jillian said.

"Hey, Jillian, good to see you," Rex said, reaching out his hand.

"Did you wash?" she jeered pulling her hand away, then jumping into his arms. They headed for a table on the outdoor patio away from the crowd. Jillian was famished after spending two weeks eating nothing but lousy tacos and cold beans.

Café Du Monde was a world famous coffee shop in New Orleans, located at the end of the French Market on the Corner of

Rexson Square in New Orleans's French Quarter. Café Du Monde has been serving crispy beignets since 1862. Jillian ordered a huge plate of the triangle-shaped beignets covered in a thick layer of white powdered sugar.

"Are the guys ordering anything?" Jillian said as she single hand-edly devoured the whole plate.

"Jillian, so what's happening?" Rex asked in a more serious tone.

"I think I found Gabriella," she said wiping the powdered sugar from her lips. "She's being held hostage at the makeshift hotel for the microdrive," Jillian said.

"Do they know we have it?" Rex asked.

"No, I don't think so. They are planning to use her as leverage against the old man," she continued. "They suspect that the micro drive is with Juan and Anna…but you really messed up their plans. Did you really take out their guys with your bare hands?" Jillian asked with a smile.

Rex just smiled and shrugged his shoulders.

"Well, let's go get her," Milton chimed in.

"Hold on. We can't just go in there without a plan," Rex said.

"This is much bigger than we thought. We have to see it through," Rex said.

"There's more…" Jillian hesitated. "Senator Bradley Stevens," Jillian said.

"What about Senator Stevens?" Rex asked.

"He's involved, not sure how or in what way…but he was at the hotel, paying the goons that brought the girls across from Panama," Jillian explained.

Senator Bradley Stevens, Rex thought back to when he was a boy, his father was part of a major cleanup in Veracruz, Mexico, after a devastating flood wiped out all their crops in the area. *My father reached out to the senator for help in the recovery effort. That was around the same time when he met Juan and Luiz for the first time.*

"Rex, you with us?" Jillian shouted as Rex's eyes stared off into the distance.

"Yes, what?" Rex said, shaking his head slightly.

"There was one more thing… The tall man, the senator called the other man…Niklas," Jillian said.

"Not Niklas Mueller, he's *dead*," Rex shouted with a bit of anger in his voice. *Can't be the same Niklas*, Rex thought as his mind wondered once again.

Rex's memories floated back in time when he and his brother Ben were in high school, how they were planning to save the world. Then to hear the tragic news that his brother was killed on a special DEA/ATF mission led by Niklas, the team leader about stolen weapons being smuggled out of Mexico. Ben was shot in the back. No leads, witnesses, or convictions, just a dead end.

"Rex, you okay?" Jillian shouted bringing him out of his trance.

"I don't know. You sure you heard that right?" Rex said quietly.

"Yes, Rex, I got a quick look at him too. It was Niklas Muller," Jillian responded quietly.

"Whatever is going on, this is a lot bigger than we thought," Milton said.

"Yes, whoever this guy is, if it is Niklas Mueller, we have to find out how the senator fits in and how it all ties to Luiz." Rex shook his head in disbelief of the thought of Niklas Muller being alive.

"We have to get to the bottom of this and end it once and for all," Jillian said.

"But how?" Milton asked pounding on the table, spilling the rest of his tea.

"I can kill him," Rex said.

"Hold on. You just can't kill a powerful, sitting US senator," Jillian cautioned.

"Oh yes, I can. If he's involved in all of this, I would rip his head off and puke down his throat," Rex said looking at Milton who was nodding in agreement.

"Just calm down," Jillian said as she took another bite out of a beignet. "There is got to be something we can do…legally, that is," Jillian said.

"We can kidnap him and make him disappear," Milton suggested.

"I said legally. You can't just kidnap a sitting senator," Jillian said sipping on a diet Coke. *What can you do to a powerful US senator?* Jillian thought quietly.

"Make him poor and unelectable," Milton mumbled to himself.

"What was that?" Jillian called out to Milton. "Make him poor and what? Unelectable?"

"Yes, make him poor and unelectable," Milton repeated, not getting where Jillian was heading with the conversation.

"Yes, exactly that," Jillian repeated it several times. "Make him poor and unelectable."

"How do we do that?" Rex asked.

"I have no idea" Jillian said.

"Are you going to tell her, Rex?" Milton said.

"Tell me what, Rex?" Jillian asked.

"We have not heard from Bruce in over a week," Rex said. "We only have bits and pieces of the last message he sent, not enough to draw any conclusions," Rex paused as Milton explained.

"Bruce was tracking the serial numbers on the guns we found in Panama. They were scheduled to be destroyed two years ago by DDR Inc., part of a plan to reduce the stock pile of older weapons in the US military. But they never made it there. The job was cancelled by DDR Inc. The funds were part of an appropriations bill approved by US Congress. From what we can tell, the funds were diverted to an offshore account in the Cayman Islands, set up by a brokerage firm in Panama under the name Kincade."

"So what about Bruce?" Jillian asked.

"This is where it got tricky. All of the transactions were made from somewhere inside the US government. Bruce figured either the State Department or the Department of Military Affairs, the encryption was definitely military," Milton explained.

"So what happened with Bruce?" Jillian asked again.

"We have not been able to reach him, not at his home or office. He's gone, AWOL," Rex told Jillian.

"Maybe he's laying low. I told him to stay off the computers for a while," Jillian fired back.

"Scooter was able to remotely access—"

"Hold on, wait a minute… Scooter? Do you mean McGowan's kid?" Jillian interrupted.

"Yes, Bobby," Rex said. "We needed a computer wiz while you were away on vacation in the Gulf of Mexico." Rex laughed.

"How did Scooter figure it was from the State Department or from Military Affairs?" Jillian asked.

"The kid wrote the program for the Defense Department," Rex told her.

"I thought that was his father," Jillian said.

"It was all on his personal computer at home," Rex said.

"That was the biggest and best computer hack anyone had ever seen," Jillian said.

"Apparently, Bruce stumbled across something that made his computer go crazy when he accessed the file with the embedded video file from the bank in the Cayman Islands. 'A tall slender man in a top coat and cowboy hat making a large deposit from the size of the cases…20 to 40 million.'"

"Scooter was working on identifying the man when his computers were hacked…in the same way Bruce's were. Scooter said that Bruce vanished or maybe even erased.

"What are you talking about…you can't be serious…erased?" Jillian thought carefully about the last conversation she had with Bruce and how scared he was. "I spoke with Colonel Jedson to see if he could check things out for us…to look into Bruce's whereabouts. I'll get Scooter to see if he can find out more on this video and this Kincade guy," Rex said. "Maybe they are all the same guy."

"Lisa and the FBI were trying to get a lead on El Jefe's money trail in Panama. Maybe Kincade is El Jefe?" Rex speculated.

"I have an idea," Milton interrupted.

"What is it?" Jillian asked.

"If the senator is this Kincade, and if he is the El Jefe that is running this whole operation, why not just take it from him?" Milton said standing up.

"What?" Rex asked.

"The best…the way to take down a powerful senator."

"And what way is that exactly?" Jillian asked curiously about what he was getting at.

"Best way to take down a powerful senator and the leader of a syndicate…is to make him poor and unelectable," Milton smiled.

"An ingenious idea," Jillian laughed.

"I am not following," Rex interjected.

"I'm not either just yet," Jillian laughed.

"Aah, come now, lads… Ya take it from him," Milton strutted around the café.

"How?" Rex asked.

"The bank in the Cayman's. I'll pretend to be Kincade and walk in and withdraw the money in broad daylight," Milton said.

"This might work." Rex looked at Milton in amazement.

"He even walks like the senator…limp and all," Jillian said, shaking her head in agreement.

"I can pull it off," Milton said gulping down the rest of his tea. "I know I can."

"Okay, I'll talk to Scooter and see if we can find out more information about this Kincade, the senator, or whoever this is at the bank," Milton said.

"I'll head back to the makeshift hotel and monitor what I can on the radio," Jillian said.

"Here, this will help." Rex reached in his pocket and tossed her a portable SAT phone with encryption; this time, he even included the charger. "Hold on, one more thing." Rex handed her a Sig Sauer P938 with an extra clip. "Try not to lose this one, okay?"

"Thanks, babe," Jillian said blowing him a kiss across the table while she slipped the elastic band up her slender leg.

Ring…ring, Rex's SAT phone rang.

"Are you calling me already?" Rex giggled, then answered the phone, his expression changed dramatically. "Yes, Colonel…" There was a long pause as Rex listened. "Yes, sir. Thank you, sir."

Rex turned toward Jillian as their eyes met.

"What is it?" she asked, knowing the answer was not pleasant.

"It's Bruce" Rex shook his head slowly back and forth.

Jillian knew that look. "What happened?" Jillian asked as a flood of tears streamed down her cheek.

"That was Colonel Jedson…from Langley," Rex said.

"I know who he is," Jillian said. "What happened to Bruce?" she asked wiping the tears from her eyes.

"Jillian, they found him in a motel room in Silver Springs, Maryland…tied to a chair…fingertips burned in both hands… throat slashed…with a garrote."

Jillian turned and slammed her fist on the table. "Bruce was onto something…but what?" she asked as she turned away headed back to the hotel.

"I'll keep in touch…and call you when I have something more," Rex said as she walked away.

*****

Jillian returned the F-150 to the alley behind the hotel, parked it, and left an envelope with one thousand dollars on the seat with a note, "Nice ride… Sorry about the glass."

Jillian walked up in the direction of the hotel. Things seemed pretty quiet as she popped open the vent and made her way back to the bathroom. It was 2:00 a.m. when she snuck back into her bed. The radio was still plugged in the phone wires, and the battery light was still glowing *red*.

"Dead battery." Fortunately, Jillian had a new toy that worked even better. She plugged the two-way radio into the wall as a faint green light came to life.

That next morning, Jillian heard the usual chatter about a guard having lost his radio to a little girl, then a second transmission.

"Pickup at airport 10:00 a.m."

Jillian pulled out her portable SAT radio/phone and sent a text message to Rex and Milton: "Possible VIP contact at airport 10:00 a.m."

"I think our girl got something," Milton said sipping his cappuccino.

"Can it wait till I get done with my breakfast?" Rex said.

"No, got to head to the airport by 10:00 a.m. Let's go," Milton told him.

Rex hated stakeouts sitting around for hours waiting for something to happen, especially on an empty stomach.

"Jillian, what do we know about this VIP?" Rex asked as he sipped on his coffee.

"Minor chatter, one guy is not a fan and called her a real bitch."

"Anything else?" Rex asked.

"Who you talking to in there?" a man yelled flinging the door open. "Nobody, sir," Jillian said in a cute little voice holding the radio just above her foot by the tip of the antenna.

"What's that in your hands?" the man shouted.

"Nothing." Jillian flipped her hands out in front of her clapping them together.

The radio dropped and balanced briefly on her heel, then lowered quickly to the floor and under the bed. Jillian returned her hands behind her back, twisted and turned a couple of times smiling at the man who was more interested in her cute little outfit than what was behind her back. Rex heard the man's voice in the background and knew he better not say a word, or anything else that might tip him off and blow her cover.

"Come along," the man said pulling on her arm.

*****

"What's going on?" Milton asked as he pulled up near the terminal.

"I don't know. The phone just hung up," Rex whispered to Milton.

"Pull up over there. Probably going to arrive in the VIP area," Rex said pointing at the private business terminal.

"And probably in a well-guarded area, away from the main terminal," Milton added.

"Like looking for a needle in a haystack," Rex said as the cruised around the VIP area.

"What do you suppose is going on over there?" Milton said pointing at a group of cars on the far side of the hangar.

Rex drove past the group, being sure to keep his distance and not look suspicious.

"Jillian did say the senator was about my heights and weight, right?" Milton said looking around the tarmac. Up ahead was a stocky man leaning on the hood of a sedan smoking a cigarette, and a second guy in the back seat of the car on a cell phone.

"Rex, this could be what we're looking for," Milton said pointing straight ahead.

Rex checked his watch it was 10:45 a.m. Rex watched as a small private plane taxied down the taxiway, heading in their general direction. The stocky man took a final drag on his cigarette, then flicked it across the jetway.

The midsized Gulfstream V jet rolled to a stop, and a few minutes later, the jet door opened, and a very sexy middle-aged woman walked down the stairs, followed by several armed guards.

"Wow," Rex said looking at Milton. "Not the VIP I expected." Maybe they had the wrong VIP.

The stocky man greeted the lady and her party, then walked to the back of the sedan where the man in the back seat spoke briefly to the stocky man. The woman walked over to the sedan, greeted the man in back seat with a passionate kiss, then got in the back seat along with her security detail.

"Was that our guy?" Rex asked Milton.

"I don't know. Maybe the VIP was a woman?" Milton said.

"I don't know. Jillian never said…just a VIP."

"Who was that in the back seat?" Rex asked Milton.

"I have no idea. Never really got out of the car long enough to get a good look at him," Milton responded.

"Did you see the way he greeted her" Rex said as they watched them pull out of the VIP area.

"Let's track her. Maybe she will lead us to the senator," Milton suggested.

"Yes, or maybe that was the senator in the Sedan." Rex looked back at Milton lifting his eyebrows slightly.

"What? No, couldn't be."

Milton sped up toward the airport exit. The sedan was heading east on I-10 toward downtown New Orleans. The sedan got off on exit 234B toward the French Quarter and downtown. Milton sped up and passed the sedan but kept a close eye on them as they made a right-hand turn. Milton turned down the next block then doubled back, hoping to get a glimpse of the sedan, just in time as the sedan made a left turn onto Roosevelt way and pulled up in front of the iconic Roosevelt Hotel.

CHAPTER 20

Rex and Milton drove passed the entrance and parked on the opposite side of the road. The man in the back seat escorted the woman into the hotel.

"Was that the senator in the back seat?" Rex asked as they pulled in the parking lot of the Wyndham Hotel next door.

"I did not get a good look at him," Milton said.

"We have to get in there and find out what we can," Rex said pulling up into the Wyndham Hotel carport.

"Let's check in here and come up with a plan," Milton suggested.

They checked into the hotel and asked for the top floor with the balcony facing the Roosevelt Hotel.

"Rex, do you remember Europe in '92?" Milton asked.

"You mean when you pulled off that rouse, and the lawyer turned over the multimillion dollar company to you and the secretary?" Rex said.

"Yes, that's the one," Milton said grinning from ear to ear.

"What ever happened with her? No, let me guess…you married her?" Rex laughed.

"Yes, for a while but got divorced shortly thereafter," Milton admitted it was a mistake.

"So what happened?" Rex asked.

"I sold the company, and she did not want anything to do with me after that…" Milton explained. "But at least I got my fishing boat and was able to retire." Milton grinned.

"Okay, what did you have in mind?" Rex asked.

"Hand me that concierge book," Milton said pointing at it on the table.

"Did you see how the porter greeted them when they walked up?" Milton said.

"Yes, kind of like they were regulars," Rex said as Milton ruffled through the pages.

"There." Milton stabbed his finger at the Gonzales Fine Suits and Tailoring ad. "Let's go," Milton said waving his hand at the door.

"Where are we going?" Rex asked.

"Shopping, my boy…shopping."

"Jillian said this guy and I were close to the same height and weight, right? Let's find out how close."

Rex wasn't quite following but went along with it anyway. "How are we going to play it?" Rex asked as he and Milton walked down the block.

"Not sure yet, just play along."

Gonzales Tailoring was a short walk, just around the corner from the hotel. Milton looked right at home when he walked into the shop.

They were greeted immediately by Phillipe a well-dressed man with a tape measure around his neck. "How can I help you, gentlemen? Aah…Monsieur Kincade, como sava?" Philippe said holding out his hand.

"Aah…Bonjour Phillipe," Milton answered cautiously in French with a slight Southern drawl.

"You…not like the suits I sent up to your suite last night, Monsieur?" Philippe said running around the shop.

"Just here to pick up a few last-minute things for tonight's festivities," Milton said as he walked over to the sales rack.

"Phillipe, can you measure my man here…for a suit," Milton said as he pointed at Rex, then the sales rack. Philippe took one look at Rex and had him all figured out without even measuring.

"Forty-two regular, sir?" Phillipe said.

"Yes, sir." Rex nodded.

Phillipe picked out a plain black suit, black tie, white cotton shirt, and all-black shoes.

"Try these on, sir." Phillipe handed them to Rex, then headed directly to the Versace imported Italian suits where Milton was browsing through the selections.

"You have really good taste, Monsieur Kincade," Phillipe said.

Milton picked out black Versace pinstripe, 100 percent silk light yellow shirt, plush leather loafers size 14, black trench coat, top hat, and umbrella. "Fabulous," Milton said heading for the dressing room. Phillipe gathered everything and followed quickly.

"Would you like me to have these delivered to your suite?" Philippe asked.

"Oh no. Just a light press, and we will wear them out the door," Milton said.

"Right away, sir," Phillipe scurried the back of the shop.

"Come along, Rex," Milton waved his hand heading for a small waiting area at the front of the store.

"Why do I get the sales rack?" Rex asked admiring the fine Italian suits.

"Rex, it suits you… You are my bodyguard." Milton winked and sat down.

"Oh, okay." Rex stood quietly nearby.

Suits were pressed, and the clothes fit perfectly.

"Philippe, put that on my tab and leave yourself a nice tip, would you?" Milton said striding out of the store with Rex following close behind. "And send the old clothes to the laundry. I'll pick them up in a couple of days."

"Rex, I told you I could pull it off." Milton strutted down the street toward the hotel with a newfound confidence.

"Now what?" Rex asked.

"Act as my personal security guard and let's have some fun," Milton said.

Milton's plan was bold—walk straight up to the Roosevelt Hotel and wing it.

It was a little after 6:00 p.m. when they approached the entrance to the hotel. Milton reached in his jacket pocket and ate a red hot chili pepper, sniffed the juice, then gagged and coughed several times.

"What was that for?" Rex asked as Milton's face and eyes turned beet red.

"Got to make it look convincing," Milton turned sneezed and coughed several times.

The two walked up to the entrance of the hotel. The doorman greeted Milton.

"Good evening Mr. Kincade. Will you be joining the festivities this evening?" he asked, slowly opening the door.

Milton pulled a crisp twenty-dollar bill from his pocket and handed it to the gentleman.

"Probably not," Milton said turning away to cough. "I think I may be coming down with something." Milton coughed several times as he walked through the lobby.

Milton walked through the lobby, slightly favoring his right leg. Something he picked up on when he watched the video feed from the bank.

"Good evening, Mr. Kincade," the desk clerk said.

He coughed and coughed, then sneezed. Milton wiped his nose with his handkerchief. "Nasty cold, I guess," he said as he turned and coughed again into the hanky.

"Mr. Kincade, your reservation not till tomorrow night," the clerk said, punching a few numbers into the computer.

"Aghhhh, last minute change. Can I still get the same suite and accommodations a day early?" Milton asked, coughing and sneezing once again.

"But of course," the clerk said handing over a set of keys for suite 2408.

"Any bags, this evening?" the young porter asked as they were escorted to the elevator.

"Not tonight," Milton said as he coughed again into his handkerchief.

The porter escorted Mr. Kincade and his guest to suite 2408. Milton palmed the kid a five-dollar bill for his troubles.

"Rex, let's find out what we can and get out of here," Milton said as he headed for the coffee service area to get some milk or cream to soothe the heat of the peppers.

Knock, knock.

"May I help you?" Milton asked, sneezing at the door.

"Your mail, sir," the porter said.

"Just slide it under the door, please," Milton told him. "I wonder what this is?" Milton walked over to the desk to have a closer look at the manila envelope.

Knock, knock. "Just slide it under the door, please," Milton said coughing several times. *Knock, knock,* a second knock at the door. Milton got up and headed for the door, catching Rex's eyes as he approached.

"Who is it?" Rex asked acting like a real security detail as he peered through the peephole.

"Who is it?" Milton whispered taking a quick peek.

"Oh, it's for me," Milton said enthusiastically waving at Rex to get out of sight. "Yup, this one is definitely for me," he said smiling slowly opening the door. Wow, a beautiful young black woman, wearing a full-length black evening gown.

"Good evening. How can I help you?" Milton asked in a scratchy Southern accent.

"Hey, baby," she said pecking him on the cheek, as she headed directly toward the bedroom.

Milton, not knowing what the senator or this Mr. Kincade guy did on these trips, just played along. Milton kinda figured she must be a high-priced call girl from her dress and must be a regular routine from the casualness.

Still feeling the effects of the red hot chili peppers, Milton sneezed a few times and got back into character.

"You okay, baby?" she asked slowly taking off her dress.

Rex cupped his ear against the door to try to hear what was going on.

Milton's eyes opened wide, as she turned around. *Hmmm...very lovely,* he thought to himself.

"Sorry, love, not today I have a terrible cold," Milton said, sneezing and coughing several times, then asking her politely to leave.

"What?" She pouted and looked helplessly at him.

"I have a terrible cold and can't tonight," pulling the top of her dress back over her shoulder, holding out her hand, demanding to be paid.

Milton pulled a couple of crisp hundred-dollar bills from his jacket and placed it on the bed.

"Next time, baby," she said as she picked up the money and headed for the door, pecking him lightly on the cheek as she passed.

"Wow," Milton said looking over at Rex who was laughing and shaking his head side to side.

"Maybe I should have taken her up on her offer," Milton grinned.

"We have work to do," Rex said carefully opening the manila cnvelope.

"What do you make of it?" Milton asked

"What? The two hundred bucks you left on the bed? Or the bunch of ads to local restaurants, plays, and other happenings in a yellow manila envelope?" Rex asked.

Milton looked at the ads, all advertisements for local restaurants and happenings nearby, all except the one on handwritten note on plain white paper stock. "Le Grande Maison, 10:30 p.m., tomorrow night."

"It could be an ad…" Rex said looking it over.

Strange way to leave a message, Milton thought.

"I guess we just have to go to the meeting and find out. Any ideas?" Rex asked.

Rex heard some voices down the hall, then opened the door slowly to have a look. "Just a couple of maids cleaning the rooms down the hall," Rex said closing the door.

"Hold on, Rex," Milton said walking toward the minibar.

Fine time for a drink, Rex thought as Milton opened a bottle of spiced rum and splashed some on his face and took a big swig.

"Pretty good," Milton said.

"What are you doing?" Rex asked as Milton took off all his clothes down to his skivvies then slipped into the bathroom, splashed some water on his face, and grabbed a towel.

"Be right back," Milton said as he slipped the towel around his waist and stepped out into the hallway.

"Where are you going?" Rex asked looking down the hall. Rex watched as Milton stumbled and wobbled down the hall, bumping into one of the maids.

"Sorry, lil lady… Can you helllp meee?" he slurred.

"Ahhhhhh," she yelled surprised by the half-naked man in the hallway. The other maid working in the room ran out into the hall and giggled when she saw the naked man. "I locked mysellslsf out of the roooom," turning and pointing down the hall.

"I will call the front desk for you," she said pulling the two way radio from her cart.

"Noooooo," Milton pleaded pulling both hands to his face, praying for her not to call.

"I'll get fireddss," he said slurring his words.

"My booosss doesn't knowww I amm here in the suiiite," Milton turned half stumbling. "I'm gonnna get firrred," he said wobbling down the hall toward the suite.

The maid giggled some more and followed Milton to suite 2406. The maid pulled the master key from her pocket, scanned the door, and opened it slowly, letting Milton in. Milton bumped her and lifted her key when he passed. Milton thanked her pulling both hands together, dropping the towel. The maid was more embarrassed than Milton, as his towel fell off and hit the floor. She quickly picked up the towel and held it in front of her eyes shielding him from view.

"Thank you, thank you," he said backing into the room.

Few minutes later, the maid left the floor, and Milton returned to the senator's suite next door.

"Nice work, old man," Rex said as he let Milton back into Kincade's room. They returned the envelope to the lobby and walked out the front door around the corner to the back alley, then back to the hotel through the employee entrance. The key Milton boosted was a master key that worked great on all the doors and service elevators.

Rex and Milton returned to the twenty-fourth floor where they were surprised by several people and security snooping around the suite next to the senators. The maid was in the hallway, explaining to the officers and the hotel manager that she had used her master key to let a customer into their suite 2406. Rex and Milton waited patiently as the security group did a complete security check of both suites.

Later they returned to the senator's suite to plant a few bugs in obvious places, lamps, cupboard, door frames.

"What are you doing, Rex?" Milton asked as he pulled the phone wires from the wall.

"Jillian showed me how to hot wire the phone so we can listen to both sides of the conversation," Rex told Milton as he replaced the phone connection to the wall.

"Hope it works?" Milton looked at Rex with a bit of doubt.

*****

The next evening, a black sedan and a small SUV pulled up in front of the Roosevelt Hotel.

"Good evening, Mr. Kincade, it looks like you are feeling better this evening," the doorman said as he opened the door.

Better…what was that? the senator thought to himself as he moved into the lobby toward the front desk.

"Good evening, Mr. Kincade, I see you are feeling much better this evening. Twenty-four-hour flu, was it?" said the young desk clerk.

The senator stared at the young man for a moment, then wondered why he and everyone else was so concerned with his health all of a sudden.

"Same accommodations as usual, Mr. Kincade?" the clerk offered.

"But of course," the senator responded.

"I see you have your bags with you this evening," the porter said as he escorted the senator up the elevator to his suite.

"Why wouldn't I?" the senator barked back, getting annoyed with all the silly comments.

Thirty minutes later, there was a knock at the door.

"Glad you are feeling better this evening, Mr. Kincade," the porter said, handing him the yellow manila envelope. "Hold on. Why does everybody keep talking about my health?" he asked the young man as he was about to open the envelope.

"Sir?" The young man turned around.

"Hold up a minute," the senator shouted.

"This envelope has been opened," he said waving it at the young man.

"Yes, sir. I delivered it to you yesterday," the young man said with a surprised look on his face.

"What the hell are you talking about, boy?" the senator said raising his voice

Tony stepped out from the other room.

"What's going on out here?" Tony asked.

"This boy said I was here yesterday and that he delivered this envelope to me."

"Yes, sir, *you were*... Check with the front desk..." the kid said backing up then running down the hall.

The senator just shook his head and slammed the door. Walking back toward the desk, he carefully opened the manila envelope. *Yup, it had been opened as he suspected but by whom?*

Knock...knock, there's a knock at the door.

"What the hell? You come back to apologize?" The senator yanked open the door yelling profanities when he realized it was his regular lovely woman in a long black dress.

"So, how are you today, baby...feeling better?" she said smiling.

The senator turned to her getting a little irritated about the whole thing. "What did you just ask me?" His eyes bugged out staring at her, waiting for a response.

"I asked you how you were feeling today, baby," she said turning toward him.

"Why did you ask me that?" raising his voice slightly.

"I came here yesterday, and you had a bad cold, sneezing, coughing," she said slowly slipping her dress off her shoulders.

"Stop... You were here yesterday?" he asked sternly.

"Yes, of course, last night about 9:00 p.m. like usual. Why so many questions, baby?" she asked. "What's the matter? No sex again tonight?" she said pouting slightly.

"What do you mean by that?" the senator snarled.

"Yesterday you had a cold and did not feel well, and you did not want to have…sex," she said, pouting like a little girl.

"I wasn't even here last night," he said sternly.

"Oh, come on, baby…you were…you gave me two hundred dollars and kicked me out," she said sitting on the edge of the bed. "No sex again tonight?"

"That is it… Get out" the senator yelled pointing at the door.

"Go on now. GET OUT," he said slapping her hand away.

"Tony… What's going on around here tonight?" the senator said now a little shaken as he walked over to the liquor cabinet and grabbed a bottle of his favorite Cajun Spiced Rum, hesitated, then examined it closely. "Damn, it's been opened," he said. He's never had open bottles of liquor in his suite before. The senator called down to the front desk.

"Bring me up a fresh bottle of my Cajun Spiced Rum," the senator yelled at the man at the concierge desk. "And make sure it's not been opened.

"Tony," the senator called out. "Here, take a drink," he said handing the bottle to Tony.

"I don't drink on duty, sir," Tony said hesitantly.

"Shut up and take a drink," the senator yelled back.

Tony took a drink and sat down.

"How do you feel?" the senator asked.

"Fine, sir," Tony responded wondering what that was all about.

"Okay, go on. Get out of here," the senator said snatching back the bottle.

There's a knock at the door. "Your fresh bottle of rum, sir," the porter said.

"My instructions are clear. I always get a unopened bottle of rum," the senator yelled at the porter.

"Yes sir, the bottle was unopened yesterday when you checked in, sir," the porter said.

"What the hell are you talking about?" the senator shouted. "I wasn't here yesterday." The senator grabbed the bottle and slammed the door. The senator opened the bottle and took a big swig of the spiced rum right from the bottle. "I wasn't here yesterday. I wasn't here yesterday," he repeated several times as he turned the bottle back for a good gulp. Then sat at the desk staring at the previously opened manila envelope.

"What's going on? Is he losing his mind?" The senator took another long drink from the bottle. "Why does everyone keep asking me about my health? Crap, I feel fine." Then took another long drink of the spiced rum.

The senator reopened the envelope and paged through the contents. Same as usual local ad, newspaper clippings, restaurant ads all the same, including the plain white paper stock note. "Le Grande Maison Hotel 10:30 p.m., tomorrow."

The senator picked up the phone, then asked the operator for an outside line.

*****

Rex and Milton were startled when the phone rang.

"We got something," Rex said, pointing a finger at Milton slowly lifting the receiver. "I told you it would work," Rex said listening to the conversation.

"I never had any doubts," Milton said as he listened to the conversation.

"Cayman National Bank, may I help you?" a lady's voice asked.

"Mr. William Morris please," the senator said.

"May I ask who's calling?"

"Kincade…Michael Kincade."

"Must be his alias," Rex whispered to Milton.

"Why are you whispering, Rex? They can't hear us," Milton said.

"One moment please." The phone went silent. "Mr. Kincade, William Morris, how can I help you?" he asked.

"Are my accounts in order?" the senator asked.

"I am sure they are," Mr. Morris assured him. "Account number and password please?"

"Account AA436525ZA…Kincade 1946."

"What a lousy password," Milton said writing down the information.

"I bet it was the year he was born," Milton said looking at Rex.

"And I bet his middle name is Kincade," Rex grinned.

"Everything is in order, sir," Mr. Wilson said.

"Two hundred and fifty million. BINGO," Milton shouted bouncing up from his chair dancing all around.

"Calm down," Rex said motioning for him to sit down.

"Anything else I can help you with Mr. Kincade?" asked Mr. Wilson.

"No, I'll be there in a couple of days to make a withdraw," the senator said as he hung up the phone.

"That is it," Milton said jumping around the room.

"What are you ranting about?" Rex asked.

"Remember what we were talking about at the café? The best way to get back at a powerful senator…is to make him poor and unelectable." Rex hesitated as Milton grinned broadly. "Yes, that we would have to make him poor and unelectable," Milton repeated it, staring at Rex who was definitely not getting it. "Don't ya see…we have both," Milton shouted.

"How? What?" Rex asked.

"We take the money right out from under his nose in broad daylight. We walk up to the bank and make a withdraw," Milton told Rex. "We have the account number, password, and Jillian even said I looked like him. I know I can pull this off. I did it last night," Milton boasted a little.

Rex finally got it.

"Okay, that makes him poor…but what about the unelectable part?" Rex asked.

"Mmmmm, I have no idea," Milton said.

"I like my idea better," Rex said.

"And what's that?"

"Just shoot him."

"Listen, most banks like the Cayman National Bank have signature cards. We don't even know what his signature looks like or what name he's going to be using," Rex said.

"Hold on, I got it… Hand me that phone book…couriers." Milton poked the page of the phone book. "Couriers Express. The fastest delivery service in New Orleans…open twenty-four hours a day."

Milton dialed the phone.

"Couriers Express, how can I help you?" the young lady asked.

"Yes, I need to have a package delivered to the Roosevelt Hotel and Bar to a Mr. Michael Kincade suite 2408 right away please."

"Manila envelope, some local newspaper clippings, restaurant ads, and a white plain sheet of paper with a handwritten note. Le Grande Maison Hotel, 10:30 p.m., tomorrow night, signature required."

Fifteen minutes later, there was a knock at the senator's suite. Tony looked through the hole.

"Special delivery for Michael Kincade," the courier said.

"Just slide it under the door," Tony said.

"Need a signature, sir," the kid said holding up his tablet.

Tony called the senator to the door and signed it Michael Kincade.

As soon as the door closed, Milton ran down the hallway and caught the kid.

"Hold up a minute," Milton called out.

The kid turned and wondered what was going on.

"Let me see that." Milton snatched the clipboard from the kid's hands.

"But I need that for my records," the kid shouted.

"I'm with the police," Milton said flashing an old inspector's badge.

"I need that signature to get paid," the kid yelled.

"Don't worry, kid. Give me a form to sign." Milton handed the kid a one-hundred-dollar bill and signed the form Michael Kincade.

"Not bad, eh, Rex?" Milton returned to the suite next door. "You gave the kid a one-hundred-dollar bill." Rex looked at him with surprise.

"Ya, it's all I had on me." Milton shook it off. "But we got the signature."

The meeting was at 10:30 p.m. at the Le Grande Maison Hotel tomorrow night. Rex and Milton had to think of something fast to prevent the senator from going to that meet.

"We could tie him up," Milton suggested.

"I'd rather just kill him," Rex said pacing around the room.

"You can't just kill a senator. It's against the law no matter how corrupt," Milton said trying to calm his friend.

"But we can make him suffer, right?" Rex said thinking out loud.

"We can give him and his bodyguard a powerful drug that will knock them out," Milton whispered.

"Yes, and when they wake up, they won't remember a thing," Rex added.

"Yes…that way, they will miss the meeting." Milton was getting excited.

"Then we go in their place and make a mess of things," Rex said quickly.

"Well, ole boy, you are certainly good at doing that," Milton said leaning back in his chair.

"I bet we can pull it off. We did it last night…right here in the lobby," Milton said.

"Wish we had the good drugs we had in the CIA," Rex said pacing around the room.

"Tulane Medical does… It's just around the corner," Milton said smiling. "They have everything we need."

"What are we waiting for? Let's go," Rex said jumping to his feet.

Tulane Medical Center is the primary teaching hospital for the Tulane University School of Medicine, one of the oldest schools in the south was about four blocks away.

"Hey, Rex, how do you want to play this?" Milton asked as they approached the hospital emergency room entrance. "You are having a heart attack. They get like all distracted. Then I'll sneak into the pharmacy and grab what we need. Simple."

"Why me?" Milton asked.

"You are older and supposed to have heart attacks," Rex said calling for a nurse.

"Help, help, doctor, my friend is having a heart attack or some-thing," Rex called out looking back at his friend.

"Come on, Milty, a little more action. Gotta make it look good." Rex laughed.

Milton clutched his chest and whined like a stuck pig. "Ohhh... Please help my friend," Rex shouted as several student nurses came to his aide.

Rex slipped into the nurse's treatment center and grabbed a doc-tor's lab coat hanging on the rack and a patient's chart, then headed down toward the pharmacy.

"Nurse, nurse," Rex called out.

"Yes, doctor?" the pharmacy nurse responded.

"My patient in room 305 did not get the medication I ordered over an hour ago." Rex slammed the chart on the counter.

"What's the patient's name?" she asked.

"Calhoun...William Calhoun," he said.

The pharmacy nurse walked over to the computer and pulled up the records, then compared them to the chart. "Sorry, doctor... There is no such order for that patient," she said holding her ground.

Rex looked around the corner at Milton who was putting on quite a show.

"Damn, there he is in the lobby, tearing up the place," Rex said as the nurse stepped out of the pharmacy to look down the hall.

"Benzodiazepine...Stat," Rex ordered. Rex quickly followed the nurse into the dispensary to get the Benzodiazepine. When her back was turned, Rex reached up and grabbed a bottle. "Let's go," Rex shouted as the two of them headed back down the hall toward Milton. Milton was surrounded by three lovely nurses, checking his vitals and trying to calm him down. Rex motioned for him to act crazy, twirling his finger in a circle around his ear. The head nurse poked him with a shot of Benzodiazepine. Milton just looked at him, wondering why it took so long as he relaxed and fell asleep.

Couple hours later, Milton was released from the hospital, and they headed back to the hotel and entered through the employee service entrance.

"Good, the key still works," Rex said as the door clicked open.

"What's going on?" Milton asked as the effects of the Benzodiazepine started to wear off.

"I never told them to give you a shot," Rex snickered as Milton went to bed to sleep it off.

It was around 6:00 p.m. when Rex and Milton returned to the senator's room, hoping they would be at dinner for the next hour or so. Rex knocked on the hard wooden door.

"Great, let's go." Rex swiped the key card. The door clicked open. "They did not deactivate the key," Rex whispered.

"Why are you whispering?" Milton asked loudly. "There's no one here."

"Why are you yelling," Rex asked.

"A few minutes longer, and they would have admitted me and poked me full of holes," Milton said heading into the room.

"They did," Rex laughed.

"Did what?" Milton looked bewildered.

"They did check you in and poke you full of holes."

Rex figured they had about thirty to forty minutes before the senator and his men returned from their dinner. Thirty minutes later, the door opened. The senator had one of his guards with him, the stocky one; others must have gone home for the night. The stocky guard headed straight for the bathroom and the senator to a small office area where he unlocked the bottom drawer of the desk and pulled out a leather satchel.

Rex was hiding behind the thick floor to ceiling curtains waiting for Milton to kill the power. Rex checked his watch. "Three, two, one." Nothing happened. Milton was supposed to kill the lights five minutes after they arrived. Rex waited a little longer, then checked his watch again. "What is taking so long?" Rex mumbled almost loud enough for the senator to hear him.

The senator got up, made his way to the liquor cabinet, and grabbed the bottle of his favorite rum and a glass, then settled in the comfortable office chair. Rex checked his watch again for the third time. "Hmmm," Rex wondered if the lights would ever go off. The lights flickered and went off.

Rex jumped out from behind the curtains, and with a quick chop to the neck, the senator was out cold. When the lights went out, Tony instinctively headed for the senator's room. When he spotted the senator on the floor, he rushed in through the doors, but it was too late, Rex wrapped an arm around his neck applying a sleeper hold.

"What took you so long to kill the lights?" Rex asked heading back into the other room.

"The main power box was in the bathroom," Milton explained. "with stocky. No telling what he was doing in there that long." Milton shrugged his shoulders.

Rex tied the senator to the chair and gave him a shot of the benzodiazepine. His eyes blinked a few times as his body relaxed. Benzodiazepine was a good substitution for a truth serum. Rex slapped him a few times to get him ready to answer a few questions.

"What is your name?" Rex asked as he stared directly into his eyes.

"Senator Bradley K. Stevens," he said half mumbling.

"Where are you now?" Rex kept a close look at his eyes, looking for any pupil dilations.

"New Orleans."

"What year were you born?"

"1956."

"I told you it was his birth year," Milton snickered.

"Are you from Texas?" Rex asked, knowing the answer to be true.

"Yes," the senator responded.

"Do you know a Michael Kincade?"

"No," his pupils constricted slightly.

Rex knew he was hiding something. Rex administered a second dose of benzodiazepine, waited a few minutes, and asked again.

"Who is Michael Kincade?" Rex asked as he started to fade.

"I am Michael Kincade," the senator whispered.

Rex slapped him across the face.

"Is there a meeting at the Le Grande Maison Hotel tonight?" Rex asked, knowing the answer to be "no."

"No…no, tomorrow night," the senator whispered.

Rex knew he was telling the truth. He changed the date. The senator started to fade. There was nothing more they could do as his eyes got heavy and fell asleep.

Milton dragged the senator to his bed, took off his clothes, and put him to bed, then dragged the bodyguard to the couch. In the morning, they would wake up and not remember a thing. Rex looked at his watch. They had about two hours before the meeting at Le Grande Maison Hotel and had to come up with a plan.

"Let's go to the meeting and cause chaos," Rex said.

Milton checked through all the paperwork inside the leather satchel, stuff like invoices from JML Corporation, notes about Luiz and La Rosa Negra, the syndicate.

How does all this fit together? Rex wondered as they left for Le Grande Maison Hotel.

CHAPTER 21

———— ⫸《◉》⫷ ————

It was about 10:00 p.m. when Rex and Milton walked up to Le Grande Maison Hotel.

"Flying by the seat of our pants again," Milton said as he rang the doorbell of the old bed and breakfast.

"This could get really ugly fast," Rex whispered back as they readied themselves for whatever.

"Good evening. Do you have a reservation?" the speaker blurted out.

Milton turned slowly toward Rex, then back at the speaker. "Yes, of course, Michael Kincade," Milton answered in a nice Southern drawl then waited hoping.

"Password?"

"Kincade 1946," Milton said moving to the side of the door, half expecting a barrage of gunfire.

The door opened slowly.

"Good evening, gentlemen," the man said inviting them inside.

The butler led Milton and Rex to the back of the lobby to a cellar door behind the vintage old bar. The stairs headed straight down two levels to the basement.

At the bottom of the stairs, it opened up into a small foyer where they were greeted and frisked by two very large security guards armed with military style assault rifles.

The place looked old and in disrepair. Down a couple of curved hallways, they stopped in front of a double wooden door to a suite. The guard opened the door, let them in, and locked it behind them.

"Some serious security, eh, Milty?" Rex said entering the room.

The suites had a rather spacious large foyer, full kitchen, two bedrooms, bathroom. The main room had a large leather sofa, facing a blank wall with a computer flashing random messages: "PLEASE LOG ON. YOUR SESSION WILL BEGIN IN ONE HOUR" with a countdown clock in the right hand corner.

"Better do what it says." Rex looked at Milton, directing him toward the computer.

Milton walked over to the computer and hit "ENTER" then login screen popped up. "I wish Jillian were here right now, I could really use her help," Milton said as he entered what he hoped was the correct login and password.

"Michael Kincade." The computer flashed then went dark. "I think I broke it," Milton yelled across the room at Rex who was raiding the refrigerator.

"Wow, they got a real nice selection of food in here. Are you hungry?" Rex asked then returned with a couple of sandwiches and ice-cold beers. "What? I'm famished," Rex said, taking a huge bite of the sandwich. "Eat something." Rex pushed a sandwich in front of Milton. "Sorry, they did not have any Guinness. Give it to me." Rex pulled the keyboard toward him.

"What are you going to type?" Milton asked, taking a bite out of the sandwich and a long swig from the bottle of beer. "Let me try Bradley Stevens." The computer was still flashing.

"Where are you going? What? I am thirsty…want another one," Rex said heading for the fridge.

"Try, Michael Kincade…" Rex said returning to the computer.

"I tried that one already," Milton snapped.

"Do you think they use middle initials?" Rex said slurping on his beer.

"What? Probably not," Milton said.

"Wonder what happens if we don't get it in time," Rex asked.

"I don't want to find out," Milton said, trying multiple variations of Kincade's name—"Mike Kincade," "Kincade 1946."

"Did you try his middle initial?" Rex said slurping on another beer.

"No," Milton said looking at the timer as it ran out of time.

"What is it?"

"Try Michael D. Kincade," Rex suggested as he munched down another sandwich.

"Why D?" Milton asked as he typed it into the computer.

The computer flashed twice blinked then flashed another message: "PLEASE ENTER YOUR PASSWORD."

"I got this one," Milton said typing in "Kincade 1946." The computer flashed and then came on.

"Nice work. Why D.?" Milton asked.

"I don't know I just guessed that he was a Dallas football fan."

"Okay, sure thing. Now what?"

"Welcome, your session will begin in five minutes," as the wall fell away into the ground, revealing a huge one-way mirror.

"Wow, this is cool. Wonder what movie they are playing?"

"Wow, it's like some sort of arcade?" Rex said enthusiastically looking forward to playing the game.

"No, looks like a stage," Milton said squinting through the darkened glass.

"There are quite a few windows out there," Rex said as he counted them out. "Fifteen."

"Check this out, Rex," Milton said pointing at the computer.

"Looks like an online JCPenney's catalog," Rex said as numbers and figures flashed across the screen. Rex read down the list. "Michael D. Kincade, that must be us." Rex kept playing with all the buttons like it was a new toy at Christmas time.

It was a little before 11:00 p.m. when the stage lit up.

"Look at that one Milton"—Rex pointed—"does that say weapons?"

Rex clicked on the pull down menu. There were categories for every weapon you can imagine on the list, mostly older discontinued models, but some of these are state of the art, even classified.

Rex flashed back to two weeks ago when he found that compound in Panama, specifically the weapons. Some of those weapons had been traced back to the straw buyers, when his brother Ben was in the ATF. When his brother was murdered…by that traitor… Niklas?

"Milton, maybe Luiz was trying to get away from the black market," Rex said as he scanned the various list of weapons.

"The reason he was murdered," Milton added.

*****

Earlier in the day, the girls were rounded up and escorted out the back entrance to an awaiting bus. A short ride later, they stopped at a second location an underground parking structure of some kind, several floors down.

The girls were moved into a big ballroom. Several minutes later, an older woman with gray hair and a strong German accent opened the door. She had several suitcases.

"Put these on and don't argue," she said throwing pretty outfits at each one of the girls.

The lights flashed onto each of the girls as they stepped out on stage with a number hung around their neck.

*****

"The auction has begun" flashed across the screen in bright green letters. Milton watched as numbers started flashing on the screen like the New York Stock Market on a trading day. Green numbers and red numbers next to everyone's names. Milton figured it out pretty quickly.

"Rex, they are bidding on these girls," Milton called out to Rex.

"Look," Milton pointed at Kincade's account as the final bid was placed and closed.

"The numbers went up on Kincade's account," Milton said.

"Did she just get sold?" Rex turned toward Milton.

"Yes, for $250,000…and I think we sold her," Milton said as $250,000 turned green.

"WE SOLD HER. I can't believe this. We just sold that girl," Rex said pacing around the room.

"Yes, Rex…but not we…him…Kincade…the senator did," Milton explained.

"I can't believe they are selling these girls at this auction," Rex said getting really mad.

"Where do you think you are going?" Milton asked as Rex stormed toward the door.

"I'm not going to just sit here and watch this happen."

"Stop. Where are you going?" Milton asked jumping up and stopping him.

"The door is locked, and there are armed guards everywhere. Now get over here," Milton said as he watched the numbers move around the screen.

"I have an idea…watch that number." Milton pointed at the total. Milton mashed a few buttons, then hit enter.

"Wow…the number just went down," Rex said in amazement. "What did you do?" Rex's eyes lit up.

"I bought something," Milton explained. "Every time you buy something, your account goes down." "Remember, the best way to take down a crooked senator is to make him poor and unelectable."

"Does that mean we can still make him poor and very unpopular…with them?" Rex pointed at the other windows.

"*Yes*. Now all we have to do is buy some stuff, charge up his account." Milton looked at the list. "Time to go shopping, Rex," Milton said.

"Jillian's going to be mad that she missed out on a chance to go shopping," Rex said pulling the computer keyboard toward him.

"Ya, and using other people's money," Milton said.

"Gotta find something that makes that number go down," Rex said looking around.

"Look, there's a list of auctions going on real time and how much time is left along with the current bids," Milton explained. Milton clicked on one of the auctions, "weapons," "automatic," "assault," "M-4."

"Look, the M-4s have a current bid of five million with one minute left," Milton said. "I'm going to bid ten million." Milton entered the amount then hit enter.

The computer updated immediately. The bid flashed red, then turned green. "Look, ten million bucks just got pulled out of the account," Milton told Rex.

Milton and Rex just sat back, all happily celebrating a victory when the ten million suddenly got added to the Kincade's account.

Milton thought for a minute. They just purchased ten million dollars' worth of weapons from themselves. "Damn. Gotta stay away from the weapons and the girls. Apparently, he owns them."

The stage door opened, and Jillian walked out, told to parade around, and look sexy. Jillian did the best she could...Sexy petite redhead, five feet two tall, 105 pounds, fifteen years old from the United States of America. She was wearing a short white miniskirt with rip away Velcro on each side, a tight little light blue blouse tied at the back.

Rex looked up from his computer screen and out the window on stage.

"Milton, it's Jillian." Rex pointed at the stage.

Rex and Milton watched the computer as Jillian made her first pass. The numbers were pretty low. Jillian clearly did not want to participate in this charade.

On her second pass, Jillian went a little crazy. Pulling off her top and performing a little strip tease when she ripped off her miniskirt and was wearing nothing but a tiny yellow two-piece bikini. She ran to the end of the runway, jumped high into the air, and landed in the splits.

The computer bids went nuts, and the offers skyrocketed. When it was all over, the final bid was 1.2 million dollars.

"Wow, I never knew we had a million-dollar gal on our hands." Rex giggled and continued bidding on different things as Kincade's total went up by another 1.2 million.

"Yea, but we need to make him lose money, not gain," Milton said looking at the totals. His numbers were going up, not down. "Buy more," Milton called out to Rex. The plan was to put him in the poor house, not make him rich.

"He has millions in the bank," Rex said lowering his head.

"Does he really?" Milton said grinning.

"Yes, he does, at least $250,000,000," Rex told him.

"Not for long. We know where he keeps his money, the password, and account numbers." Milton leaned back and smiled. "Now all we do is take it." Milton leaned back on the couch.

"How do we do that exactly?" Rex asked.

"We take it right out of the bank in broad daylight." Milton smiled.

"But now we got to buy more and get him in all sorts of trouble with these guys," Milton said as the computer flashed a warning. "Auction will end in one hour… All accounts will be settled upon its conclusion." Rex looked up at the computer and the totals. Kincade was in the green for just over 100 million dollars.

Rex and Milton started bidding on anything they could think of that would bring the total down. Unfortunately, you never knew who owned what till the auction updated the computer, and after the bidding was closed, you could not go back.

"How we doing, Rex?" Milton asked as he finished another bidding cycle.

"It's $130,000,000 in the green," Rex responded looking at his friend in desperation.

"Ten minutes and counting, still a bit short," Milton said as he hit enter.

"How much do stingers go for on the black market?" Rex asked Milton.

"No idea" Milton said.

"Ten million apiece," Rex said hoping it was not something they controlled or owned.

"I just bid on forty of them at ten million apiece," Rex said. "Auction will end in less than a minute… What is taking so long for the computer to update?" Rex said as the timer ran out.

"Did it go through?" Milton starred at the computer screen.

"I don't know" Rex said.

The auction was officially over and totally out of both of their hands.

"Please settle all your accounts at this time. A huge *red* number popped up on the computer screen: 330 million dollars.

Milton looked back at the screen again. The Kincade account had a total of -330 million dollars.

"We did it." Rex jumped up and threw a fist into the air.

"Ohhhh yes, we did," Milton hooted a few times.

Beeep…beeeeep…beeeep… "Please enter the proper account and bank routing codes to settle your account," the computer continued flashing the same message over and over again.

"Hey, Rex, we are not out of the woods yet." Milton pointed at the screen.

"Time to go," Rex said heading for the door, but the door was locked. "Now what?" Rex looked at Milton.

There was a click at the door.

"Be cool," Milton said as Rex backed away from the door.

A man with a clipboard walked in with two guards carrying automatic weapons.

"There seems to be a problem with your account. We have not received your bank account or routing numbers," the man said.

"I realize that, sir, but my computer will not accept the codes," Milton said punching numbers in as fast as possible into the computer.

"I need you to relog onto the system, sir," the man said as he approached.

Milton watched Rex as the guard walked by with a nod Milton shook his head and knew what was coming next. Rex flipped the rifle from the guards hand, and the butt of the rifle slammed into the bridge of his nose. The blood gushed out as he hit the floor hard. The second guard reacted too slow as Rex turned and front kicked him across the room.

"You call that cool?" Milton yelled out heading for the door.

Rex shrugged his shoulders and quickly disabled both weapons.

Rex slowly opened the door and looked both ways.

"Coast is clear. Let's go." Rex waved his hand at Milton. "Let's play it cool," Rex said as they headed down the curved hallway.

"Okay." Milton nodded his head in agreement.

Up ahead by the staircase, they spotted a guard letting one of the VIPs out the exit.

"Stop right there," the guard called out. "You have not been cleared to leave," he said walking toward them.

"Oh my, I thought we were," Milton said as he casually looked over at Rex, then stumbled toward the guard. The guard reached out awkwardly to catch Milton but was met by the handle of the umbrella right in the jaw. Milton grabbed the rifle and removed the receiver, rendering it useless.

"That was cool," Milton said, looking back at Rex motioning for him to get a moving up the stairs.

They ran passed the VIP and into the main lobby. The main alarm had gone off as additional guards ran up from downstairs. Milton blocked the door with several chairs as Rex clotheslined the lobby guard running toward them from the main entrance. They both made a mad dash across the street to the parking lot and sped away just in the nick of time.

CHAPTER 22

Jillian was taken out back to an awaiting minivan along with several other girls, then driven several miles to the marina where they boarded a one-hundred-foot private yacht with a funny name, *The Adara*, which in Arabic means "virgins." Jillian had a bad feeling about the whole thing, realizing that she was now the property of some wealthy Saudi Arabian king or prince. The thought did not settle well with her either way.

Nobody was watching the door as Jillian turned to the other girls and told them to stay put and keep quiet, that she would be right back. It was pitch-black outside with the new moon obscured by the clouds. *A perfect night for hunting*, she thought as she ventured out on deck.

There was one guard a hundred feet away having a cigarette at the end of the walkway. Jillian took off her shoes and snuck around behind him and pounced on him like a cat. It took only a few seconds for the choke hold to take effect as the guard's eyes fluttered and passed out.

She continued down the walkway and heard faint conversations up ahead. She grabbed the guardrail above her head, and like a gymnast, she did a kip, up and over the railing, a perfect ten in her mind. From above, she could easily see the two guards talking below.

Jillian dropped down between the two guards, grabbed one by the hand turned, and kicked the other up and over the rail. Still holding the first guards hand, she turned and clipped him in the throat, shocking his trachea.

She moved around to the other side of the deck a guard, a much taller man stood in her way. Jillian took off running toward the man and at the last second slid down between his legs snagging his left foot as she passed, tripping him up.

The big man stumbled and fell, face first on the deck. Jillian held his ankle and rolled over his back, thumping him in the back of the head with her elbow. Jillian gathered up his weapons and flicked them over the rail. Jillian looked back as the girl's faces were squished against the small windows of the galley.

Three guards approached running down the gangway heading toward the bow with the lights dimmed you could barely see Jillian as she hid in the shadows.

The first guard ran passed. Jillian jumped out and punched the second guard in the face, then grabbed him and twisted him toward the third guard closing the gap from behind using him as a blocking dummy. The guard took two punches, hitting the guard in the face both times. Jillian held him up by his arms from behind and threw a front kick, knocking him back a few feet. The guard fell to his knees, drew his gun, and got off two rounds, hitting the second guard twice.

The first guard spun around to help, pointed his gun, and let off a few shots that barely missed Jillian and hit the third guard, killing him instantly. Jillian pushed the now lifeless body of the second guard toward the first one, who emptied his magazine.

From behind and under the guards arms, Jillian threw multiple kicks, once from the right side then from the left, quickly doubling him over. Jillian pushed the second guard forward toward the ground using his weight to catapult over his back, knocking out the first guard. Jillian pushed the two guards overboard, and when she approached the third, he jumped up. The girls screamed as the gunshots went off and watched as Jillian and the guard disappeared out of sight. Seconds later, there was a huge thud that could be heard through the bulkhead, then another a slight pause and a splash. The girls let out a cheer as Jillian jumped into view with both hands raised high above her head, jumping around like a heavyweight boxing champion who just won the world championship.

The sirens could be heard as the NOPD and the New Orleans coast guard responded to the shots fired and rescued the girls from the yacht and the makeshift hotel. No one even knew her name, but when the police questioned them, all the girls could remember was the little girl in a white miniskirt and a bright canary yellow bikini top kicked ass and disarmed all the bad guys.

One of the girls while being treated for her wounds looked over the EMT's shoulder into the darkness and spotted Jillian lurking in the background. The little girl waved then smiled as Jillian disappeared.

CHAPTER 23

——◦«◉»◦——

Later that night, Jillian pulled up in front of the Roosevelt Hotel in a powder blue 5.0 liter Mustang Convertible, handed the keys to the valet, and walked into the main lobby still wearing the mini-skirt and the two-piece yellow bikini.

"May I help you, young lady?" the desk clerk asked.

"That is quite all right, my dear," as she pulled off her oversized sunglasses and looked around the hotel lobby.

"There's our multimillion-dollar girl now," Rex said as Jillian scampered over to the table and gave Rex and Milton a big hug.

"Did I hear you say million-dollar girl?" Jillian asked, looking at Rex as he grinned broadly.

"Actually, 1.2-million-dollar girl," Milton corrected his colleague.

"At the auction, you were sold for 1.2 million dollars," Milton explained as Jillian slugged Rex in the arm for the remark.

"So how was your night?" Rex asked.

"Maritime disaster for some," she said with a grin of her own. "What about you?" she asked as the waitress approached to take the order.

"Good evening, Mr. Kincade, would you folks like to place an order?" the older waitress asked smiling.

"Yes, of course," Jillian said. "Two double cheese burgers, filet of fish with pickles and extra fries. Oh, and a banana split sundae with extra chocolate syrup," she said looking at the waitress.

"Anything to drink with that?" the waitress asked.

"Yes, I forgot an extra-large margarita."

"Can I see your ID? You have to be twenty-one to drink."

"What? You are kidding, right?" Jillian said. "That's okay, just make it an unsweetened iced tea. I am trying to watch my weight," Jillian said patting her tummy. "Are you guys eating?" Jillian asked looking around the room.

"I'll have a burger and fries with a Sam Adams Lager," Rex said.

"And your usual, Mr. Kincade?" she said looking at him strangely.

"But of course," Milton said with a nod.

"Will that be on your room account, sir?" she asked.

"Yes, just put it all in my account," Milton said nodding slightly.

"What was that all about?" Jillian asked when she walked away. "The way she looked at you and called you Mr. Kincade?" Jillian looked at Milton.

"Oh dear, yes, Mr. Kincade," Milton said looking at Rex.

"So what happened to Kincade?" Jillian asked. "Rex shoot him or something?"

"No, he wanted to," Milton said, looking around.

"I wanted to rip his arms and legs off too," Rex said slamming his fist on the table.

"No, he's taking a nap. But right now, we have to get out of here," Milton said.

"What? Why?" Jillian asked.

"I think we've been made…the waitress," Milton said.

"What about the food? I haven't had a decent meal all week. I'm starving," Jillian said.

"Gotta go now," Milton said, "before she gets back."

The three of them headed out the front door around the block to the back of the Roosevelt Hotel.

Rex pulled the master key from his pocket and swiped the door. *Click.*

"Here ya go." Rex tossed Jillian a bag of chips when they passed the service cart.

"Geez, thanks. I always knew you were a cheap date," Jillian said as they headed up to the twenty-fourth floor.

They slipped into the adjoining suite. "There's food and cold beers in the fridge," Rex said, taking a seat on the comfortable sofa.

"So why were you in the restaurant?" Jillian asked.

"Wanted to see if we could spot that VIP we saw at the airport yesterday," Milton said.

"We have the information on the microdrive and the files Lupe gave us. What else do we need to take him down?" Jillian asked.

"Well, like you said before, the best way to takedown a powerful senator is to make him poor and unelectable," Milton said. "We've done part of that already," Milton said.

"What do you mean?" Jillian asked, looking across at the Roosevelt from the balcony.

"Milton and I went to that auction...where you were sold and made a mess of things," Rex said.

"What kind of mess?"

"While you were on your adventure," Rex paused, "we were able to make him poor at the auction," Rex explained.

"What are you planning now?" Jillian asked.

"Now he's a wanted man," Milton said. "Just have to see who comes after him."

"Milton and I went to an auction and jacked up his account... He owes the syndicate or whatever this is 330 million dollars...and to the best of our knowledge, he only has one account with a balance of 250 million dollars in a bank in the Cayman Islands. Soon to be zero, that is," Rex stopped and grinned at Milton.

"Okay, what are you planning to do?" Jillian asked.

"The next part of the plan is to make him poor, really poor," Rex continued. "That is where Milton comes in." Rex turned toward Milton who took over.

"You said it, love... I look like the man, and yesterday we proved it...and even tonight," Milton hesitated.

"But tonight you blew it," Jillian said.

"But, did I?" Milton asked.

"The lady at the bar saw you and recognized you," Jillian said, not quite grasping at what Milton was saying.

"Yes, and what did she see… I was in the hotel with a lady and another man," Milton hesitated.

"Now they are onto you. They suspect something is going on," Jillian said, still not getting it.

"Wait and see," Milton said. "They need to know that he is in the hotel, and the waitress will make sure they know it," Milton explained.

"She's with them?" Jillian said nodding her head.

"But right now…we have a bank heist to plan."

"What? We are going to rob a bank?" Jillian said. "That is your big plan?"

"Not exactly, just a major withdraw in broad daylight, totally legit," Milton told her.

"But we have to get there first," Rex interjected.

"Get where?" Jillian asked.

"Cayman National Bank," Milton said.

Ring….ring. The senator's phone rang. *Ring, ring.* The room phone rang.

"It's for you," Rex said handing the receiver to Jillian. "Now we can listen in," Rex said picking up the other receiver.

"I showed you how to do that," Jillian said, listening in to the conversation.

*****

"Hello, this is Kincade," the senator sat up in bed. His head was spinning and felt a sudden urge to vomit.

"Mr. Kincade, as you well know, you are required to settle all your accounts before leaving the auction," the voice said in a broken Spanish accent.

"What account and what auction are you talking about?" the senator said shaking the cobwebs from his head.

"Last night, you acquired a vast amount of merchandise and did not settle your account within the allotted time frame," the man explained on the phone.

"What are you talking about? That auction is tonight?" the senator stood up too quickly as the blood flowed from his brain almost falling over.

"The auction is tonight. I have it right here." He looked closely at the date on the sheet of paper. "The auction is not until tonight," he repeated several times.

"Your account is overdue and owe the syndicate a very large sum of money," the man said.

"What large sum of money?" the senator raised his voice angrily.

"It's 330 million dollars, sir," the man said on the phone.

"What the *hell* are you talking about?" the senator yelled.

"I did not go to any auction and spend 330 million dollars," he yelled. "It has to be a mistake," the senator barked on the phone.

"Well, sir, we have all the correct approvals username, log on, passwords, signature verification, even a video of you and your associate at the auction," the voice explained.

"I made no such purchase," the senator said.

"Sir, may I remind you of the rules of the syndicate."

"No, you may not… I am totally aware of the rules of the syndicate… I wrote them," the senator yelled.

"Well, sir, we will be over immediately to collect," the man said as he hung up the phone.

"Geno, Geno…where the hell are you?" the senator yelled out. "Geno." The senator walked out into the main room. "Geno, is that you?" He walked up and kicked the man several times sleeping on the couch.

"What the hell is going on?"

Geno rolled off the couch onto the floor, clutching his head with both hands.

"What's today's date?" the senator asked.

"What?" Geno asked looking at him, wondering about the question.

"What day of the week is it?" the senator yelled.

"Friday, sir…I think," Geno said shaking his head.

"Friday?" the senator wondered as he called the front desk for confirmation.

"What's today's date?" he asked the clerk.

"The thirteenth, sir," the clerk responded.

"Day of the week?" the senator yelled.

"Sunday the thirteenth, sir."

The senator hung up the phone.

"Sunday the thirteenth…that is impossible."

The senator opened the desk drawer and pulled out the plain white handwritten note. "Friday, 10:30 p.m. Le Grande Maison Hotel." The senator sat at the desk and stared at the note, rolled open the bottom drawer of the desk. His hands shook as he took a long drag from the bottle of rum. "What's going on? Why is the syndicate after me?" Then took another drink from the bottle.

"Geno, we gotta get out of here. Call the guys," he yelled, realizing they would be coming after him.

"Geno, we have to go *now*," the senator called out to Geno as he grabbed his briefcase and headed into the next room.

There was a knock at the door. Geno walked slowly toward the door.

"Stop, don't open it," the senator called out as the door crashed open, knocking Geno back and off his feet. Geno fell back instinctively, pulling his weapon from his belt and firing three shots at the intruders.

The first two bullets hit the lead man's center mass, the third was wild and to the right. The second man through the door returned fire, hitting Geno in the chest. The third man grabbed the senator who was cowering in the corner and threw him into a chair.

"I give up. Don't shoot. Don't shoot," he cried out.

"Where is the money, Kincade?" the man demanded.

"I don't have that kind of money," Kincade yelled back. "I didn't even go to the auction," he pleaded with his attackers. "I don't have that kind of money," he shouted at the thugs.

"Well, you better get it," the man slammed the phone in front of him, jamming the receiver into his ear.

"Do you know who I am?" the senator yelled at the man.

"I don't care who you are," as he pistol whipped him across the face. "I am here to collect the money you owe the syndicate."

"I am a senator in the US Senate," he cried out.

"Well, get it…Mr. Kincade."

The senator picked up the phone and dialed.

The phone next door rang twice. Milton picked up the phone.

"Here we go…"

"Cayman National Bank, I am sorry the bank is closed at this time. We will reopen at 9:00 a.m. Monday morning. Thank you." The senator hung up the phone.

*****

"Who was that?" Jillian asked.

"The senator," Rex said. "He made a call to the bank in the Cayman Islands," Rex said smugly.

"Looks like he had some visitors," Milton added. "Looks like they are headed to the Cayman's…but so are we and got to get there first," Milton said.

*****

"So you heard it. The bank is closed till Monday morning," the senator said smugly.

The man walked up to him and slugged him once in the gut, then again across the face. "We will catch a flight to the Cayman's and be there when your bank opens on Monday morning," the man said.

The three of them took the express elevator down to the back service entrance where Jillian barely had enough time to get to her powder-blue five liter Mustang. The senator and his companions came through the lobby a few minutes later. Jillian peeled out burning off about an inch of rubber as she made it around the block to the entrance of the Roosevelt Hotel just as the senator's sedan rolled down the road.

"Jump in," Jillian shouted.

"Keep an eye on the senator's sedan. Make sure not to follow too close as to raise suspicion," Rex said with authority.

"Sure thing, Rex," Jillian responded then floored the multiport fuel-injected engine, leaving a forty-foot skid mark and a cloud of smoke.

The senator's sedan took off north then west on I-10, heading toward the airport, then up to the international departures area.

Jillian watched as they got out and headed into the terminal. Jillian got out and followed them inside to the main ticket counter.

"Hi, how are you today?" she said taking off her oversized sunglasses.

"Just fine, and you?" the senator said gently tipping his hat like a proper Southern gentleman.

Jillian was standing directly behind them when they made their purchase.

"Oh, are we on the same flight?" Jillian said peeking at the flight number.

"Yup. Cayman Island, flight 2234 at 2:00 p.m.," she said with a huge smile. Looks that way," the senator said, looking deeply into her bright blue eyes.

Jillian smiled and greeted the other two men with the senator, but they did not respond and pushed the senator along to the security checkpoint.

Jillian's seat was four rows back and off to the left, close enough to keep an eye on the senator but not too close to suspect anything.

Rex and Milton walked into the terminal a few minutes later and booked a flight for later that night. The five-hour flight landed on time at the Cayman International Airport. The senator and his two guards headed for the AVIS rental car stand. Jillian followed close behind and stopped at budget car rentals a couple of stations away. After a few minutes of negotiating, Jillian had her 5.0 Mustang GT convertible, this time in a dark royal blue.

The two rental car company garages were about one hundred feet from one another, which made it easy to depart at about the same time. Traffic was kinda heavy as they exited the airport complex onto Robert's drive, which made it hard to tail someone without raising suspicion but also easy to get lost in the crowd.

At the first stoplight, Jillian pulled up right next to the sedan but never even looked over.

Jillian put on her oversized sunglasses, opened the convertible ragtop, and floored it when the light changed as her long dark red hair fluttered in the wind. After few turns, she fell back, trying to figure out where they were headed. They made a right on N. Sound Road and into a mini roundabout but kept straight on N. Sound, approaching the second mini roundabout. Jillian pulled up right behind them, close enough to be seen. The sedan quickly exited onto the Esterly Tibbetts Highway. Jillian floored it around the round-about onto the Eastern Avenue exit then on to West Bay Road where the two roads run parallel for a while. At one point, the roads come close enough for her to see inside the sedan.

Jillian sped up and turned right on West Bay passed Calico Rex's Bar and Grill. Up ahead, she spotted the sedan rolling through the roundabout heading north, then northwest up the coastal road, Jillian followed from a distance.

The sedan finally turned left into the CoCo Condos luxury townhouses in the Caymans. Jillian, continued down the road to the Cayman Sunset at Coconut Bay right next door to the CoCo Condos Resort, overlooking the beach.

Jillian parked the Mustang and walked toward the CoCo Condos resort. She spotted the sedan, parked behind a bungalow about one hundred yards from the beach.

Rex and Milton landed a few hours later and called Jillian.

"Where did they end up?" Rex asked as he picked up his luggage.

"The CoCo Condos luxury townhouses," she told him.

"How about you?" Rex asked.

"The Cayman Sunset at Coconut Bay, next door about one hundred yards away, just over the next burn," Jillian told him.

"I bet that's going to blow our budget?" Rex said jokingly.

"Did not know I had one. But not for you, Rex… I got you a great hammock on the burn overlooking the CoCo Condos," Jillian said.

"Milton can stay with me at two thousand dollars per night with free ocean beach view, internet, coffee, free breakfast in the morning." Jillian laughed.

Rex and Milton pulled up later that night in a dark blue sedan, same make and model as the senator's group.

"Hey, Jillian," the voice was unmistakable. "Can you make room for me?" Milton asked giving her a big hug.

"I got you covered." Jillian smiled than pointed outside to Rex and his hammock. "It's just over that burn." Jillian pointed.

The plan was all set. Milton would enter the bank, disguised as the senator, and make a sizeable withdraw. Jillian and Milton went over the tapes several times, even picked up a couple of tips from his campaign speeches, when he ran for Senate for the fifth time. They would go in assuming he was Mr. Michael D. Kincade. Milton had the bank part down including the slight Southern mannerisms.

What they really needed was a way to slow him down, long enough to get in and out of the bank.

"I got the perfect plan…been setting it up all day," Jillian said as she pulled open a road map of the island. Jillian pointed out a few chokepoint along the route and knowing the senator's love for sexy young ladies and helping damsels in distress. "I'll slow him down."

CHAPTER 24

A̶t the break of dawn, Jillian relieved Rex who spent the night
watching the senator at the CoCo Condos.

"Good morning, Rex. How was your night?" Jillian asked.

"Apart from a few sand crabs, pretty quiet."

"Milton is all set. You better head on into town," she said.

"Okay, see you later."

Jillian set up a vantage point between the two resorts keeping
an eye on the bungalow but enjoying the early morning sunrise with
a fresh cup of coffee. Shortly before eight o'clock in the morning,
the senator and his party left the resort heading SE on Pointe Road.
Jillian gathered her stuff and headed down the road in her royal blue
Mustang Convertible.

Jillian knew the only way into town from the north was the
Pointe Road, if all went according to plan she would stop him at the
chokepoint.

Jillian took her time catching up to the dark blue sedan. When
it was in sight, she punched the accelerator as the *tack* redlined, and
the Mustang roared past the senator's car at over one hundred miles
per hour, weaving in and out of traffic passing two or three cars in
the process.

Jillian drove her Mustang to the intersection of NW Pointe
Road and West Bay Road in front of the Renaissance Resort Hotel,
where she hit the brakes and spun out just short of the roundabout
with the intent of blocking any traffic heading south. Before leaving
the condo, Jillian placed a smoke bomb on the inlet manifold that

would go off when it reached a certain temperature. She had timed it perfectly.

Jillian stood there in the middle of the road, wearing nothing but a bright green bikini and a shear yellow summer wrap, frantically trying to call someone on the phone as smoke billowed out from under the hood.

A quarter of a mile back there's an ever-growing traffic jam.

"Why are we slowing down?" the senator called out to the driver.

"There is a lady in the middle of the road blocking the traffic. Some kind of car trouble," the driver said as the car came to a stop.

"Go around it," the thug in the passenger seat told the driver.

The driver pulled out against the flow of traffic around some of the stopped cars. There was a rather large truck blocking the thruway traffic closer to the intersection.

"Go around," the thug in the passenger seat yelled, as the driver tried to go around on the soft sandy shoulder and spun out.

The senator looked up from the back seat of the sedan and spotted the commotion in the road ahead.

"Is that the royal blue Mustang that flew passed us back there?" the senator asked urging the driver to just stop.

The senator got out of the car and headed up toward the intersection recognizing the lovely young lady as he approached.

"Where are you going?" the thug asked the senator.

"Just gonna see if I can help the lil lady," the senator snapped back. *Yup, that's that sexy lil redhead that was at the airport ticket counter in New Orleans*, he thought to himself walking up to the intersection, checking out her tight little body.

"Howdy, lil lady. Can I help you?" the senator called out.

"Oh, it's you," she said turning around at the sound of his voice. "Ahhh...I saw you at the airport," she said crying and sobbing, wiping the tears from her cheek. "I'm Jillian," she said frantically, trying to call someone on the phone.

"I'm Senator Stevens. Just settle down now. It will be all right," he said reassuring her.

"I thought you looked familiar when we met before," she said smacking the phone with her hand. "I don't know what happened... It just started smoking," she said dialing the phone again.

"I bet it was probably that little piece of driving back there," he said sarcastically. "What's the big hurry?" asked the senator.

"My phone, it's not working," she said hitting it several times. "My husband is waiting for me at the airport...and he will be furious," she said crying.

"That's all right, you can use mine," the senator offered.

"I have to call my husband. He's waiting for me," she said whimpering.

"Now come on. Let's get you out of the road. You can call from my car," he said leading her toward the sedan.

Jillian got in the back of the car and called Rex.

"Hey, honey," she said, wiping the tears from her eyes.

"Where are you? You were supposed to pick me up a half hour ago," Rex said loud enough to be overheard by the senator sitting next to her.

"Yes, but I was in an accident and can't get there..." she said crying.

"I can't believe you... If it's not one thing, it's another. What am I going to do now?"

"But the car broke down. I am going to have to get another one," she said crying.

"Get another car and get over here," Rex said hanging up the phone.

"He's not very nice, is he?" the senator said quietly.

"What am I going to do now?" she said crying.

"Are you staying on the island?" the senator asked.

"Yes, the Cayman Sunset at Coconut Bay," she said.

"Why, that's up where I'm staying. How about I give you a ride up there? You can call the rental car company from there," the senator offered graciously.

"Well, I don't know. I don't want to be a bother," she said smiling passed the tears.

"No bother…no bother at all. It would be my pleasure," he said smugly.

The trip back to Cayman Sunset took about twenty minutes, plenty of extra time for Rex and Milton to get in and out of the bank.

CHAPTER 25

⟫⟨⟨◉⟩⟩⟪

At exactly 9:00 a.m., Milton walked gingerly across the lobby of the Cayman National Bank, limping slightly on his right leg, just like he saw on the video footage.

"Hello, Isabella," he said, tipping his hat like a true Texan. From the bank video footage provided by Jillian of his past bank visits, he always hung out at the desk and appeared to be flirting with Isabella.

"Hello, Mr. Kincade. How are you today?" she asked smiling.

"I'm afraid I have a bad cold," he answered reaching for his handkerchief coughing slightly. "I can barely talk. Mr. Wilson, please?" he asked softly coughing and blowing his nose.

"Would you like some coffee?" Isabella offered.

"Only if you get one for yourself, my dear," he said in his best Southern drawl. "Same as usual, cream with extra sugar."

"Actually, make that a tea, Earl Grey hot with a slice of lemon," Milton said. Milton hated the flavor of coffee.

"Good morning, Mr. Kincade. How are you this morning?" Mr. Wilson asked, reaching out to shake his hand.

"Sorry, I have a terrible cold," Milton said waving off the handshake.

The two headed to the back for Mr. Wilson's office.

"I'll bring your tea in a minute," Isabella said.

"Thank you," Milton mouthed as he walked by.

Minutes later, Isabella brought in the tea.

"Thank you, my dear," Milton said with a nod of his head.

"How's your tea?" Mr. Wilson asked as he sat back in the plush leather chair.

"Perfect, just the way I like it…hot with lemon," Milton said.

"So how can I help you today, Mr. Kincade?" Wilson asked.

"We spoke—grrrrr, yester—rrrr," Milton grunted hoarsely reaching for his throat. "I can't talk, laryngitis," Milton said taking a sip of his hot tea, then handed Mr. Wilson a note. "I would like to close my account and would like that to be in cash, US dollars." Milton sat back and tried to relax.

"Account number please?" asked Mr. Wilson.

"AA436525ZA." Milton wrote it down and handed it to him.

Mr. Wilson pulled up the account and verified the amount 250 million dollars then pulled out a small signature tablet.

"That is quite a large withdraw. Please verify your signature." Mr. Wilson swung the tablet around for him to sign.

Milton grabbed his favorite pen from his breast pocket. "Mi—" the L started to come out but made a nice recovery. "Michael Kincade," just like he practiced all morning.

"With a transaction this size, I have to verify the signature," Mr. Wilson said getting up from his seat and heading into the next room.

"Yes, of course," Milton nodded.

"Would you like another cup of tea…is it?" he asked.

"Yes, of course. That would be nice," Milton said.

"Isabella, another cup of tea for Mr. Kincade, please," the intercom squeaked on Isabella's desk.

"Right away, sir," Isabella answered.

An old man sitting near the desk overheard the request for tea.

"Isabella?" the old man interrupted "Yes, sir."

"I work for Mr. Kincade… I was waiting for him in the lobby," he said, looking around kinda puzzled.

"The tea. Is that for Mr. Kincade?" the old man asked.

"Yes, it is. He's in Mr. Wilson's office right now," Isabella said heading back to the office area.

"Your tea, sir," she said with a smile.

"Sir, you have an associate in the lobby…waiting for you," Isabella said quietly.

"Is that right? Did he say who he was?"

"No, sir, just that he worked for you."

"I see, thank you." Milton sat there wondering who was in the lobby waiting for him. He knew that Rex would never come in and jeopardize the plan or even Jillian; it was way too early for her to arrive anyway.

Several minutes passed as Mr. Wilson finally returned to his office. "The signature checked out," Mr. Wilson typed out a few things on the computer. "Can you enter your password on the key-pad please?" Mr. Wilson asked. Milton punched in "Kincade 1946." The computer blipped a few times as Mr. Wilson got up and stepped out the back door without saying a word.

Milton sat there for what seemed like an eternity, wondering if his goose was cooked. The door opened, and Mr. Wilson walked in with two very large security guards.

"Okay, just take me away," he mumbled and almost passed out till he realized they were holding some very large duffel bags.

"Would you like to count it, sir?" Mr. Wilson asked.

Milton unzipped the bags and looked at the money.

"No, I trust you," Milton said with a sigh of relief.

"The security guards are protocol and for the banks protection. When you step outside the bank, you are on your own," Mr. Wilson explained.

The guards escorted Milton through the lobby toward the old man.

"Hey, boss," the old man called out as they approached.

The security guard stepped in front and pushed him away, blocking him from coming any closer. Milton looked briefly at the old man and wondered who he was without acknowledging him. The security guards handed Milton the four bags at the door and wished him good luck.

*****

A dark blue sedan pulled up outside the front entrance to the bank. The senator casually stepped out of the back seat, along with the two thugs and headed for the bank.

"Hey, boss!" the old man called out staring at the senator

"Pablo, what's the matter?" the senator asked.

Pablo looked at the senator in disbelief, then at the man that walked out of the bank crossing the parking lot, then back at the senator.

"Hey, boss. Did you just walk out of the bank a minute ago?" the old man asked.

"No, I just got here a second ago," the senator said watching as a dark blue sedan drove slowly passed him. The senator almost fainted when he saw the man in the back seat staring at him. It was him. It was like looking into a mirror.

The senator turned and rushed into the bank lobby.

"Hey, boss," Pablo called out as he followed the senator into the bank and across the lobby, followed closely by the two thugs.

"Good morning, Isabella," the senator said, nodding his hat as usual.

"Mr. Kincade, how can I help you? Did you forget something?" Isabella asked looking strangely at the senator.

"Hey, boss," the old man tried to interrupt but was pushed away by the two thugs.

"No, I didn't forget anything. Why do you ask?" the senator looked at her briefly.

"I am here to see Mr. Wilson," he said.

"Mr. Kincade...boss," the old man shouted and pushed his way passed the two thugs.

"What is it Pablo?" The senator turned around.

"I've been trying to tell you, you were just here," Pablo said with a confused look on his face pointing at the exit.

"What are you talking about? I just got here five minutes ago," the senator shouted.

"But, sir, you just walked out of here a second ago," the old man said.

"Isabella?" The senator looked at her.

"Yes, sir, about 10 minutes ago," she said smiling.

"Isabella, call Mr. Wilson right away," he said raising his voice.

"Mr. Wilson...Mr. Wilson...Mr. Kincade is here to see you," Isabella called out over the intercom.

"Mr. Kincade, is everything all right?" Mr. Wilson asked concerned running from the office into the lobby.

"I am sure everything is all right. I just need to make a withdraw," the senator said smiling.

"Another withdraw, sir?" Mr. Wilson asked with a puzzled look on his face. "Sir, it is against the rules of the bank to take out more than one major withdraw on the same day," Mr. Wilson explained.

"I beg your pardon? More than one withdraw?" the senator looked at Mr. Wilson. "I just got here five minutes ago to make a withdraw," the senator explained.

"Okay, I am sure we can figure this out. Come back to my office, and we can talk about it. Would you like another cup of tea?" Mr. Wilson offered.

"More tea? I don't drink tea," he said shaking his head.

"I apologize, sir. This morning, Isabella brought you Earl Gray tea hot with lemon," Mr. Wilson said pointing at the empty cup on his desk.

"That is impossible," the senator said.

"I hate tea and am allergic to lemon."

"Mmmmm, okay. How can I help you, Mr. Kincade?" asked Mr. Wilson.

"I would like to make a withdraw like I mentioned on the phone?" Mr. Kincade said.

"Well, sir, like I explained already… It is against bank rules to take out more than one major withdraw on the same day. I cannot approve another withdraw at this time, especially in that amount," said Mr. Wilson.

"What are you talking about? I did not make a withdraw from this bank this morning," he yelled pounding his fist on the desk.

"Listen, the two men in the lobby are expecting me to hand them 250 million dollars. So let's get on with it," the senator said, slightly panicking at the thought of not having the money.

"What is the account number and password?"

"AA436525ZA, Kincade 1946." He punched in the codes.

"Sorry, sir. That account was closed this morning," Mr. Wilson informed him.

"Closed? Now you listen, and you listen carefully. I spoke with you last night. You told me I had 250 million dollars in that account. Who closed the account?" the senator asked.

"You did, sir, this morning, when the bank opened at 9:00 a.m.," Mr. Wilson explained, calling for the head of security.

"That is impossible. I was stuck in traffic at nine o'clock this morning," he shouted demanding an explanation.

"I can show you, sir. We have security footage of you when you came in this morning." Mr. Wilson pointed to his security specialist who turned on the monitor, closed the door, and ran the tape.

"Mr. Kincade, you walked into this bank wearing the same outfit you have on right now, including the cowboy hat. We sat down at this desk, you sat in that chair, drank tea, and made a cash withdrawal of 250 million US dollars, in cash. My two security guards walked you into the lobby and out the front door. Just before you walked out of the bank, you looked up at the camera."

"What did you say?" the senator asked.

"You looked at the camera."

"No, I drank tea?"

"Yes, you were complaining about a sore throat and laryngitis and asked Isabella for some tea." Wilson looked at him, then pointed at the empty cup of tea.

"What did you say?" the senator interrupted.

"What?" asked Wilson.

"You said I drank tea…"

"Yes, the cup of tea." Wilson pointed at the empty cup of tea.

"Does it sound like I have a sore throat?" the senator barked. "Not only that…I hate *tea*."

The senator's mouth fell open as he stared at the image on the monitor. It was him as plain as day. It was Michael Kincade. The senator's face turned white, and his stomach turned as a bead of sweat rolled down his cheek.

"That was impossible. I was on the road at that time…stuck in traffic," the senator called his driver into the office.

"Where were we at 9:00 a.m. this morning?" the senator told his driver to speak up and tell him.

"On the road, sir, stuck in traffic."

"Well, that wasn't me," the senator repeated several times.

"Mr. Kincade…anything else I can get for you?" Wilson asked.

"Yes, my money…and I want it now," the senator shouted.

Mr. Wilson, feeling uneasy, pushed the security button as two large bank security guards stepped into the office.

"Would you please escort Mr. Kincade to the front door?" Mr. Wilson directed his guards.

The guards passed Pablo in the lobby.

"Do you have a car?" the senator whispered as he passed. "Get it now."

Pablo walked out the front door and waved at his two nephews waiting in the car.

"Where are you going, Kincade?" the one thug asked as the guards moved toward the front door.

"We gotta get out of here…fast," the senator told Pablo heading out the door.

"Where are you going, Kincade?" the one thug asked.

"Get my briefcase."

"Your car is this way." The thug pointed, moving quickly toward the senator.

"Kincade, where are you going?" the second thug asked as he followed them out the door.

Pablo waved his hand, signaling for the nephews to pull up.

"Hey, Kincade, where is the money?" the second thug demanded getting out of the sedan.

"The money, Kincade," the first thug yelled, running across the parking lot at the senator and Pablo as they hopped into the moving car.

The senator barely got in the back of the sedan when the shots rang out and peppering the back of the car with bullet holes.

"Where are we going, boss?" Pablo shouted as the car accelerated.

"Anywhere but here," the senator shouted as a hail of bullets shattered the back window.

*****

Rex and Milton figured they had been followed from the bank and needed to get to the Canadian National Bank as soon as possible. Riding around the streets with this much money was dangerous.

Rex waited in the car and kept a lookout for the senator and his men. Milton knew he had been made the minute he walked into the bank. He looked too much like the real Michael Kincade. The word was probably out to all of his associates to lookout for the imposter with a large sum of money.

Milton opened the account and deposited $245 million, thanked the manager, then signaled for Rex to bring the car around the back.

"Is there a rear exit?" Milton asked as he headed out the back and immediately noticed two very large islanders shadowing him.

Milton signaled Rex to go around the block and meet him in the back alley since there were too many people and potential witnesses on the street. Milton slowly made his way down the street toward the alley, then turned and ran all out half a block where he was cut off by a third islander.

The two men following him caught up and pushed him into a nearby brick wall. When Milton's right shoulder hit the wall, he reached inside his suit coat and pulled out a six-inch baton, a weapon of choice for close quarter combat situations and social malcontents in his days as Scotland yard's chief inspector on the streets of London. With a quick flick of the wrist, the six-inch hardened steel rod extended to just over eighteen inches. Milton spun to his left and delivered a devastating blow to the outside of the man's left knee. His partner, following close behind, never saw it coming as Milton continued his spin in same direction and popped the man right below his left ear, knocking him out cold.

Milton turned back toward the third man who threw a few punches that were quickly blocked with the baton. Milton hooked the man's right arm and rammed his head into the brick wall.

"Who do you work for?" he asked, applying upward pressure on the arm causing extreme pain.

The first islander slowly got up and advanced toward Milton who spotted him coming from the side, turned and swung the baton at the man's right kneecap, shattering it into several pieces, then turned back toward the third islander, locked the baton in his arm once more, and slammed his head into the brick wall.

"What was that? I did not hear your answer. I believe I asked you a question?"

The islander hesitated, but the upward pressure on the arm was too great and finally spoke up.

"Senator Stevens," he mumbled under his breath.

"Give your boss a message… 'Remember Luiz De La Cruz,'" Milton whispered into the man's ear, then clubbed him over the head.

Milton sauntered down to the end of the alley humming some old Scottish tune.

"Are you okay?" Rex shouted stretching to a halt.

"Ran into some locals, but I think they got the message," Milton continued whistling the old tune as he jumped into the back of the dark blue sedan.

Minutes later, a dark blue sedan pulled up to the islanders.

"Where's the old man with the money?" the senator yelled.

The three islanders moaned and groaned on the ground.

"Get up, you bums," the senator yelled. "I thought you said you had him. Where is he?" the senator yelled again.

The third islander got up slowly, hobbled over to the senator.

"He wanted me to give you a message, mon. 'Remember Luiz De La Cruz,'" he whispered quietly.

"What? What did he say?" the senator was clearly startled and felt his stomach turned when he heard that name.

"Remember Luiz De La Cruz," the Islander repeated.

What did this have to do with Luiz? Why here? Why now? he wondered as he got back into the sedan.

*****

Rex called Jillian a few minutes later.

"Do you have him?" Rex asked.

"Yes, heading toward the airport," Jillian responded keeping a good distance behind the car.

"Do you think he got the hint?" Rex asked Milton.

"Yes, I think so," Milton said as they drove down the street toward the airport.

"Where do you think he will go?" Rex asked curiously.

"Somewhere he feels safe. He's broke and on the run from his own syndicate. Can't go to the authorities," Milton said as they pulled up in front of the terminal. "He's got to go somewhere he feels safe and can lay low" Rex added.

"Do you still have him in sight?"

"Just inside the door," Jillian said pointing Rex in the right direction.

The senator was on a call when Rex walked by. Three men were with him. Rex could tell these guys were professionals. The way they dressed federal, definitely federal, probably his regular security team as a senator.

"We have to move fast," the senator told Mike, his head of security.

They headed down the escalator to the lower departure level when Mike noticed a group of men off to the right who appeared to be looking for someone. They made eye contact, and the group split up and pulled automatic weapons. Mike pushed the senator to the side, crouched over him, and fired at the oncoming man, two shots center mass. The second and third men engaged the other two agents in a gunfight, but the agents 9 mm handguns were no match to the automatic firepower from an M4 assault rifle. Mike ran with the senator in tow, but the chase was short lived as the bullets ripped through Mike's back from behind.

The battle lasted only a few minutes as the senator was hooded and tossed into the back of a black minivan.

"Did you see that?" Rex called Jillian who was waiting outside. "Keep an eye on that minivan… The senator is in it," Rex yelled as he slid down the escalator. The two agents were dead, but Mike was still alive, barely.

"Who are you?" Rex asked as the life drained from his body. Rex ran outside to meet up with Jillian and Milton.

"Where's the senator?" Rex asked as he jumped into the back of the Mustang.

"We never saw him come out," Milton said.

"The black minivan. It has to be around here somewhere," Rex said frantically looking around.

Rex called Scooter.

"Hey, kid, the senator was just taken from the departures area by three men. Can you hack or whatever you do and find out which way they took him?"

"I'll see what I can do. I might have to hack into the airport security system," Scooter told Rex.

"Go ahead, kid. Jillian's got your back," Rex said looking at Jillian who gave him a dirty look.

"I don't care, just find the senator," Rex said laughing.

"Sure, Rex, but you will owe me big time for this one," Scooter said as his finger flicked across the keys

Scooter hacked into the airport security system, pulled some recent video feeds from several exits.

"Scooter, do you have anything?" Rex asked as Jillian slowly drove around the airport grounds.

"Rex, I have three men shoving a hooded man into the back of a black minivan," Scooter told him.

"Can you track the van and see where it's headed?" Rex asked still looking around.

"Yup, sure can," Scooter snickered. "Look behind you."

Rex turned as the minivan slowly passed them on the left. The minivan headed toward the warehouse district, about fifteen miles away. They hung back far enough to see the senator get dragged into one of the abandoned buildings.

"We going in?" Milton asked

"No, don't think that would be a good idea, just yet," Rex said wondering what they were doing. Rex could care less what happened to the senator, but he was more concerned about how to find Gabriella. After all, the senator was their only lead to her whereabouts.

The senator was tied to a metal chair.

"Mr. Kincade, or should I say Senator Stevens?"

The senator recognized the voice behind him.

"I am very disappointed in you," he said walking around to face him. "To think you are trying to run out on your debts." The man slapped him across his face several times with the butt of the gun.

"Niklas...you know me... I would never," the senator squirmed in his chair.

"Why would you do such a thing?" the man said slapping him again across the face.

"I am here to collect the $335 million you failed to pay or make arrangements for at the auction," Niklas said pacing around the room.

"Look, it wasn't me. I never made it to the auction," he said pleading to Niklas.

"But you did go to the auction. I have an informant at the Roosevelt Hotel that saw you with your accomplices the night of the auction."

"But I haven't lied," the senator said in a trembling voice.

"But you have," Niklas said calling over one of his men. "Dimitry here remembers you when you were at the Le Grande Maison." Niklas opened a computer laptop and played the video.

"I have you entering the suite, logging on, and making purchases totaling $335 million. I have it all on camera." Niklas looked at the senator.

"I tell you that was not me," the senator cried out.

"You lied, just like you lied today at the Cayman National Bank when you told us that you did not have the money." Niklas pointed at Dimitry who played the second video.

"You withdrew $250 million this morning," Niklas paused. "You claim that is not you?" Niklas stopped the security tape on the part where he is looking straight at the camera.

"But it wasn't me... I tell you... I never made it to the bank," the senator still pleading with Niklas.

"Senator, you know who I am," Niklas asked, "and who I answer to?"

"Yes, of course... La Rosa Negra," the senator answered right away.

"And you know what happens when you cross me or lie to me, right?" Niklas hesitated.

"Now, Dimitry knows the consequences for failure to tell the truth. Now, if you are telling me the truth, that means Dimitry is not," Niklas said pulling a Colt .45 from his waistband, shooting Dimitry in the head.

"What…that's not me… I swear it… It's not me," he cried out.

"We have you running out of the bank claiming not to have any money… Are you saying you were not at the bank this morning?" Niklas said pointing the gun at his head.

"No… I mean, YES, I was at the bank…later after I got robbed… by that man in the video," the senator said as Niklas pulled the trigger, shooting him in the leg.

"Ahhhhhhhhh," the senator cried out.

"Well, Senator, my employer wants the money," Niklas said pointing the gun at his head.

"No, no, wait…wait. I have the girl," he grumbled in pain.

"What girl?" Niklas asked.

"The De la Cruz girl. She has the microdrive," he whispered.

"The microdrive that will take down the whole syndicate. The one Luiz had. The one you failed to get," he said, almost passing out. Niklas stepped away and made a phone call, too far for him to hear it and all in Spanish, which he did not understand.

"Si, Señora." Niklas hung up the phone. "Where is she now?" Niklas asked.

"The hacienda. I'll take you there," the senator said.

"Patch him up. Let's go." Niklas pointed at one of his men.

The senator was clearly limping when he was shoved into the minivan. They left the warehouse district and headed for the airport to the private jet concourse.

Shortly after takeoff, Rex called Scooter.

"Hey, Scooter, this is Rex…need another favor right now," Rex asked hearing a lot of background noise.

"I'm infiltrating a castle… Can it wait?" Scooter pleaded.

"No, it can't. Now turn it off and track this flight out of the Caymans…now," Rex asked nicely.

"Ok, mmmm, you said it just took off?" Scooter asked.

"Yes. I'm watching it gain altitude right now," Rex said watching it disappear into the clouds.

"I'm checking the tower flight control logs. There's no clearance from the tower. There's nothing there. No departures of any aircraft from that airport," Scooter said.

"Hold on, I have an idea." *Beep.*

"Can you believe it? He put me on hold," Rex said holding the phone away from his ear.

"Rex, It's Scooter."

"Yes, what do you have?" Rex asked.

"I called one of my buddies at NOAA who tracks weather patterns in the Gulf via satellite. With his access code, I hacked into the satellite—"

"Scooter, Scooter," Rex interrupted. "Just tell me were you able to track the aircraft?" Rex asked taking a deep breath.

"No, not yet. The satellite was facing the wrong way. I think I can get a better picture from NASA," Scooter said.

"NASA?" Rex asked.

"Ya, right now it is orbiting over the Gulf of Mexico. I can hack into the Skylab computer and get great aerial footage of it leaving the airport, all in HD," Scooter explained.

"Stop right there. I don't want to know. Just track that jet, stay on it, and let me know where it lands." Rex hung up the phone.

"What's going on, Rex?" Jillian asked.

"Scooter's going to hack into NASA's Skylab computer to get a better look," Rex said.

"What? I really need to talk to this kid," Jillian said with a little jealousy in her voice.

Few hours later, Rex received a call.

Beeep, beep.

"Yes?" Rex answered his phone.

"Rex, it's Scooter…"

"Of course, it is… What did you find out?" Rex asked.

"I tracked the jet as it crossed the Caribbean Sea on a heading of 110 deg S by SW," Scooter explained.

"That would put it somewhere in Central America," Jillian said.

"Yup, try Panama near the Panama Canal," Rex said thinking of the compound.

CHAPTER 26

———⟫«(◉)»⟪———

Several hours later, a private jet landed at France Field, an abandoned airstrip just outside of Colon, another hour by a truck on a dusty dirt road on the side of a mountain lies the hacienda, a private compound deep in the dense jungle of Panama.

The senator was greeted by several members of the La Rosa Negra Cartel, including their leader a beautiful woman in her early fifties who took over the family business after her whole family was gun down by a rival cartel.

Since then, she was on the most wanted list of criminals in several countries, including the United States of America. Up until a month ago, no one even knew her real name…except Luiz. They only knew her as the "La Rosa Negra."

The next day, Rex got a call from Juan.

"Rex, are you there?"

"Yes, Juan, what is it?" Rex asked.

"I got a video from someone," Juan said holding back the tears.

"Who, Juan?" Rex asked listening intently.

"No, se…ransom video. They have mi Gabriella and Sr. Stevens," Juan said crying.

"Did they say what they want? Make any demands?" Rex asked.

"They want the microdrive and the files that Luiz had," Juan pauses

"Juan, don't worry. I'll take care of it," Rex said calling Scooter immediately.

"Scooter," Rex yelled into the phone over the background noise.

"Rex, is that you?" Scooter asked holding his ear tightly to the phone.

"What now? Another conquest of a castle?" Rex asked loudly.

"No, just listening to a little music," Scooter yelled back moving into the other room.

"Juan has a ransom video. I need to know where it was transmitted from and gotta have it yesterday. Got it…very important," Rex said

"Right now?" Scooter asked.

"Yes, ASAP. Now *go*." Rex hung up the phone.

The video lasted about fifteen minutes. The senator and Gabriella were tied to small metal chairs with black hoods over their heads. A man with a back stocking cap over his head peered into the camera through the eye holes, explaining what would happen to the senator and the little girl if their demands were not met. Rex watched and listened to the video several times, and each time, something about it kept bothering him, but he did not know what it was about the tape.

*****

The man walked over to the senator and pulled off his hood. The bruises and swelling were still visible from the warehouse beating.

"Tell them what I want," Niklas demanded as he poked the barrel of the .45 into the senator's bandaged right thigh.

The pain shot up his leg straight to his head. His expression changed as if he actually feared for his life. This was never supposed to be a real torture, just a play act to get Juan to give them the microdrive and the files.

The man walked over to Gabriella, pulled off her hood, slapped her several times till the blood flowed from her lower lip.

"Tell them what I want," the man screamed.

The senator cringed in his seat at every blow as the video ended the senator is seen pleading with Juan to give them what they wanted.

The camera pulled in on Gabriella's face.

"Ajuda me papa," she cried.

The video was uploaded and sent to the corporation and Juan De La Cruz with a ransom demand: "Give us the microdrive and files on Luiz De La Cruz, or this will not end well for the senator or the little girl."

*****

Rex watched the complete video several times. But every time, Rex would stop it at one point, then play it over and over again.

"What is it, Rex?" Jillian asked.

"Not sure," Rex rewound it again several times. "What do you see?" Rex asked as Jillian reviewed the video.

"A gun…a .45 caliber revolver," Jillian said looking at Milton, not knowing where he was going with it.

"No, that." Rex pointed at the emblem on the gun. Rex stared at it for several minutes.

"I've seen that gun before…that emblem, but where?" Rex sat back and closed his eyes.

"Niklas Muller… That was Niklas Colt .45." Rex sat up quickly "That's Niklas Muller's .45. The one with the gold tint and white pearl handles, with the little skull and crossbones on the heel." Rex shook his head. "Niklas Muller was dead."

Rex's mind flashed back to a time before the agency and even further back to his senior year at Georgetown University where he was approached by the CIA for a special project they were working on. Actually, it was his friend and classmate Niklas Muller who were working in the foreign intelligence department who recruited him. Later after, Navy SEAL training and special warfare class. Rex was assigned to Niklas's team, along with a young female operative named Jennifer P. Campbell, US Army. The mission was to infiltrate and disable a nuclear reactor that was being constructed by the Iranians. Iran, for over a decade, had been developing the ability to produce and enrich high-grade uranium intended for one purpose and one purpose only, nuclear weapons. The Iranian government had always claimed that it was for energy production. But satellite pictures would show a lot of activity moving to and away from the site.

UN inspectors could never get access to parts of the plant that was always under construction. The plan was to cause a minor leak, forcing the Iranian government to comply with the UN inspectors. But during the extraction from the facility, a massive explosion occurred. The explosion left several team members dead including team leader Niklas Mueller. After several months of diplomatic negotiations, the Iranian government returned the body of one of the team members. The subsequent autopsy revealed that the cause of death was one shot to the back with a .45 Cal. bullet. Only one man carried such a weapon as a backup, known only by other members of the team—a gold-plated .45 with a white pearl handle with a skull and crossbones emblem, Team Leader Niklas Mueller. Niklas Mueller's body was never found nor was his .45.

Rex's phone rang.

"Scooter, what's up?" Rex asked wondering why it was so quiet in the background.

"I got him," Scooter said.

"Got who?" Rex asked half in a daze.

"I was able to isolate the IP address and with a special home-made algorithmic program, back trace the signal through several satellites extrapolate the info, and locate him."

"Scooter, Scooter, stop… Just give it to me in English. Who do you have?" Rex asked.

"Him, the guy, in the mask that sent the video," Scooter said taking a deep breath. "I triangulate the signal—"

"Stop," Rex said. "Just tell me again that you got the son of a bitch," Rex said.

"I got him," Scooter responded without the extra expletives.

"Do you have a location?" Rex asked enthusiastically.

"Yes, of course."

"Panama, right?" Rex said.

"I was just getting to that," Scooter explained.

"Well, get to that sooner next time," Rex said sarcastically, then thanked him for a job well done.

"It's some sort of compound, perimeter fencing," Scooter went on and on.

"Scooter, can you get some close up shots of the building and the surrounding area?" Rex asked.

"Yes, I can hack into the weather satellite, demodulate the digital signal."

"Scooter, Scooter… I got it. Don't tell me. Just do it. Pretend that you are infiltrating a castle and get back to me ASAP," Rex said hanging up the phone.

CHAPTER 27

＝＞◈◈◈＜＝

It was early in the morning when the 727-200 broke through the heavy clouds as it descended into Tocumen International Airport Panama City, Panama. The storm front had arrived earlier than expected as the plane buffeted its way through thick clouds, heavy winds, and an occasional air pocket. After WWII, Milton hated flying, especially in this kind of weather. His preferred mode of transportation would have been by sea, a ship or submarine would do nicely.

Jillian was too busy going over last-minute operational plans with Scooter who provided top-notch intel on the compound to worry about a little turbulence. Rex, on the other hand, slept like a baby the entire flight. Once on the ground, they rented a small pickup truck and headed into the mountains toward the compound.

For the plan to succeed, they needed a diversion of some kind, something big enough to cause a ruckus all over the area including the compound. Rex was talking things through like he always did before a big mission, making sure everyone was on the same page.

"We need a diversion," Rex said as they motored down the dusty road. "I wish Buster was here. He would just blow something up and make it look like a natural disaster," Rex thought out loud as they approached the compound.

"A shocking one," Jillian said as the night sky lit up with a lightning strike. Rex stopped talking and looked over at Jillian pointing at something on the map Scooter provided.

"What is that?" Rex asked.

"The main electrical feed for the hacienda runs through this substation, about a mile from the building," Jillian said.

"If we cut the main power, that should give us ample time to get in and out without any undue delays." Rex was thinking out loud again.

"Scooter," Rex called out over his speaker phone. "Can you hear me?" Rex shouted over the background music.

"Sure, no problem, you don't have to yell," Scooter said. "Just a little pick-me-up music before the big raid."

"Do you have a location for the electrical substation? Things are not well marked out here," Rex asked.

"Ya, it's coming up on your left, right about now," Scooter said smiling, as he took a bite out of his hoagie sandwich. "Did you find it?"

Rex looked up into a grove of trees. There was a small brick building steel door with a chicken wire fence around it. "Not much of a substation," Rex said as he pulled up next to the tiny building.

"All you needed was a pole to put up a transformer, why all the brick and steel?" Rex said as he walked up to the locked steel door.

"Maybe they wanted this one to be a little more secure," Milton said keeping an eye out for any unwanted visitors.

Rex pulled out his trusty lock-picking kit he just purchased online, the one that would open any lock, any type in under a minute guaranteed.

"Sure you want to do this?" Jillian asked as he eyeballed the tiny lock.

"Oh, I got this," Rex said as he got to work.

After several minutes, Jillian peeked over his shoulder.

"Hey, Rex, need a hand getting that lock open?" she asked checking the time.

"Ahhh...no, I think I got it, just need another minute or so," Rex said as he fought with the tiny lock.

"Hey, Rex, we don't have all day, lad," Milton said, trying not to look too worried about the time. Rex mumbled something under his breath then handed the tools to Jillian.

"Click, click, and not very secure," Jillian said as she picked the lock in under ten seconds "I think that's a new record," Jillian said handing the kit back to Rex.

"Did you get instructions with that kit?" Jillian asked.

"Yes," Rex mumbled.

"You might want to read it next time," Jillian said as Milton giggled in the background.

"I prepped it for you. That's all," Rex said shaking his head.

Once inside, Rex looked around and found what he was looking for—a solid black cable from the transformer heading south toward the compound. Rex reached in his pocket and pulled out a clear bottle of hydrochloric acid then taped a blasting cap and a small receiver/transmitter to it and placed it on top of the cable.

"That should do it," Rex said turning back toward Milton and Jillian. Rex had seen Buster do it a million times. They synchronized their watches and waited for the go signal.

Milton took off to the overwatch position about five hundred yards out on an adjacent hillside with "Betsy," his trusty, accuracy international model L115A3 sniper rifle, with the 30X Schmidt and Bender nightscope. Milton had a clear view of the front and both sides of the compound.

It was a perfect night for a raid. The new moon provided the darkness, and the approaching thunderstorm a nice diversion. Scooter called Rex on the SAT phone.

"Rex, you will have a two-hour window to get in and out with Gabriella and the senator before I lose the satellite feed. The satellite will be in range at 10:00 p.m."

"Okay, it's a *go*," Rex called out over the comms. "Wait for the signal." Rex checked his watch one last time. It was 9:55 p.m. when he dialed the number and set off the mini charge, breaking the vile of hydrochloric acid over the cable.

Rex figured he had five minutes before the fireworks began.

The approaching thunderstorm was right on time as a lightning bolt struck and lit up the sky. The thunderclap exploded just as the acid hit the live wires, and the sudden surge of power overloaded the transformer sending a power surge through the wires toward the house, cutting off the power to the compound.

The distraction worked perfectly as the tangos all moved forward to the front of the house to see what all the commotion was about.

"Patience," Milton said to himself as more guards moved forward. At first count, there were four tangos on the second floor and two more patrolling the grounds.

Milton sighted in "old Betsy" with the nightscope the targets popped out of the darkness. A slight pop was all you could hear as he slowly pulled back on the trigger, clearing the top floor working his way down to the ground floor. Milton took out six men in under a minute, clearing the way for Rex and Jillian to get into the compound.

Rex and Jillian would use the dark of the night to make a stealth approach and enter the building from the back, then rely on their hand to hand and blade skills the rest of the way. They both carried a 9 mm Sig Sauer model 226, and a 6-inch KA-BAR combat knife.

Jillian approached the back door and was surprised by one of the guards heading outside. Jillian's reflexes were fast, and her strikes efficient, incapacitating the guard without a single whisper.

"Rex, I have one of their radios. All clear, go," Jillian said as she plugged in a portable headset.

Rex headed for the other entrance.

"Rex, you have two tangos approaching you from the right. Take cover," Scooter squawked in his ear, cranking up the music in his head phones as he watched the battle unfold on his computer.

"Copy...taking cover," Rex said slipping behind a large overgrown bush.

"They are ten feet away. Stand by," Scooter said.

Rex heard a faint buzzing above his head.

"Hornets," Rex squawked.

"I have about ten pissed-off hornets about a foot above my head. Do I have a clear path?" Rex asked quietly, trying not to disturb them.

"Stand by, Rex, one more minute. I think they are about to turn," Scooter told him.

"I don't think I have that kind of time," Rex whispered as the hornets swarmed in on his CO_2 emissions.

"Hold on, Rex," Scooter told him.

What could be worse? Rex wondered, considering his options. *Two fully-loaded M-4 automatic rifles or a squadron of pissed off hornets?* Too late, the hornets had their target in sight and went in for the kill. Rex held his breath as the barrage began, and in less than a minute, he had been stung several times on his face and neck.

"Rex, all clear, you can go now," Scooter squawked in his ear.

"Too late. They got me," Rex said as he made his way to the door.

"Rex, you okay? Who got you?" Scooter yelled.

"The hornets," Rex said.

"Hornets? Rex, you okay?" Jillian squawked in.

"Fine, okay." Rex entered from the back and caught up with Jillian on the main floor of the compound.

"What happened to your face?" Jillian asked staring at the multiple bumps.

"The hornets…never mind." Rex waved her off.

Once inside the main building, the satellite feed and comms to the outside were useless. Scooter provided them with detailed maps of the interior of the surface building. As far as the tunnels go, that was a different story.

They had exactly two hours to locate Gabriella and the senator. Jillian did what she did best and made her way into the ventilation shaft and worked her way around the maze of ducts. It was amazing how much you could hear inside a ventilation shaft. Jillian heard faint conversations coming from up ahead. As she moved in closer, she could hear a man calling over the radio.

"What is going on up there?" he yelled.

"Niklas, the lightning took out the main transfor—" the man's conversation ended abruptly as a high-powered bullet ripped through his chest.

"What name did the man use on the radio? Niklas?"

Again, there was that name from the past, but it had to be a different Niklas. The earlier video of the gun and now this. That Niklas of the past was dead, Jillian was sure of that.

"Why hasn't the backup generator kicked in?" Niklas yelled over the radio, but there was no response. Niklas stepped out into the hallway and down the hall toward the generator room.

Jillian moved closer and spotted two figures tied to metal chairs. They were gagged and blindfolded, one a man, and the second a little girl.

There was a man standing guard near one of the ventilation grates. Jillian slid her way around to the vent and with both feet kicked out the grate, hitting the guard in the head, knocking him to the floor. Jillian jumped down, and with a straight palm strike to the nose, the man was out cold.

Rex headed down into the basement or the catacombs as he liked to call them. Rex was vaguely familiar with these tunnels. He had been there about a week ago where he found and rescued Anna. *But where was Gabriella? Was she here the whole time? How did I miss her?* Rex thought back to the video and the bruises on her face.

Was she raped and tortured like Anna? Could I have stopped or prevented that from happening? The thoughts kept popping up in his head.

I could have rescued her... Why did I stop looking for her? Knock it off, Rex, he scolded himself. *This is not the time or the place for that kind of talk.* He had a new mission and that was to find Gabriella.

Jillian pulled the hood off the senator and Gabriella, cutting them loose from the chairs.

"Who are you?" the senator asked, looking at her strangely. With her hair pulled up into a bun and covered with a black beanie, he did not recognize her.

"Never mind that... I am here to rescue you," she said hustling them to the exit.

"What's going on? Who are you?" the senator asked again squinting to see who it was.

"Here, to get you out of here," Jillian said smiling. "Hold on, it's you...the gal from the Cayman's," the senator said.

"Quiet, shshhh, I'm here to rescue you," Jillian grabbed him by the arm and led him down the hall. Jillian heard voices up ahead. She turned and shoved Gabriella and the senator into a small broom closet.

"Stay put. I will come back for you when the coast is clear," Jillian closed the door.

The senator opened the door slightly and watched as Jillian encountered the two men. Jillian slid up against the wall as the two men came around the corner, then punched the first man, spun down on one arm, kicking the legs out from under him. The second man reached for his gun, but Jillian caught him with a devastating side kick to the abdomen, knocking him and the gun up against the back wall. The first man got up, pulled his gun, pointed it at Jillian, who with two hands moving in opposite directions disarmed the man, pulling it from his hand. The second man started to get up, but Jillian took a few steps and kicked him in the head with a spinning side kick, slamming him again into the back wall. The first man got back to his feet and pulled a knife, waving it back and forth, trying to intimidate her. Jillian casually pulled the six-inch KA-BAR strapped to her leg, flipped it several times in her hand, then motioned with her fingers for him to make the first move. When they clashed, it was his last as Jillian made a quick slashing move across his jugular. The man stood there expecting her to keep fighting, but Jillian turned and walked away.

"What the hell?" the senator said closing the door quickly.

"Rex, I found Gabriella and the senator," Jillian said over the comms.

"Where are you?" Rex squawked in her ear.

"Southwest corner of the compound," Jillian responded.

"Great I'm in the catacombs, the basement. I'll see you in a couple of minutes," Rex said.

"Rex, he's here," Jillian said softly.

"Yes, I got that. The senator is here," Rex said pulling his hand up to his ear to hear clearly.

"No, Nik—" Jillian said as her comms crackled and went dead.

"Jillian, Jillian, come in." Rex tapped his earpiece a couple of times. *Must be the catacombs*, Rex thought heading for the southwest corner of the compound. Rex came around the corner and ran into the two dead guards. *It's got to be Jillian's work*, He thought with a grin as he searched for her.

"Hey, Rex," Jillian whispered.

Rex looked around then up.

"Rex, up here," Jillian said quietly. It was coming from above his head. "Yes, up here," she said again.

"What are you doing up there? Rex asked.

"Waiting for you," she said squirming away, hopping down from the vent.

"Where are Gabriella and the senator?" Rex asked.

"Safe. They are in the broom closet," Jillian said pointing straight ahead.

"Let's get them and get out of here," Rex said as the main lights flickered and came back on.

Jillian looked up.

"Damn, what happened to your face?" she asked almost laughing.

"The hornets got me. I'll explain later," Rex said as he reached for the door.

"It's locked," Rex said.

Jillian reached over and tried to open it. "Electronic lock, must have kicked in when the power came back on," Jillian said.

"Darn it. I didn't bring my electronic key card," Rex said in disgust.

"Give me a boost," Jillian said pointing at the open vent. Jillian crawled several feet through the shaft into the other room. "Good thing there are no locks inside the ventilation shafts." She giggled as she kicked her way into the room. Jillian pried open the lock mechanism and crossed a few wires. The latch popped, and the door opened.

"We gotta move fast," Rex said as the door swung open.

Jillian grabbed the senator's arm and led him past Rex.

"Do I know you?" the senator stared at Rex for a few seconds.

"Never mind. We gotta go now," Rex said pushing him and Gabriella down the hall to the back stairwell.

"Where did you learn how to fight like that?" the senator asked, staring in disbelief at the petite gal.

"Detroit," she said.

A shot rang out when they reached the top of the stairs, hitting Jillian in the upper back, throwing her to the ground. Rex spun and kicked the gun from the man's hands as a shiny gold-plated Colt .45 with a pearl handle slid to a stop.

"Jillian, are you okay?" Rex called out.

"Yes, I'm okay," she responded faintly.

"Go get the senator and Gabriella out of here. I'll take care of this myself," Rex said as he pointed his gun at the man.

"Niklas?" Rex stared in disbelief at the man standing in front of him.

"Yes, Rex, it's me… Your old friend Niklas," he said smirking.

"The Niklas Mueller I knew died in that explosion in Iran," Rex said cocking back the hammer. "I always suspected we had a mole. The plan was a secret, a quick in and out. Only a few of us knew the real plan was to disable it long enough to get the UN inspectors in to prove they were building a nuclear bomb, so we could impose the sanctions and eventually shut them down," Rex paused thinking about the chain of events. "But somebody told them we were coming. They waited for us and ambushed the whole team," Rex hesitated. "We lost some really good men that day… Buster, my brother Ben, even *you?*" he continued, still pointing the gun at his friend.

"When they recovered the bodies, Ben was shot in the back… with a .45 caliber bullet," Rex said looking at the .45 laying in the floor. "Was that your gun that killed Ben?" Rex looked into his eyes for the answer.

"That rat… He was too smart for his own good," Niklas explained. "We could not take that chance. The plant had to be destroyed… But your brother Ben was going to expose the syndicate to the FBI. We had to take him out," Niklas said smirking proudly.

"We…who's *we?* Niklas?" Rex yelled.

"The people I work for wanted it that way," Niklas said.

"The syndicate? Who are they?" Rex asked.

"Some very powerful people you don't want to mess with," Niklas said.

"People in the government. The syndicate is tied to the government?" Rex was trying to put all the pieces together. "You killed all these people…for what? The syndicate?" Rex pondered the question. "The syndicate was tied to guns, drugs, money laundering, and prostitution… What more could it be? Why blow up the Iranian nuclear plant?" Rex asked still pointing the gun at Niklas's head.

The microdrive? What is on that microdrive? Rex wondered. "The senator…is he involved? Was he the man looking for the microdrive… Oh my, Jillian," Rex called out as Niklas lunged forward, knocking the gun from his hand.

The two old friends pulled their knives at the same time in what would be a deadly dual to the death.

The clash of knives echoed in the hallway as blocks turned to strikes. Rex blocked several blows, then plunged the knife deep into Niklas's upper torso, then front kicked him across the room.

Niklas reacted as is if nothing happened, not even an inkling of pain. There was no pain for Niklas that is for he suffered from a rare disease, congenital insensitivity to pain with anhidrosis.

While at Georgetown University, Niklas would make extra spending money on gullible underclassmen, playing terrible tricks daring them to stab him with a knife. Later, realizing he could use the disease to his advantage, joining the CIA with the Special Operations Department. At the academy, he would pretend to be tortured, driving cadets and instructors crazy. The CIA eventually made him into not only a great agent but an extremely dangerous one too.

The knives clashed again and again…attacking and defending. As the two collided, Rex came in a little low. The blade slashed across his cheek, spewing blood across the floor. Rex crouched low and spun on to one knee, hooking Niklas's ankle with his arm, sweeping him off his feet. The two scrambled for position trading blows, arm locks, leg locks in a vicious ground attack. Rex inflicted as much pain as he could, striking sensitive nerve centers with every blow, to no avail.

Rex scrambled to his feet as Niklas threw a devastating round-house then a step behind side kick, slamming Rex up against the concrete wall. Niklas advanced and attacked with an overhand stabbing move. Rex caught the knife with both hands. The tip of the knife stopped just inches from his throat. Rex rolled backward, kicking Niklas up over his head slamming him into the back wall. Rex twisted the knife from his hands and tossed it to one side.

Rex rolled out and turned toward Niklas who was struggling to get up.

"Why Niklas, why did you do it?" Rex demanded as he lay into Niklas with a barrage of attacks. Right cross, a crescent kick to the head followed by a spinning side kick, knocking Niklas back. Niklas advanced. This time with weak right hand punch that Rex blocked, then stepped in with a right hip judo throw smashing him to the ground.

Niklas scrambled on the ground toward Rex's gun as he turned to shoot.

Rex was already heading toward him, throwing a running side kick to Niklas head, snapping it back violently. Rex walked up to Niklas who was bleeding from the nose and mouth.

"Why did you do it?" Rex yelled.

Niklas lay there, grinning as blood filled his lungs slowly suffocating to death.

Rex fell to his knees and let out a yell, "NIKLAS!"

With the power restored all over the compound, Jillian, Gabriella, and the senator made a run for the surface. As they opened last door leading outside, they were met by two armed guards. The first man pointed the gun at Jillian, who spun down on her good arm, kicking his legs out from under him shooting a bullet straight into the air. She rolled over him, elbowed him in the jaw, then grabbed his gun and discharged two shots at a second man coming in from her right.

Gabriella and the senator headed for the tree line, as she trained the gun on the third man, pulled the trigger, and nothing happened. She lay there looking up the barrel of a gun pointed at her head as her whole life suddenly flashed before her. You could hear the swoosh of the high-powered bullet as it hit the man center mass. The impact knocked him back three feet. Jillian wondered if it would hurt any more or less if you never saw it coming.

"Thanks, Milty," Jillian said as her comms came back to life.

"Mmm, I have another bogie coming your way approaching from the hacienda," Scooter told her in her ear.

"Milty, do you have a shot?" Jillian called on her comm's.

"No," Jillian heard someone coming up behind, but in the dark, it was hard to tell who it was.

She hoped it was Rex.

When the figure came around the corner, it was a rather large guard. Under normal circumstances, this would have been a breeze, but with her right shoulder all shot up, she would have to rely on her legs. The first strike was to the inside of the right knee, the second inside the left. The big man's legs buckled as he fell to his knees. Jillian kicked up on her good arm and swung her leg around his head in a figure four headlock then flexed her legs and arched her back. The pressure on the neck was too great as the man's neck snapped.

Jillian crawled over to Gabriella.

"Where is the senator?" she asked pulling her into the grove of trees.

Gabriella pointed off into the darkness.

"Where is Rex?" Milton squawked in her ear.

"Ran into an old acquaintance… It's Niklas. He's here," she said turning toward Gabriella.

"Scooter, the senator is gone. Do you have a bead on him?" Jillian asked.

"Sorry, I don't."

"What about you, Milton?"

"Sorry, my dear. My position has been—" *Bzzzzzzz*…Milton's comms went dead.

"Milton, are you there? Milton, come back," Jillian called out but silence.

The bullet deflected off the slide of the sniper rifle, rendering it inoperative. Milton quickly scanned the horizon to get a vector on where it was coming from. *Whhhooosh*, a second bullet flew by

Milton's head as he rolled out of his "hide" into the deep grass. With his position compromised, the only thing he could do is to use the dark of night and disappear.

Milton rolled over and spotted two jeeps, and several men heading in his direction. Milton rolled slowly down the hill to a slight indentation in the ground, a nearby fallen tree branch, and foliage offered great cover. Two small teams of men and dogs searched the area but quickly gave up because of the ferocity of the weather.

Jillian heard some rustling in the bushes behind her.

"Mmm, it's Rex coming up behind you," Scooter whispered into her ear.

"Thanks, kid," Jillian said.

"Jillian, is that you?" Rex asked ruffling through the dark bushes.

"I could have killed you. How did you know it was me?" Rex asked.

"Little birdie in the sky told me…" Jillian laughed pointing up.

"What about you? How did you know where to find me?" Jillian asked.

"I just followed your handywork. Did you do all that with one arm?" Rex said looking around.

"Yes, mostly, but I had some help Milty," Jillian said with concern.

"I heard a sharp noise. Then his comms went dead," Jillian said.

"Yes, I heard that too. Where's the senator?" Rex asked.

"Ran off when we got ambushed," Jillian said.

"Scooter, do you have eyes on Milton?" Rex held a hand to his ear.

"No, his comms went dead, but there is lots of activity in the area of his hide. I think they are looking for him," Scooter said.

Rex and Jillian headed back to the extraction point about one hundred yards from the power station, where they stashed the truck. The plan was to wait at the extraction point until midnight, then head back with or without all the team members. Rex hated this part of any operation, not knowing if all your friends would return, safely or have to leave them behind.

Rex looked anxiously at his watch, 11:50 p.m. Then again five minutes later. *Where are ya, Milty?* Rex thought to himself quietly as they waited in the truck.

The rain had stopped, and there was a heavy fog across the road in the distance through the fog was a tall figure walking down the middle of the road, whistling some old Scottish tune.

"Nice night for a walk, wouldn't ya say?" Milton said as he approached.

"I am glad you're all right," Jillian said reaching out to give him a hug.

"Oh, what happened to you, my dear?" Milton asked with concern.

"Just a scratch," Jillian said giving him a left-handed hug.

"Look what they did to my Betsy," cradling the rifle like a wounded warrior.

Rex shook his head in deep despair for the wounded rifle. "But did she save your life?" Rex asked.

"Yes, that she did, lad. More than once, I'd say…more than once," Milton said looking up at Rex reaching out to give him a hug.

"Hold on there," Milton said backing away from Rex cautiously. "What happened to your face?" Milton asked, looking closely at the bumps.

"It's a long story. I'll tell you all about it on the way to the airport," Rex said hoping into the truck.

That next morning, a limousine pulled up to the hacienda along with two SUVs, one in front and one in the rear. Several men exited the SUVs with automatic weapons and stood guard as the driver of the limo got out and opened the door for the passenger in the back seat, a lovely woman in her early fifties, standing five feet eight, jet black hair. Señora Rosalinda De La Rosa Sanchez, also known as "La Rosa Negra."

Several years ago, her husband, Rodrigo Sanchez, was captured and extradited to the United States and to this date still being held in a max security prison in Texas. Since then, she took over the family business under protest from several group leaders. At one of the meetings, she was challenged by one of the other leaders, told her she had no right to be in the business, and that she should stay barefoot and pregnant. She turned to the man, pulled a Colt .45 from her purse, and shot the man in the head. That was her cousin Mauricio Sanchez. From that day on, no one ever challenged her again.

"Roberto…Donde esta Sr. Kincade?" she asked walking around the carnage from the night before.

"Señora…Niklas esta muerto, tambien," Roberto responded.

"Who is responsible for all of this?" she yelled kicking some of the dead bodies.

"We may have something on the people that did this," Roberto said cueing up the security feed.

"It shows him escaping, willingly with these two and the girl," Roberto said.

"Who are these people?" she demanded waving her hands around in despair.

"We don't know who they are at the moment," Roberto said. "We think it might be the same ones we ran into in Panama, and he took out four of my men, plus the doctor and his two guards," Roberto explained.

"Find out who they are. I want them. *Dead* or *alive*," she yelled.

CHAPTER 28

They caught the first available flight back to Veracruz, and the entire flight was spent hearing about Rex's encounter with the hornets.

"So, Rex, tell us again what you fear the most, two fully automatic M-4 assault rifles or a squadron of pissed-off hornets?" Jillian laughed.

"Hornets," Rex said sulking a little.

They stopped by the Santa Maria Hospital and met up with Anna and Juan who were in the special care facility at the hospital. Anna was still recovering from the trauma and abuse in Panama, smiled when she saw Gabriella for the first time in over three weeks, a little beat up but in overall good shape.

Juan's injuries, on the other hand, were too severe his right leg had been amputated just below the hip. The infection from the bullet wound and the ensuing torture had spread to the rest of his body, slowly shutting down his vital organs.

Anna leaned over and whispered something into Juan's his ear. Juan's expression changed suddenly. The heart monitor alarm went off as his pulse rate skyrocketed, and his blood pressure spiked then flatlined.

"Help," Rex yelled down the hall as nurses and doctors came running to help. But after several minutes and repeated attempts to restart his heart, Juan was declared *dead*.

Several days later, JML Corporation and prominent members of the board of directors voted and later designated the two girls

Anna Ramos and Gabriella Maria Fernando De La Cruz as the new CEOs of JML Corporation.

"One more thing," Rex interrupted the festivities.

"Jillian, can I borrow your computer laptop?" Rex typed in a few codes Scooter provided for him.

"Hey, Rex, it's all set?" Scooter told him.

"This is for Juan and Luiz De La Cruz," Rex said pointing at Anna and Gabriella, handing them the computer laptop.

"Just hit enter," Rex said. They all put a finger on the button and hit enter.

"What happened?" Jillian asked curiously looking around the room.

A small electronic signal shot straight up into the air bounced off a couple of satellites then back down to a transmission tower in the middle of the Panamanian jungle one thousand miles away, setting off a chain of explosions that ripped through the underground catacombs below the compound.

The explosion was so large, leaving a three-hundred-foot crater where the hacienda once stood, setting off seismic readings in Mexico City. The Panamanian government had no real explanation for the explosion and made a statement to the media that it was a natural gas leak.

"When did you come up with that idea?" Jillian asked giving him a thumbs up.

"Just before I came out of the catacombs."

FINALE

Several weeks later, Jillian and Scooter along with the cybercrimes division of the US government released a computer bug that would locate and shut down any and all programs, websites, and accounts tied to the case. Over the next several weeks, thousands of churches and schools were brought up on charges of human trafficking and other crimes. Several leaders of foreign governments were questioned and arrested on racketeering and money laundering charges.

Several major US and international corporations were shut down, and billions of dollars seized. The US Senate Judiciary Committee opened an investigation into Senator Bradley Stevens involvement and his participation in the syndicate. Senator Bradley Stevens disappeared the night of the raid, and he never appeared at his hearing or returned to the US Senate.

Later that year, in a small house on the shores of the Rio Negro "Black River" in the city of Manaus, Brazil, while sitting at the dinner table, a young lady handed a manila envelope to an older lady then turned toward the door as a man walked in.

"Holla, Papa," she said smiling.

"Holla, Anna," he said, giving her a big hug.

"Holla, Rosalinda, como estas?" he said, walking up to her.

"Holla, Michael," she said, giving him a kiss.

ABOUT THE AUTHOR

John N. Iung, a.k.a. Jack Nelson, is a former US Air Force staff sergeant that has traveled throughout the United States, Europe, and parts of South America. As a young man, he grew up in the southernmost state of Brazil, Rio Grande Do Sul, with parents and brothers and sisters. John worked as a technician at a major corporation in the Atlanta Metro area and was called a renaissance man by one of his supervisors. John enjoys fine dining, golf, and a taste of Glenlivet scotch on occasion.

CPSIA information can be obtained
at www.ICGtesting.com
Printed in the USA
LVHW091535300120
645337LV00001B/97